Sue Heath lives in Ch working, she can often l courses with her spaniel, cook and spend time with f

Sue has also written fourteen *USA Today* bestselling romcoms under the pseudonym Zara Stoneley and has sold over half a million copies of her stories worldwide.

You can find out more about Sue on her website.

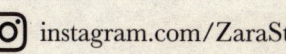

www.sueheath.co.uk

instagram.com/ZaraStoneley
facebook.com/ZaraStoneley

Also by Sue Heath

The Secret Ingredient

THE STORYTELLERS

SUE HEATH

One More Chapter
a division of HarperCollins*Publishers* Ltd
1 London Bridge Street
London SE1 9GF
www.harpercollins.co.uk
HarperCollins*Publishers*
Macken House, 39/40 Mayor Street Upper,
Dublin 1, D01 C9W8, Ireland

This paperback edition 2025

1

First published in Great Britain in ebook format
by HarperCollins*Publishers* 2025

A catalogue record of this book is available from the British Library

ISBN: 978-0-00-875654-3

This novel is entirely a work of fiction. The names, characters and incidents
portrayed in it are the work of the author's imagination. Any resemblance to
actual persons, living or dead, events or localities is entirely coincidental.

Printed and bound in the UK using 100% Renewable Electricity
by CPI Group (UK) Ltd

To you, if you're waiting for the right day to start writing that novel of your dreams — I hope this story inspires you to make a start today!

INTER-LIBRARY WRITING COMPETITION

WHAT'S YOUR STORY?

As part of our centenary celebrations, we are launching our biggest writing competition yet! For this year only, the short-story competition will be replaced with a collaborative project – a novella-length story!

Can your writing group create a story that will capture our imagination?
Large teams welcome (minimum 3 people).

** THEMES **
Love. Loyalty. Lies.
choose one or combine!

** PRIZES **
1ST PLACE:
The winning story will be published and made available in all our libraries. All contributors will be invited to the centenary party. Extra funding will be made available to the winning library to improve their café area.
2ND & 3RD PLACE:
Inclusion in the publication and an invitation to the centenary party.

More information and rules can be found online, or from your librarian.

Chapter One

HATTIE

Don't Judge a Book by its Cover

Hattie liked a competition almost as much as she liked a Bourbon biscuit. That was partly why she'd returned to the library after her first, rather nervous and disastrous, visit. Because of the biscuits, that is, not the competition.

On that first day she had gone to the library, not to read a book, but to find out how to use the computers.

Her neighbour, Margaret, had given her the idea, and she'd not been able to shake it out of her head. Margaret had been wittering on to her friend about a website on the computer where you could trace people and find your ancestors. Hattie didn't have any ancestors she wanted to dig up (if she'd wanted them in her life, she wouldn't have been so careless as to lose them, would she?), but she did want to find Peter.

She'd pushed Peter right to the back of her mind after

she had married Harold. He'd been filed away into a small, sealed box in her heart. Because that was what you had to do, wasn't it? But he had always been there, because banished had not meant forgotten.

Hattie didn't make a habit of eavesdropping, and now she wasn't sure if she was glad that she had, or not. Because the more she thought about the fact that it might be possible to find him, the more important it had become. As she drank her cup of tea, her heart had pattered in a way it hadn't done for years. This could mark a turning point in her life. A chance to wipe out regrets.

To wipe out the resentment of Harold that had grown over the years.

Hattie hadn't got a computer, and she didn't want to ask Margaret for more information because she could be rather nosy. They all could be, where she lived in the retirement apartments. It was full of busybodies, they wanted to know your business, which, after a lifetime of being with Harold and shunning the rest of the world (*they're all stupid*, he used to say, *stupid nobodies*), was a step too far.

And then she'd seen the poster about the library in the post office. Use it, or lose it, it had said. It had also said, more importantly, that there were computers. Free to use.

It was as though she was being sent a message, telling her to do it.

There were leaflets in libraries, they'd tell her what to do, and she'd be doing the community a favour. Saving the library.

Hattie's heart had started to beat so rapidly, she'd walked

out of the post office with the letter she'd wanted to post still in her hand – forgotten.

The thought of using one of the machines, and making a fool of herself, had been quite daunting, but Hattie was nothing if not determined. When you got to her age, it was too late to let nerves stand in the way. There were too few opportunities, too few hours left.

Unfortunately, when she had walked into the library fifteen minutes later, it was to discover that all the machines had been prebooked. All the bravado had been knocked out of her.

For a moment she had been confused, knocked off balance, but before she had time to leave, the young librarian, Will, had introduced himself. He had been quite insistent on her trying out the new comfortable chairs and the coffee machine – and what was a drink without a biscuit?

After that, it had been much easier. She'd still not got to grips with using the computer, which had been her reason for coming in the first place, but it didn't seem quite so urgent. Instead, she'd discovered that novels really could be quite engaging – it would have been churlish to ignore the books when she was surrounded by them.

She had in fact settled into a nice routine of visiting once a week. It wasn't that she was lonely, or at a loose end – oh, good heavens, no, she had more than enough to occupy her time – but the library was a nice change of scene. And it was quite interesting to watch some of the people who came into the library – much more interesting than the lounge at the retirement apartments, where the book selection was sparse and there was a good (a very good) chance that somebody would try and engage her in conversation.

It was interesting to see what the visitors liked to read, or whether they were there for the coffee and newspapers. You could watch, without being interrupted or expected to chat.

Not so long ago, Thursday had just been another day to endure. It was the day that Harold had always insisted they walk into town together to collect their 'old age pensions' – that's what they called it when she had qualified for the payments, in the days when you had a 'pension book' that you had to take into the post office. A coupon to swap for cash.

They called it the State Pension now. No mention of age, nobody liked being called old, did they? She often thought that nobody liked being called *anything* now, but that was progress for you, she supposed.

Harold had a lot to say about it – none of it good – when the letter had arrived, telling them that the system was changing. They wouldn't have to go and collect their money; it would go straight into their bank account. Harold hadn't trusted banks, or change. He was a creature of habit, he didn't like his routines disrupted, so he'd told her that they would still go for a stroll, for coffee and cake.

It wasn't that Hattie didn't like walking round the town, or cake (she certainly liked cake), it was that Harold had turned it into such an ordeal. He'd liked her to look smart – Sunday dress. And nobody did that these days, did they? She couldn't put it past him to insist she go and change if he didn't think what she'd put on was suitable, and then he'd be tapping his watch and tutting because he was being kept waiting.

What exactly would they be late for?

He would be horrified if he could see her now. Throwing caution to the wind.

She'd abandoned her smart skirts (which had got longer each year as though they had to keep pace with her ever-growing earlobes and eyebrows) and replaced them with M&S trousers (much more practical) and she'd abandoned the routines that he had inflicted upon them. She didn't even go for her weekly hair appointment. She'd cancelled her appointment the week after his funeral, because she didn't want to face the sympathy. And then it had been easier not to go back at all, because she'd never really liked the place, it had been noisy. Nor did she really like the old-fashioned cut. It had been Harold's idea of who she should be. But it was too late to ask them to do it differently, they just automatically did it 'Harold's way' and she really didn't know how to explain what she really wanted – because that was just to feel younger, to feel more 'Hattie' and less Harold's 'Harriet'. It was easier to not go at all.

Harold had been too bossy, too full of his own opinions and importance to take her thoughts into account.

She could have left him, but he had control of the money, it was just how it was when they'd got married, and with each passing year it had become harder to do anything about it.

But then she hadn't had to. Leave him, that is. Because he had left her. He had died.

A massive, sudden heart attack had rudely interrupted

him mid-rant, leaving a strange silence that she'd always longed for, but now didn't know quite what to do with.

Until the thought of finding Peter had lodged itself in her head and wouldn't let go.

What would her life have been like if she'd defied her father and Harold, if she'd waited for Peter. Followed her heart?

That was why she'd had to go to the library. Take this opportunity before it was too late.

Now, Thursday was Hattie's favourite day of the week. It had crept up on her unnoticed until one morning she had been eating her breakfast and suddenly realised that even though she'd just spilled tea down her favourite blouse, she wasn't bothered. It was Thursday, the day she went to the library.

The library was another of the many things that Harold hadn't liked. He'd always scoff and say libraries were 'full of clever dicks who think they're better than us'.

They probably are, she'd thought to herself at the time, but been wise enough not to say out loud.

She wondered now if the idea of a place filled with words, with knowledge, had made Harold nervous, insecure. He hadn't been a man who liked to feel inferior. He liked what he knew, and he knew what he liked, as he used to say. She nearly put that on a stone in the memorial garden, but it had seemed too friendly, too anecdotal, something that would make people smile. And Harold had never been a man who would make you smile.

Two weeks after he'd died, Hattie had put their house up for sale. It was too big, too dusty, too full of the type of memories she'd rather forget. It echoed with his voice, smelled of his beer.

Six weeks later – while she was waiting for a buyer – her solicitor had pointed out that there was enough money in her savings account to buy an apartment. She didn't have to wait.

A week after moving into her new home, Hattie had gone to the library in search of a computer. It had been an act of defiance.

***

'Not another poster!'

Will, the librarian, was stretching to push a pin into the noticeboard, and blocking her view of it. All she could see was something about a centenary, and the word 'competition', which made her curious, although she tried to keep that out of her tone of voice. It didn't do to let people know that you were too interested in things.

'And rather a big one. The bigger the notice the more boring the subject in my experience.' She tried again to peer round him, but despite his slight build, it was impossible to see properly. 'What is it this time? Preserve Making for Pensioners?'

'Well, if it was,' he paused as he pushed the pin in a bit more firmly, 'it might be just up your street, Hattie.'

She harumphed. Hattie did not think of herself as old, definitely not the eighty-seven she was, unless there was some benefit such as a discount to be had.

'You shouldn't smirk,' she said.

'I've got my back to you, how can you——?'

'It's your tone.'

He turned round, a good-humoured smile on his face. She liked Will. How different would her life have been if she'd met somebody like him, not Harold, all those years ago? Will was everything her husband had not been. Gentle, mild-mannered, polite and thoughtful. But he also had a twinkle in his eye that suggested he might have a wicked sense of humour under that librarian outer shell.

She liked wicked, when it wasn't malicious. She would quite like to crack that shell, Will was too young to lead the serious life he appeared to.

'My tone is because I'm happy to see you, and the poster is large because the powers that be sent it.'

'Ah, well, it must be important, then!'

Will sighed. 'Or they want you to think it is.' He shook his head, but moved to one side of the noticeboard so that she could take a step closer. When posters were as garish as this, they were hard to decipher at a distance. 'You are bossy at times, Hattie.'

'I'm not sure you should speak to your clients like that!' she said tartly, finding it hard to suppress her smile. From that very first time she had met him she had felt like Will *saw* her. A real person, not an invisible old woman. He hadn't judged her on that first Thursday, he'd looked beyond her grey hair and failing eyesight, had ignored her dithering and instead offered her the greatest gifts of all. Time, and a listening ear. Hattie didn't want charity, or sympathy, but she did like a nice Bourbon biscuit. He'd noticed her looking and opened a new packet even before he'd poured her coffee.

After Harold died, Hattie hadn't really had anybody to talk to. Not that Harold had been chatty, but he had been there. Even if he didn't listen, or like her chatting to anybody else. They had kept themselves to themselves, and it had been more than a habit, it had been her life. But here in the library, it felt different. It wasn't the world she had inhabited with her husband; it was hers. Just hers. She felt like she was *allowed* to express herself, and Will's inviting manner made talking to him feel natural. Normal.

She liked the hushed atmosphere, the unassuming Will, the free Bourbon creams that were in the kitchen area, and the people here weren't snobs or intellectuals at all, they just seemed to be ordinary. She liked to watch them, because as an old woman she knew she was practically invisible to most folk. Except Will, of course.

He'd also offered an introduction to the computers, when there was one free. Not because she might struggle, he'd said, but because everybody had to have the demonstration before they were allowed to book a slot.

Will, she surmised, was probably wiser than his years suggested because he was a reader. He knew better than to judge a book by its cover, because he knew that sometimes the dullest wrapper could hide an interesting story. Not that she was an interesting story. But … well, this could be!

'Goodness me, your powers that be are right, this *is* important.'

'Sorry?' He frowned.

'The competition!' She tapped the poster. He was being

unusually slow on the uptake today. 'If we win, we will be published, and'—she paused, smiling at him—'we can have one of those posh coffee machines that does frothy coffee! How exciting.'

'I seem to remember you saying that you didn't like fancy coffee when I first met you and offered you a cappuccino.'

Hattie hadn't even known what a cappuccino was. Harold had thought coffee was frivolous and always ordered them a pot of tea. But she'd studied the menu in the café that the local supermarket housed the other day and thought that this might be another habit she needed to break.

'I don't like the way cafés have a confusing menu of coffee, these new-fangled skinny, frothy lattes with extra syrup and a cherry on top. What happened to coffee with milk? And they put you under so much pressure with their clattering about, you don't have time to think.' She shook her head. She'd gone in fully intending to try something different, but had been flustered and settled for her normal pot of tea and scone, which had left her feeling like a silly old woman who had yet again missed an opportunity. Life was so over complicated at times. 'But there's nothing wrong with a bit of froth!'

'Indeed,' he answered gravely.

Hattie pursed her lips. 'So, I would like some, please, William.'

Will frowned. 'Froth?'

He really was being a little bit dense today. He must have things on his mind.

'More information. I should like some more information.

It says that I should ask the librarian, and that is you.' This time she was not going to miss out.

'It is. Well, if you'd like to settle in down in your normal spot, I shall print it off for you. But'—he paused—'there is one rather obvious problem, Hattie.'

'There is?'

'We don't have a writing group, do we?'

'*Pfft.* We're not going to let a little thing like that stop us, are we?' She narrowed her eyes and studied Will. He seemed a bit, well … reticent was probably the word. 'Unless you don't want us to enter?'

'If you want to do it, then of course I want you to.'

'Hmm.' If there was one thing Hattie was good at, it was spotting a fib. She'd had plenty of experience.

'I just think it might be difficult, this is aimed at writing groups, and you can't do this by yourself, can you?' His tone softened. 'I don't want you wasting your time, when you've got your own little project on the go.'

Will didn't know much about her search for Peter, but he did know she was trying to trace somebody. Somebody important.

'I am sure I will find a way,' she said. 'Nothing ventured, nothing gained. Right, I shall be in my normal seat, young man.' Harriet took a firm grip of the handle of her shopping bag on wheels and set off towards the seating area at the back of the library.

This was very interesting. Why on earth would a librarian not want his library to win such a wonderful, in fact she'd call it prestigious, competition?

Chapter Two

AVRIL

A New Chapter

It was a Thursday. Avril had left home at her normal time of 7:55am and caught the 8:36 train that would arrive in town at 8:51am. As she always did.

The service was reliable, dependable. In the ten years that she'd been taking this journey to work she could only remember a handful of times when it had been cancelled or running late.

The train was never very crowded as she was travelling in the opposite direction to most of the commuters, who were heading into the city. Avril was travelling to Knutsford, which most definitely was not a city. It was a town. A very nice town, but very much smaller, smarter and more self-contained (her stepmother Lisa sometimes added 'smugger') than her hometown of Altrincham.

Lisa often asked her why she hadn't found a job nearer home, or in Manchester. Lisa questioned – criticised – everything Avril did, in that passive-aggressive way she seemed to reserve just for her. She was never outwardly nasty, but it was always dig, dig, dig.

But Avril liked the smaller town. She liked the fact that faces were familiar, that there were quirky buildings and that she could sit and feed the ducks on her lunchbreak.

So, this morning she was sitting where she always did on the train. Second carriage, third row, window seat.

It was predictable. Like the rest of her life.

Except this morning was different. Her stomach flickered with nerves, but they were intermingled with something else. A good feeling.

This morning, as she watched the clouds scud across the sky and the countryside fly past the window, they added to her impatience. Her need to do something. Although, right now she had no idea what that was going to be.

Once you've sown the seed, there's no un-sowing it. That had been one of her grandfather's favourite sayings when she was a child. She hadn't really understood what he'd meant until a few weeks ago. For her, the seed was one of doubt. A doubt that she wasn't living the life that she really should or could. A doubt that couldn't be ignored, that grew into a certainty. She had to leave the job that she liked but didn't love, she had to change her life. Now. Not in five years', ten years' time.

She was already twenty-eight years old, so what was she waiting for? Marriage, kids, somebody else to tell her what to do?

She didn't want life to be something that just happened to her. So, two weeks ago she'd made the decision to text her boss – before she had time to change her mind – and tell her she wanted to hand her notice in. One brief text and that chapter of her life was over.

Avril stared out of the window again. Unseeing. Had it been the right thing to do, handing her notice in? She had enough money in the savings account her mother had set up for her to support herself for a few months, and she'd thought she would have four weeks' notice period to put aside more money. To think about what she wanted to do next, which direction she really wanted her life to take. Which jobs to apply for.

But she'd forgotten about the eight days holiday that was owed to her. Before it had even properly sunk in that she'd actually done it, that she'd taken the plunge, she was jobless. She had nowhere to go. Today, for the first time since she left school, she was officially unemployed.

Lisa, would be furious when she found out.

And her stepsisters? Chloe and Dawn. Oh, they would have a field day.

Her father would be worried. And he was the one she was really bothered about. Her only blood relative. The only one who really mattered. She didn't want him to worry.

They'd all say it had been rash, and maybe it had been, but sometimes you had to take a chance in life, didn't you? She didn't want to look back on a life full of what ifs and if onlys. Surely it was better to regret making the wrong decision, than not make one at all. Just let life happen to you.

This was her act of independence, of doing what she knew was right for her. Not what was expected.

She'd not felt she could just stay at home, because then

Chloe, who lived up the road, would see her, she'd have to explain, and she wasn't quite sure she was ready for the showdown yet. She needed some time.

The train started to slow, and the announcement of the next stop pierced the silence of the carriage. Her stop.

The train pulled to a halt and Avril stepped off, hesitating on the platform for a moment.

What on earth was she going to do all day? It wasn't that doing things on her own was a problem, Avril was used to that. Being brought up by a single father had set her apart from the other girls when she was little. At the start, after her mother's death, he'd retreated. He had withdrawn from all the groups that her mother had taken her to. Moved house. Sent her to a new school where she didn't know anybody. It had meant that joining in was difficult, so it had soon become a habit to do things on her own. She hadn't been one of the gang, and she didn't know how to be. As she'd got older, she had made a few good friends, but she had never been one for a crowd. Crowds made her uneasy, she felt like she stood out as different and she didn't like that at all.

So spending the day on her own wasn't the problem. It was the feeling that she was doing something wrong. That she'd be found out.

She could only sit in a café for so long, and even doing that might not be the brightest of ideas – somebody she knew might see her, might mention it to Lisa.

Avril pulled her coat more closely around her body, to protect her from the cool fingers of the morning breeze, and the brief shiver of nerves. She hadn't had time to think this through, her only motivation had been to act as normally as possible. She'd have to risk going for a coffee. There was less chance of somebody she knew spotting her if she went to the small café at the bottom of the road, and then she'd decide what to do for the rest of the day.

Avril walked the short distance through the familiar small car park to the roadside. Normally, she turned right, walked up the steep hill, strolled along the near-empty streets that were lined with boutiques that didn't open until ten o'clock and looked into the estate agents' windows, at the photographs of houses that she'd never be able to afford. She would continue along the street, taking the ten-minute walk that it took to get to the hair salon.

Today, after a moment's hesitation, she turned left instead and headed down the hill, before turning left again onto King Street. She found herself marching at a pace that left her slightly out of breath, and it was a relief when a few minutes later she could sink down onto a seat in a quiet corner at the back of the café.

She stared at the drink and pastry in front of her. Normally she'd tuck in with relish, but she felt uneasy, jittery. It was impossible to relax, not because she regretted leaving her job, but because she was being deceitful. Lying by omission, and that wasn't good, was it? That was why she'd caught the train this morning. Pretended nothing had changed.

But it had, and avoiding a lie was nearly as bad as telling one.

She should have gone into Manchester. Big cities swallowed you up, offered a hundred and one places to explore. To hide.

With a sigh she picked up the knife, to cut her pastry into two, and a glint of colour caught her eye.

It was a book, abandoned or forgotten, on the seat next to her.

The title made her smile – *The Lost Bookshop*. More like the lost book.

She had never been much of a reader; at school she'd been put off by the poems and stories that they had to find *meanings* in. She didn't get the clever answers that some of her classmates spouted. It was just a story, right? How could a teacher, an exam board, know what was in the author's head? Surely there couldn't be a right, or wrong?

But it wasn't the kind of thing you said out loud, was it? She didn't want to be ridiculed, she had enough of that at home. From her stepsisters. So, she'd learned to keep her lips sealed. To keep the things that she was thinking in her head, not to allow them out of her mouth.

She picked the book up out of curiosity, flipped open the cover. It was a library book. She half lifted it to catch the attention of the waitress, then something made her slowly lower it back to the table. Closing the book, she stared at the tagline on the cover: *How far will you go to find your story?*

She wasn't getting far with her own story, but the book had given her an idea. She could go to the library. She was pretty sure that they had coffee, desks, Wi-Fi.

It was somewhere to hide, use the internet, make a start on planning her future. Nobody she knew read books. *She* didn't read books.

With a grin she lifted her cup and took a sip of coffee.

A library. Who'd ever have thought that she, Avril, would be going into a library voluntarily?

She couldn't remember ever going into a library before, but it – or the idea in her head of what it would be like – was kind of nice. A refuge; like a church, but without the religion. A place to hide.

A building full of books, now that was a daunting thought. But she wouldn't be expected to read, to analyse one, so it would be fine. Quiet.

The fluttering sensation in her stomach, that had been there since she left home, eased, and the sweet smell of the pastry tingled at her nostrils. She was actually quite hungry. A quick look on her mobile phone confirmed that the library didn't open until 10am – not much did in this town – but that was perfect. She'd have her breakfast and then it would be just the right time to wander down the road.

She glanced back down at the book. Then, with fingers slowed by hesitation, she opened it again. Turned the pages. Read the heading saying 'Prologue'.

Could the library be her prologue, the start of *her* new story?

Chapter Three

STUART

A Blank Page

There were times when Stuart would quite like to have pulled a second chair over and put his feet up. Except that wasn't 'the done thing' in a public library.

When he read his newspaper at home, he quite liked to pop his feet onto the small footstool. But he wasn't at home, it wasn't an option.

He sighed and turned to the next page, glancing over the top of his glasses at the elderly lady who was there every week with her large bag, and eagle eyes. He wasn't sure if she'd tut or encourage him if he ever dared to move one of the chairs. Now, though, she seemed to be berating the young librarian, who, as usual was taking it in good humour.

He supposed he shouldn't call people elderly. But despite the fact he'd hit retirement age – *early* retirement age – himself, she most definitely had quite a few years on him. She was possibly old enough to be his mother.

The reminder of his retirement paused his other thoughts.

He hadn't wanted to retire. The day he had found out was one he wouldn't forget for a long time. He'd felt something that he could only assume was panic – he'd never panicked in his life because he had always known who he was and where he was going. And in one fell swoop everything that he'd taken for granted was gone.

He had felt lost since he'd left his job. He'd liked going to work, he liked the routine, the structure, and since leaving he'd felt at a loose end.

His wife, Jo, had told him he needed to get out more, get a hobby. But he'd never really been a 'hobby' kind of person. She meant well, she wasn't being nasty, because she had no problem at all with filling every available hour of the day. And she was right, if he had a hobby, he might have something more interesting to chat to her about. He had his golf of course, but she wasn't exactly riveted when he told her he'd 'beaten the dogleg on the fourth and settled just on the edge of the rough for the third week on the run'. Her eyes glazed over when he started talking about the state of the greens, and talk of the bunkers usually resulted in a 'I've just got to put the washing machine on, dear, but keep talking, I'm listening.'

He couldn't blame her. He'd be the same if she'd started talking about knitting or pruning the roses. But she wasn't that kind of woman. Oh no, Jo talked about the *fascinating* tattoo just above the hip bone of the latest life model she and her friends had been drawing. He tried to supress the tiny shudder. An art class was one thing, but immortalising nude bodies was another – and in their living room! He wasn't a prude, and if she found pleasure in painting then he was happy for her. But when she'd offered to host the class after their usual venue had been temporarily shut for restoration work, because they had the perfect, bright, front room, how could he object?

Well, he wished he had. Everything was rosy, until one morning he'd forgotten it was 'art day' and wandered into the front room to look for his spectacles. He was glad he hadn't got them on, because as it was, he'd never be able to look at the leather armchair in the same way again. Apparently, it was the perfect prop, just the right height. They had draped it in a tartan throw – which was perfect, Jo said with a laugh, because the model was Scottish. Stuart would have been happier if they'd draped it over the Scot. He didn't hang about to examine the tattoo; he left so quickly he pulled a muscle in his inner thigh. A part of his body that was considerably less toned than the Scot's.

And that was why he'd ended up at the library. He had to make sure he wasn't at home the following Thursday. How could he concentrate on his newspaper and the state of the economy when there was a naked stranger in the next room? It made him feel uncomfortable. The library was a much better option.

If he was honest, it slotted in quite nicely between golf practice day on a Monday, and a round or match day with the over-sixties on a Friday. He wasn't old enough to be filling his days with trips to the supermarket, or cafés, but the library was comfortable enough. He could read in peace and be surrounded by people without feeling the need to chat or explain himself. He could try and keep the grey matter exercised, and he could think.

The problem was, he knew that he probably should do more to keep his mind, as well as his body, active. His life really was a blank page these days, which was quite unnerving. He'd never had to deal with a lack of direction. A lack of routine. He could remember a writer friend of his once saying that the scariest thing of all was a blank page, because it was overwhelming. There were just too many possibilities. Which was a little bit how he felt. Where did he start? How did he fill it? How did he make himself interesting again?

'We might not have a writing group, but we do have lots of lovely people with too much time on their hands.' The elderly woman, who had just sat down in her usual spot, was saying to Will, the librarian.

Stuart couldn't supress the smile. She was right, of course. He wouldn't be here if he didn't have time on his hands.

'That's a bit dismissive, Hattie.' Will laughed. 'I like to think some people come to find a good book or two, and for my wonderful company.'

'Oh, you know what I mean. They sit in here and peep over their newspapers, just like I do.'

Stuart tried to sink down further behind his and eavesdrop less obviously. Hattie was, however, in full flow and hopefully not even aware he was there.

'They're readers and people watchers, the perfect people! You're being uncharacteristically negative, Will. I don't know why.'

'I'm not—'.

'I'm going to get to the bottom of it, you mark my words.' Hattie wagged a finger at him. 'Now I think you need to print off some more of those leaflets with the competition rules on, then I can hand them out to people. Just think how exciting it will be to win, to go to the party! I've never been to a party with the mayor before, will it be like a royal garden party?'

'I've no idea, Hattie. I don't mix with royalty.' Will paused. 'Or the mayor. That's left to the head of the main library.'

'Well, I think we need to put that right, because you're a splendid librarian, isn't he, dear?' she said, seemingly directing the last at Stuart.

He started guiltily and peeped around the side of his newspaper. Worried that he'd been spotted. But Hattie wasn't addressing him. She was talking to a young girl who Stuart had never seen in the library before.

'Oh, what? Who? Well, I'm sure he is, he looks very nice.' The girl's cheeks coloured as she looked from Hattie to Will and back again. 'But I've never been in here before so I can't really…'

Stuart sat up a bit straighter in his chair. Well, this could be interesting. He'd stay exactly where he was, and find out what Hattie was up to, and how the mayor was involved. Jo would be happy to meet the mayor. He wasn't sure she'd be impressed exactly; she judged people on what they did, not who they were, but she'd be interested. *He'd* be at least a tiny bit interesting.

He might even take one of the leaflets home with him, and then he could raise it when they were having their tea.

Chapter Four

HATTIE

Everybody Has a Story to Tell

Hattie was on her second Bourbon biscuit and wondering if she'd bitten off more than she could chew, when the solution appeared in front of her very eyes!

She glanced from the vaguely familiar girl, who was looking slightly lost, to Will. Who seemed mesmerised. A situation he rapidly remedied with a blink and cough, when he realised that she had noticed.

She couldn't blame him. Most of the library visitors were either in their dotage, or with toddlers attached to their hips. The library was not a place to search for love, unless you were happy for it to sit between the pages of a novel. Not that it was for her to assume he was looking for romance, but he seemed to work very long hours and despite seeing him in the town now and again, he'd always been alone. It was a shame; he was quite a catch.

'You are correct, dear, he is very nice. But I'm surprised

you've not been in before, you look familiar.' She frowned at the girl. She was positive she knew her, although maybe not in the library as she'd definitely never seen Will pretending not to stare at anybody, in the way he was doing now. Indeed, she hadn't seen him looking quite as animated in all the time she had been visiting the library. The girl was rather striking, particularly now that she had a rosy glow in her cheeks that clashed slightly with the pink streaks in her hair.

'I was just wondering,' said the girl. 'Can anybody just come in and use the computers?'

'I do know you, don't I?' Hattie interrupted.

The girl nodded. 'Yes, Mrs Jamieson, you do. It's Avril from Summers, the hair salon.'

'Of course it is!' The moment she said her name, Hattie remembered who she was. How could she forget those wonderful, green-flecked hazel eyes, and the colourful hair? She shook her head in frustration, how could she have forgotten her? She'd visited that salon every week for months, years. Although these days if she met people in an unexpected location, it quite often threw her. It was lucky, she supposed, that they'd had no children. What could be worse than not recognising a daughter because you met her where you didn't expect to?

'Shouldn't you be sweeping hair up? Is it your day off?'

'I don't sweep hair up, the juniors do that,' said Avril. 'But I don't work there anymore.'

'Oh, that's a shame. You weren't as nosy as some of them.' Hattie had liked the young woman. She'd always been polite and friendly, but with none of that incessant chatter, and questions that you couldn't hear above the sound of the dryer. Why did they do that? It was like the dentist; he'd fill her mouth with instruments then ask her a question. Ridiculous.

Will chuckled. 'High praise.'

'Did they let you go?'

'No, Mrs Jamieson, I decided to leave.'

'Well, that's nice.' Hattie paused. 'And you have no need to call me Mrs Jamieson, you're not at work now. Call me Hattie. Harold liked everybody to call me Harriet, he said Hattie was frivolous, but I like it.' She gave Avril a challenging look.

'I like Hattie, as well. It suits you.'

This really was perfect. 'I suppose you've got plenty of spare time on your hands then?' A hairdresser would have stories to tell, they listened to other people's business all day – the gossip and scandal. And a youngster would be full of ideas, and know what was 'on-trend', as she believed they said these days.

Will had, of course, been right when he'd suggested that the competition would distract her from her own project. She had come to the library on a fact-finding mission, but it wasn't as straightforward as she'd expected. She was beginning to wonder if she'd made a mistake. Each time she left the library a little voice in her head said that maybe there was a reason for her lack of progress. Maybe she shouldn't be doing this. It wasn't right. It wasn't meant to be. She was a silly old woman, whose time, whose chance of love and happiness, had passed her by.

It was a voice she didn't really want to listen to. She didn't want to face up to a future that held no excitement or hope. It was the hope, the dreams, that got her up each morning.

But maybe this competition was the answer? This new project was far more achievable, even if Will was being rather negative. Maybe it would be a more constructive use of her time to investigate this competition, and to work out exactly what was bothering him.

And it wouldn't be a waste of her time, or anybody else's, she was sure of that.

'Not exactly,' Avril said in answer to her question.

Hattie couldn't help it, she felt her eyes narrow at Avril's response.

'I mean I came in here to use the Wi-Fi, to look for a new job, actually,' Avril continued, her tone apologetic. 'It's only the first day I've not been at work. That's why I wanted to use a computer. Do I need to fill in a form, or anything?'

Avril was looking at Will now, who still seemed slightly dazzled, and tongue-tied. Hattie was tempted to answer for him, but this was interesting. This was like watching one of the soaps. And it would be rude to speak for him, she, of all people should know that.

'No, no, you don't need to be a member of the library, though it does mean you get the first hour free; otherwise you need to pay. So it's worth it if you're going to come in again?'

Hattie raised her eyebrows at the question at the end of Will's sentence.

'I'm not sure yet. I just need to do some, er, research,' Avril said.

'I'm afraid they are all booked up today. You can book

online, or I can do it at the desk for you.' Will waved an arm in the direction of the entrance. 'I'm Will by the way. Oh, are you bringing that book back?'

'Oops, I nearly forgot I had it!' Avril glanced down at the book in her hand and grinned. She had a lovely smile, thought Hattie. Impish was the word.

'What's it about?' asked Hattie. Maybe the book would give them some inspiration for their competition entry?

Avril shrugged. 'I don't know. I found it in the café, so thought I'd bring it back.'

'Thanks.' Will smiled. 'I'll have a look and see who borrowed it. And I can show you the booking system, so you can book on for a different day if you like?' Avril seemed to hesitate. Will felt it in the same way that she did, thought Hattie. 'I can give you the password for the Wi-Fi. And feel free to grab a coffee, or a book while you're here.'

Hattie tried to supress the smile that was threatening to break out, at the look on Avril's face. The young woman looked positively terrified. But just because she wasn't much of a reader, didn't mean she didn't have a story to tell, did it?

Hattie decided that it was time to step in, before Avril was out of the door, and she'd lost her first writing-group member. 'Oh, do sit down dear, you're making me dizzy towering up there above me. I want to show you something I think you'll like.' Hattie pulled a chair out slightly. 'You can give me some advice about my hair, as well… And give her one of those leaflets, Will.' There, she'd mentioned it so casually it couldn't frighten Avril off. 'You can pop it in your bag and read it later.'

Will looked down at the leaflets, and there it was again.

His reluctance, she was sure of it before, but now she was convinced.

'It's a competition between the libraries,' she explained. 'And we can't let the next town win it as they won "In Bloom" last year. Pipped us to the post, didn't they, Will?' He nodded. 'And "Best Book Display"!' There it was again, he positively flinched. 'They cheated. They always cheat.'

'I'm not sure it's fair to say that, Hattie.'

Hattie harumphed. 'Even Harold said so.' He'd grumbled about it often enough when he'd read the articles in the local newspaper. Either that, or he'd say their own town was a washout. It depended on his mood.

Hattie smiled triumphantly as Avril took the leaflet. 'We need your help. We need to write the beginning! That's the most important part, isn't it?'

And, she thought, we need to work out the riddle of Will's reluctance.

Chapter Five

AVRIL

Start at the Beginning

Grab a book? Avril's stomach had lurched at Will's words. She glanced at the row upon row of bookcases, crammed full of, no doubt, all the classics, poems and plays that had haunted her school days and made her feel as though she was shrinking away.

And then Will held the leaflet out.

'Great, er, thanks,' she said, taking it as his fingertips brushed hers, and this time the hiccup in her stomach was altogether different. She was nervous, that was all. But so was he. In fact, he looked quite uncomfortable.

'We need to write the beginning.'

She tore her gaze from his at Hattie's words. A new beginning. Wasn't that why she was here? 'What do you mean?'

'The leaflet.' Hattie pointed to it. 'It's a competition. Haven't you been listening?'

Avril stared at it blankly. A writing competition. What on earth did that have to do with her?

'We need a writing group.'

Avril laughed. A laugh that faded at the deadly serious look on Hattie's face.

Other than not being a big reader – unless you counted magazines, Avril most definitely was not a writer. She paused. 'Oh, I can't write. The thing is, I think I'm dyslexic. I never told Dad, so nobody ever checked.'

'I thought schools were supposed to be on top of that kind of thing these days?' said Hattie with a frown, but Avril shrugged.

'It didn't matter, I managed.'

'Hmm, well, anyway … you do watch television, I presume?'

'Yes, but…'

'Well, there you go. What's the difference between some show on the TV and a story in a book?'

'Well, spelling, and describing things in a fancy way, and—'

'Nonsense, you don't need fancy. And somebody else can do the spelling, I'm sure Will knows all kinds of long words, don't you?' Hattie raised her voice in a way that made Avril smile, and Will glance up. He shook his head ruefully, but there was a hint of a smile there, too. They were funny, Will and Hattie, they obviously got on well despite the age difference. 'I don't know a split infinitive from a part participle,' Hattie went on, 'but I do know a good story can change everything!'

'But I don't know anything to write about.' Avril laughed. 'I don't do anything exciting.'

'That's the point, you make it up! It's a story, dear, it's why they call it fiction.'

Avril felt bombarded, but it was funny to see Hattie so enthusiastic. In the salon, Mrs Jamieson had been known for her sharp tongue, apart from when Harold, her husband, had been there. Then she was as quiet as could be, subdued. She'd never been like this, lively, chatty. What on earth had happened to her?

'You can make anything happen; you can put people through hell.' Hattie's eyes were twinkling. 'Haven't you wanted to do that at some time?'

'Maybe!' Avril laughed. 'Look, I don't want to be a spoil-sport, but I really don't think I'll be much use in your writing group. And I don't know if I'll be coming back to the library.'

'Oh, you definitely have to come back. You need to use the computers, you said so!'

'True.' Avril nodded. Being honest, the main reason she had come to the library was to hide. She didn't need to use one of the computers to start her job search – she had her phone to do that – but it would make the task easier, having a bigger screen. And it was easier to agree with Hattie about that, than explain what had really brought her here.

What harm could it do, coming here until she found a new job? Here was as good a place as any.

'Thursday is a nice day to come, you can book one for next Thursday. But…' Hattie chuckled. 'I might let you use mine for a bit today, if you'll help me out. I've booked one.' Hattie's eyes were still sparkling in a mischievous way that made Avril smile.

'Really?'

'Yes, I have a project that I am struggling with.'

So do I, thought Avril. But it was a project she wasn't particularly enthusiastic about right now. She didn't want to jump into a new job that she didn't want – she needed time to think about her future. What she really wanted.

She sat down on one of the plastic chairs that reminded her of school.

'We can help each other, and in the meantime if you have a wonderful idea for the story, you can tell me,' added Hattie.

'Don't let her boss you around!' Will, who was walking past with a pile of books in his hands, grinned at Avril. His broad smile transformed his features in a way his shy smile hadn't. He looked boyish, his eyes glinting with fun.

Avril was pleasantly surprised that Will was the librarian here. Come to think of it, the last time she'd been in a library, her hazy memory was that all the adults seemed old, and the librarian was a woman with steely eyes peering over her glasses and putting her finger to her lips in a silent 'shush'. Will didn't look shush-y at all. His eyes were blue, but they weren't steely. His hair, unfashionably wavy, curled at the nape of his neck. He had an open, friendly face, and dimples. She tried not to stare at him, which would have been weird. But when he smiled, his dimples were deep and he had subtle wrinkles fanning out from the corners of his eyes. He was actually quite sexy, in a studious kind of way. And he was nice, kind, she could tell that by the way he spoke to Hattie. She liked that.

He most definitely was not fuddy-duddy.

'I won't, don't worry!' she told him. The tension that had been in her jaw when she'd stepped into the library – into the unknown – had gone, and as Will returned to the front desk Avril admired his broad shoulders.

She really was staring now.

'I think he's quite taken with you.' Harriet smiled mischievously.

'I think he's just doing his job,' Avril said firmly. She glanced back down at the competition leaflet. 'What's this story about, anyway?' she said to deflect Hattie's attention. What was it about old people and their need to matchmake?

'Whatever you want, that's the fun of it. We haven't started yet.' Hattie paused, then leaned in close to Avril, and her next words were a loud whisper. 'I don't think Will wants us to do it. But at the moment, there's only me and him in the group. Though he doesn't know that yet.'

'Doesn't know what?'

'That he's in the group. But I can't do it on my own, can I? And Will's the one that knows most about books.'

'I see what you mean.' Avril frowned. 'Why doesn't he want you to do it?'

'I don't know, he didn't actually say he didn't. But I could tell. I think you have more chance of getting the truth from him, than I do. You can find out.'

'Hattie.' Avril laughed. 'Honestly, why would he tell me?'

'Because he likes you.' She pursed her lips. 'He was a little bit prickly before you came in, and Will is never prickly. I think it's to do with the other library, in the next town. The big one.'

'Or maybe he's got something else on his mind?'

'No, it was definitely the competition.' Hattie suddenly pointed at the clock on the wall. 'Oh, my goodness. Look at the time.' She pushed herself to a stand. 'Come along dear, we shall look at this later.'

'We shall, shall we?' Avril lifted an eyebrow. 'And where are we going?'

'There!' Hattie gestured triumphantly at the computer, a few metres away. 'It's my turn. So while we're trying to come up with an idea for the start of our story, you can help me use this machine. I was thinking I may not bother today. But seeing as you're here to help, it would be silly to give up.'

Avril didn't normally let anybody boss her around, but something about Hattie's determination buoyed her spirits. She wondered what had happened to transform her from the cantankerous, but quiet Mrs Jamieson who used to come into the salon. Did the library have some strange powers lurking in its depths? The thought brought laughter bubbling into her throat – which burst out when the large trolley bag that had been parked next to Hattie's seat lurched to one side of its own accord.

She stared, and Hattie grabbed the handle.

'Can I help with that?' Avril reached for the bag but was brushed away.

'No, no, I can manage.'

Avril paused, but only for one second, as the question

had to be asked. 'What on earth have you got in there? Your bag just moved.'

'It may have done, or it may not. I didn't notice.' It was Hattie's turn to look slightly uncomfortable, as she dragged it closer to her.

'Is there something inside it?'

'Shh.' Hattie glanced around guiltily. 'I'll show you, if you promise not to tell anybody.'

Avril nodded.

'Promise. Say it.'

'I promise. I won't tell.'

'He's not a something, he's Nutmeg.' Moving around, so that her back was to Will, and shielding his sight of the bag, she opened the zip a couple of inches.

Something small and black pushed its way through. Avril blinked. 'It's a nose.'

'Of course it is.'

'A dog's nose?'

'Well, yes, what did you think it was?'

'A cat?'

'Well, that would be stupid, who would be daft enough to take a cat out in a bag? If it got out, I'd never catch it. You've heard the expression "don't let the cat out of the bag"?'

'Isn't that to do with not telling secrets?' Avril's head was starting to spin.

'Exactly. So don't, or the dog for that matter.'

Avril decided that being direct would probably help. 'Hattie, why have you got a dog in your bag?'

'Because dogs are not allowed in the library.' Hattie's

tone suggested that she thought Avril was being stupid. She unzipped the top a few more inches, and a whole head popped out. The little dog gazed around, slightly bemused.

Hattie stroked his ear. 'Oh dear, I suppose you need the toilet, do you? We have been here rather a long time.' Her tone was quite different, the sharp edge of a moment ago had been replaced by something gentle, and her gaze was soft as she stared down at Nutmeg. Avril swallowed down the lump that had lodged in her throat. This was yet another side of Hattie she'd never seen before. A caring side.

'Will he be okay to walk if I get him out?'

'Of course he will, he's got legs, hasn't he? But you can't just take him out, you must take the bag. Outside.'

Avril smiled at the return of Hattie's tart tone. 'Are you sure dogs aren't allowed in the library?'

'I am, there's a sign. Though if they'd discovered him, I was going to say he was my assistance dog.'

'He's not assisting much at the moment, is he?' Avril raised an eyebrow.

'It's not a full-time position,' Hattie retorted.

'Maybe you should have taken him out and told Will that. It would have saved the poor little thing being in the dark.'

'We're all in the dark in one way or another, dear,' said Hattie mysteriously. 'Right, off you go and take him out while I sign into this machine and then I'll tell you my secret if you tell me yours. We shall start at the beginning.'

'But I haven't—'

'Of course you haven't, dear, but you can make something up, we need material for our story!'

Avril took the handle of the bag and pulled it a bit closer. 'Well, we will have to make something up, I'm far too boring.' The last thing she wanted was for her family life to feature in some story.

Hattie grinned. 'So, you'll do it!'

'What? I never—'

'You just said we! You said *we*'ll have to make it up. Oh, talking about wee, that reminds me, Nutmeg is rather fond of that lamppost on the corner. He likes a little sniff to check out the opposition, then to leave his mark.'

'I'm sure he does.' Avril shook her head ruefully, but Hattie just smiled back at her. Hattie, she realised, had turned into one of those old people that wouldn't take no for an answer. But she guessed it couldn't hurt. She needed time to think, she needed a place to sit and do it — so why not here, and why not help?

'How about a story about finding somebody? You know, somebody that's disappeared and you don't know if they've run away and don't want to be found, or drowned, or don't realise people think they're missing? I like stuff like that on the TV.'

'So do I. That's perfect.' Hattie agreed.

'Really?'

Hattie's smile broadened, and the wrinkles round her eyes deepened in a way that told Avril she really did like the idea.

The swirl inside Avril's stomach spread, and then she smiled, too, and found she couldn't stop. She wasn't being laughed at, or told her idea was daft. Hattie actually liked it.

'Now, if you could take Nutmeg for his constitutional,

afterwards we can get cracking! We will leave sharing secrets until next time, we will "brainstorm" – is that the word, dear? – our entry. Oh, and when you pass the desk, you can tell Will he can fill in an entry for us. It says on here that we have to register. Now we have a team of three, we're the three musketeers!'

Chapter Six

WILL

Red Herrings

'Thanks for bringing the book back.' Will glanced up as Avril walked towards the desk. He felt the need to talk to her, to find out who she was and if she was going to come back. It was daft, he knew it was, but there was something about her. She wasn't the type of girl he normally dated: she didn't read, her hair was a mass of colour, she was wearing heavy, black, thick-soled boots, and a summer dress that should have looked a weird contrast – but strangely worked – and she had the high cheekbones and full lips of a model. And she was more than a match for Hattie's sharp tongue. Not his type at all.

Except, how good had he been at knowing his 'type' in the past? His last girlfriend had dressed conventionally and had been really quite bossy. Sharp. Had she always been like that? he wondered, or had it happened over the course of their relationship. Had his gaze, at the start, been drawn constantly to her as it was now to Avril?

His mind was probably just unconsciously casting Avril as the main female character in the book he'd always thought he'd write but not yet got round to. She seemed interesting, and nice. Nice enough to give old ladies and geeky librarians her time. The perfect empathetic character.

'Hattie's never trusted anybody with her'—he paused—'*bag* before.'

Avril gave him an impish, almost naughty grin. 'You know about the'—it was her turn to pause, her eyes sparkling—'the *bag*.'

'I'd never seen a bag fidget until Hattie came in,' he said, and laughed.

'You could tell her you know.'

'And where's the fun in that?'

Avril tipped her head on one side, studying him. 'You two just like to tease each other, don't you?'

'I like Hattie.' He put his forearms on the desk and leaned forward slightly, lowering his voice so that his words wouldn't carry to Hattie. Although, despite her denials, he knew that her hearing probably wasn't as sharp as it had been. He didn't want to risk upsetting her, though. 'She was fairly quiet and reserved when she first came in, as though she was scared of being here, but she's coming out of her shell. It's nice,' he added simply. He sensed that underneath her crust outer, Hattie was fun and daring.

'Harold, her husband, was pretty grumpy,' Avril said. 'I think he told her what she could and couldn't do. A bit like Lisa tries with me.' She finished with a smile.

'Lisa?'

'My stepmum.'

'But I bet you don't let her boss you around.' There was something about Avril, thought Will, that was similar to Hattie. Underneath he was sure they were strong, like his own mother. That was why they seemed so comfortable with each other, Avril would be good for Hattie, he was sure.

'Never, although it is because of Lisa that I'm here, I guess.'

Will raised an eyebrow.

'I needed to be somewhere she wouldn't find me,' Avril explained. 'I needed to do some thinking without her interfering. I haven't told my family I packed my job in, and they won't be happy.'

'It's not their life, though, is it?' he said softly. But who was he to talk? He'd packed in the life he loved in Cambridge, the bookshop that he'd always wanted, and come back here. The place where he'd been brought up, where his parents still lived. But it had been his choice. In fact, his family had been strongly opposed until he'd pointed out that he'd go back at some point. When the time was right. When he knew they were okay – although he hadn't voiced that last bit. They'd brought him up to be independent, to live his own life, and would hate to feel a burden. They weren't a burden. And working in the library was fine. As a fill-in. He still had books, and he was on the doorstep if his parents needed him. He'd been back two months now. The time had flown – would the twelve-month break he'd had in mind be enough?

'I guess not.' The doubt rang out in Avril's tone.

'And now you've got Hattie and her competition instead of just a job search to deal with.' He smiled.

'She's fine. She said you don't want us to do it, though?'

'I haven't got a problem at all, if she wants to.' He shrugged. 'I don't want her to be disappointed, though. It could be a tough comp, and we've not even got a writing group, that's all.'

Deep down, Will knew those weren't the reasons that made him so reluctant. He'd rather have just ignored the competition; it threatened to bring too many complications back into his life, his head. It brought Lucy. Lucy and Jake. He tried to stop the grimace creeping onto his face, but from the look Avril was giving him, he'd failed. 'She did come here desperate to find somebody, though, so we'd probably be better helping her with that?'

Avril shook her head. 'I think she really wants to do this competition. Maybe she needs some time to decide if she really want to find whoever it is.' Her last words were soft. 'Maybe she just needs to be able to do whatever grabs her right now. Something to take her mind off the scary stuff.'

'I think *you* grab her right now! But I'm pleased she's engaging in something and chatting to people. Honest.' He was. 'I've not seen her talk to people before, let alone let them take her bag out.'

'Ah, yes. I better get on with wheeling it around. Have you seen inside?' She grinned when he shook his head. She lowered her voice to a whisper. 'Come on, come outside with me and have a look at Nutmeg, he's cute!'

She was cute, thought Will. How could he not take up her invitation? It was quiet in the library; nobody would miss him for a few minutes. He was a bit curious about the contents of Hattie's bag and he wanted to chat to Avril, find out more about her job search, what she was looking for. He could help her, that was all, he told himself.

'So you don't' object to us doing the competition?'

'Us?' He raised an eyebrow.

She tutted; she wasn't going to be distracted. 'I might help, it seems mean not to and she said you'd be one of the three musketeers.'

'Oh no.' He shook his head. 'No, I can't do it.'

'But we need a minimum of three.'

'I work in the library, I can't; it's in the rules.'

Avril's hand stilled on the zip of the bag. 'You're the head librarian?'

'Well, no, she doesn't come in on a Thursday, so it's my day in charge. I'm just part-time here.'

'But you're not the head librarian?' she asked again, her voice firm. He tried not to smile; she'd make a good teacher. Was it wrong that it sent a little tingle down his arms?

'Well, no—' He wasn't the head librarian, he wasn't even a permanent member of staff. Just the guy covering maternity leave.

'That's fine, then, you can do it. I had a quick look at that leaflet, and it says in the rules that it's just the people in charge that can't.'

'You're as bad as Hattie! You two are ganging up on me.'

'I will take that as a compliment.' She paused, looked at him with such a direct gaze it was impossible not to listen to her. 'Look, Will, she's an old lady and she wants to do this. I can't write for toffee, I don't even read books, but I said I'd help her, so surely you can, too? Until we find somebody else?' She fluttered her eyelashes in an obvious way that made him laugh. 'She's very persuasive.'

'So are you.'

'Is that a yes, then?' She grinned. 'We've got a team of three, so you can fill in the form for us to enter? It says on the leaflet the librarian has to apply.'

'Ahem.' The cough to his left made Will turn. It was the gentleman who tended to sit in the far corner of the library and read his newspaper, acting completely out of character. He was hovering, almost nervously, almost … deferential, which is not how he normally appeared at all. He was heavy-set, in a way that suggested he'd spent his life sitting behind a desk enjoying good food and wine. Not that Will should judge, he knew it was wrong to jump to conclusions, but the man wasn't typical of the type of person that spent time in the library. He also, according to Hattie, often came across as very assertive, bossy and loud.

Will had never seen the man pick up a book, and he had a very set routine. He arrived ten minutes after the library opened, announced his arrival with a booming 'Morning!', which added to Will's impression that he was a businessman, a man used to taking charge. But a man who was probably in his late fifties, or sixties, now retired. Then he would collect a coffee and settle down with his paper.

You could just see the top of his head, with its greying hair, and have an occasional glimpse of his blue-grey eyes as he turned the pages. But he would barely move until 11:45am, when he'd fold up the paper, check he hadn't left anything on the seat, and with a brief nod in Will's direction, leave.

'Sorry to interrupt'—he was definitely stepping out of his comfort zone—'but I couldn't help overhearing. I'd rather like to have a leaflet, if you'd have me on the team? I did a creative writing course a while ago but have never found the time to knuckle down and start writing a book. I'd quite like to get stuck in with you, if you'd allow me to join?'

'Of course we will have you!' They all turned as Hattie's voice rang out. 'You strike me as the type of man who bosses people around, not writes stories, but you've done a course! Splendid.'

Avril gave her a critical look. 'Have you been listening in, Hattie?' she said, before glancing at Will, who smiled at her and gave the slightest shake of his head. He was pretty sure that Mrs Jamieson hadn't heard anything up until that point.

'Of course I've been listening,' said Hattie, then turned to the man. 'And you are?'

'Stuart,' he said. 'Wonderful, thanks for including me. I'll read the information and confirm next week, shall I?'

'Yes, yes. Give the man a leaflet, Will! Four is much better than three, don't you think?' Harriet beamed.

'Of course it is.' He rolled his eyes, and Avril laughed.

'The fab four!' she said.

'I can't wait to meet the mayor!' Hattie rubbed her hands together gleefully. 'We shall have a meeting next Thursday, if that is convenient for everybody, to make sure we know what we are doing.'

'I think we're all supposed to write our own bits,' said Avril, 'not…'

'Collaborate?' Stuart was studying the leaflet as he spoke.

'Yeah. See, there…' Avril pointed at the second paragraph down.

'Of course, but we still need to meet,' said Hattie. 'So we can confer on what we're all doing. And then Will can do whatever he needs to do to sort our entry out. I'm sure there are lots of forms to fill in, there always are.' She paused to catch her breath. 'Shouldn't you be doing something, young lady?' She stared at Avril, who blushed.

'I'll hold the door for you, shall I?' asked Will, ushering Avril out as quickly as he could as he wasn't sure how long he could keep the laughter inside.

What on earth was he getting involved in? And how was he going to keep his head down and stay uninvolved? He'd just about got his head and heart straightened out, and he wasn't going to let this derail him.

Chapter Seven

STUART

Every Picture Tells a Story

It wasn't until Stuart was getting ready for bed that night that he remembered about the competition. The leaflet crinkled in reminder as he slipped his trousers off. He'd been planning on whipping it out as they were finishing their dessert, but Jo had unveiled something that had left him speechless.

'I've got a surprise to show you.' She had put the plates of cheesecake on the table but didn't sit down. 'I've treated myself! Tony in the gallery has given our art club a discount.'

'You've bought a painting?' He picked up his spoon but let it hover over his dessert. He was slightly surprised Jo had purchased something like that without talking to him first, but to be fair she did have excellent taste and was probably a much better judge than him of what would look good on their walls.

'Oh no, no. I wouldn't do that without asking what you thought. No, I've had one of my own paintings framed! I know it's a bit indulgent, but—'

'It's not indulgent at all! Your paintings are wonderful, it's about time you let other people see them, put them on display! That one you did of the fox was particularly—'

Jo laughed; it was more of a giggle, if he was honest, and should have been a warning. 'Oh no, I've not wasted my money on one of those chocolate-box paintings.'

'Who on earth called them that? I bet it was Celeste, wasn't it?'

Stuart was angry on Jo's behalf, but he wouldn't put it past the woman who taught the art class. She reminded him of a fortune teller, all waving arms, bright jewellery and flamboyant clothes. She was very fond of telling her students that they had to 'let go of their inhibitions'. Celeste liked abstract art and self-expression. Stuart had made one (admittedly brief) attempt to understand the attraction of a painting that consisted purely of coloured stripes but represented the shades of life (what on earth was one of those?) when they'd visited the Tate Modern, but it was beyond him. He could understand poetic, or artistic, licence, but not the idea that it was the viewer's, not the artist's, job to use their imagination. He liked a good painting, a realistic painting. A *proper* painting.

'They're excellent, all your pictures are.' He smiled.

Jo picked up a tissue-wrapped item that had been propped up against the sideboard and walked round to his side of the table. She kissed his cheek.

'Thank you, darling. They're not all excellent by a long way, but I'm proud of one or two of them.'

'We can put it in the hallway, or the lounge, or even here in the dining room where everybody can see it. You know I'm proud of you, don't you?' He put his hand on her waist. He was proud of his wife, and he loved her. A lot.

He'd enjoyed looking after Jo over the years, providing for her and their family, which was why now that he'd retired, he felt at times that he was no longer the man he should be. The man she'd married.

'I do, but think you better wait until you've seen it…' she warned, then carefully folded back the tissue paper, and with a slightly self-conscious smile turned it round and propped it on the table in front of him.

Stuart's spoon clattered onto the table. The words of congratulation that had been on his tongue deserted him. He was speechless. With an effort he closed his open mouth and swallowed, in an attempt to bring some moisture, and the ability to talk, back.

'Can you tell who it is?' Out of the corner of his eye, he could see his wife's worried frown, but he couldn't drag his gaze away from the picture. The masterpiece.

'Oh yes,' the words struggled out, 'I'd recognise that meat cleaver anywhere,' he finished weakly.

'Celeste says it's my best yet,' Jo said cheerfully.

Stuart blinked, he couldn't think of a single appropriate thing to say, he was just turning the strange taste in his mouth over.

'She wants to put it in the summer exhibition, isn't that exciting!'

Oh, my God. Stuart finally managed to work his mouth again. 'The summer exhibition?' he echoed weakly.

'Yes, I told you,' she chided gently. 'In the library. Celeste does it every year. We have a display board near the entrance for a whole week! Isn't that amazing?'

'Amazing.' In the library? He was sure she'd not told him. 'Are you sure your life model, George, won't mind having all his wares on display, for the whole town to see?'

From the art in front of Stuart, George was as naked as the day he was born, but hairier. Very much hairier.

'Oh, he said he wouldn't mind.' Jo leaned in, lowering her voice conspiratorially, 'I think he's a bit of an exhibitionist, actually. He loves the attention.'

'I bet he does.' Stuart hardly recognised the strangled tone as his own. And he found that wherever he tried to look, his gaze was drawn back to the painting. He couldn't help himself, however much he didn't want to see what he was seeing. George's florid cheeks, his pallid chest. The cleaver…

And what were they going to do with a framed original of the local butcher, with only a carving implement preserving his modesty? There was no way Stuart could eat his meals in here with that, literally, hanging over him.

Perhaps he could arrange for somebody to steal it when the exhibition was on?

'Half the group painted George.' Mercifully Jo put the painting down on the floor, where he couldn't see it without craning his neck. 'And the other half painted a still life, a rabbit that George had hanging in his shop.'

'A rabbit,' Stuart repeated. He couldn't say he had a

liking for dead rabbits, but it might have been marginally better than a frankly indecent painting of George.

'The exhibition is about life and death. Light and dark. You know?'

He didn't know. But he would very much like it if this exhibition were to be in the dark – preferably total darkness – so that nobody could actually see the paintings.

Stuart pushed his plate into the middle of the table. For some reason the rich cheesecake no longer appealed. In fact, it was making him feel slightly nauseous.

'Sophie didn't fancy either – you know, the rabbit or George – so she just did a charcoal of his hand curled round the cleaver. She said it was symbolic.'

Stuart cleared his throat. 'Sounds an, erm, good representation, the hand and instrument of death.'

'Celeste is very good at exploring themes and meanings. The exhibition is going to have the two sides, so that it leads you from one to the other.'

Had the whole town gone mad? How could he ever look the butcher in the face again? He'd have to buy his sausages from the supermarket. And how would he ever face Will and his writing group if Celeste filled the library – his refuge – with naked images of George – one of which would have his wife's signature along the bottom?

What on earth would Hattie think?

The groan escaped unbidden. He wanted to bury his head in his hands.

'Are you okay, darling?'

'Fine, fine, a touch of indigestion I think.'

'You don't want your dessert?'

Stuart looked across at his happy wife, who picked up her spoon and tucked into her cheesecake with relish.

'Have you had a nice day, darling?' she asked, her mouth half full.

'Not bad, not bad. Not as exciting as yours, though. Would you like me to pop that up on the wall later?'

'Oh no, no, don't worry about that. I've got Steve coming around tomorrow as there's also that shelf in the bathroom that's gone a bit wobbly.'

'I could—'

'It's fine. Steve's very good, and tidy. And he's got all the tools.'

Stuart's gaze strayed back in the direction of the painting. So, it seemed, had George.

That was the problem with his retirement. Neither of them had adjusted. Jo had already found her DIY man, and her gardener, and somebody to fix almost anything, while Stuart was working. He'd always been too busy to do jobs around the house when he was employed. Jo had been uncomplaining, and practical. She'd coped. She'd found a 'man' to do the things she couldn't, or Stuart couldn't, do.

Stuart hadn't done anything around the house for years, he realised. Was he still capable of using a drill? Was it like riding a bicycle and you never lost the skill once acquired? If he was honest, without his job Stuart felt that he wasn't useful, not good at anything. Redundant. Had he ever been good at anything? There was a time when he was at least good, successful, at his job. But he hadn't felt that was true towards the end. Before he was pushed into leaving, before he felt ready. And he still wasn't sure if they'd known, if his failing had been part of the reason he'd been on that list. He had been too driven, too involved in his work, too desperate to still feel valued for his experience at a time when the average age of workers in the company was getting younger by the day. He'd lost sight of who he was, what he should value. The health of his workers.

He'd failed. It hurt. It was on his mind however many hobbies he thought of taking up, however much he tried to occupy his time.

His failure was inescapable. He had let a member of his staff down. He had forgotten, if he'd ever known, how to listen.

He couldn't find a way to explain to Jo how he felt – and he didn't want to lumber her with his problems – but he could be there for her. Be a better husband.

He wanted to listen to Jo. He didn't want to let her down.

He wanted to be that man now, the one who could do the jobs she needed do. The person she turned to. A provider. He'd lost his role, and his purpose.

He also felt like he was losing Jo.

'I think I need to work out how to use a drill,' he said, trying to make light of it.

'I'm not sure that's you, dear.'

He wasn't sure either. But what *was* him? He didn't know anymore.

There was one thing that he did know, though. There was no way he could take part in the writing group and enter the competition. If they won, it would be an embarrassing disaster.

Unfortunately, the leaflet about the competition fell out of Stuart's trouser pocket as he got undressed ready for bed. And even more unfortunately, Jo spotted it, and it was in her hand before he could react.

'Oh, what's this?'

'Nothing, just something somebody put in my hand when I was leaving the library, needs to go in the bin.' He reached out to take it, but Jo was quicker and snatched it away. She looked it over.

'It's a competition, to write a story! You've always said you'd like to write a book, Stuart. This is perfect, how exciting.'

So much excitement, all in one day, he didn't know if he could take any more.

'I don't think it's really up my street,' he said. 'It's for a writing group. We each write a different chapter that must follow on from the one before. It's not as if I'm writing a novel of my own, I'm afraid.' He held his hand out, but Jo clutched the piece of paper close to her chest.

'Oh no, Stuart, you're not wriggling out of this one. You wanted a challenge and now you've got one. And look, you can win entry to the mayor's garden party!' Her eyes were sparkling in her gentle, teasing way.

'You're making fun of me.'

'I most definitely am not. Oh, Stuart, this could be wonderful.' She sat down on the bed next to him. 'Who knows, this could put you on the path to writing your own book. It couldn't do any harm could it?' She leaned in to him. Her warm body against his. The back of her hand resting against his. 'Wouldn't it be wonderful to do something together, well almost together, at least in the same place. Your writing, and my art?'

'You think it would be a good idea?'

'I do. You've always told a good tale, and you're a natural organiser, you could take charge.'

'I think they've already got somebody for that.' Despite his mood, Stuart felt the smile tug at the corner of his mouth.

'Oh, really? A proper author?'

'No, I don't think anybody who has been published before can enter. It's an elderly lady.'

'How elderly?' He could feel Jo's gentle laughter vibrate through his body.

'More elderly than us! She's quite a character, I think.'

'I am imagining Miss Marple,' said Jo. 'Is the story going to be a murder mystery?'

'I wouldn't put it past her! Although everybody writes their own bit, so you have to go with the flow, I suppose. She's roped in this young girl who says she doesn't read, let alone write.'

'How young?'

'Twenties I suppose, pretty.'

'I can see I'm going to have to pop into the library and keep an eye on you all. What a group, how can you fail?' Jo was chuckling and Stuart found himself joining in.

'How indeed?' he said, thinking about Hattie, Avril and Will. They were quite a motley crew, not at all what you'd expect from a writing group – well not what he'd expected.

But maybe it would give them an edge. Maybe they'd come up with something more original than any more traditional set of writers would. And that's what this competition was about, according to the leaflet.

Not perfect prose, but originality.

'You are going to do it, aren't you, darling?'

He nodded. Smiled. 'I am. Yes,' he said more forcefully, 'I am. You better start to look for a suitable hat, you don't get invited to the mayor's garden party every day of the year you know!'

Chapter Eight

AVRIL

Ghosts of the Past

Avril had begun to wonder if she was going a little bit crazy, if she'd lost her grip on reality.

Hattie had been right: she did have secrets. Like leaving her job. That had been impetuous, and she was being dishonest – well, lying by omission – not daring to tell her family. And then there was her diary. That was a secret she wasn't going to share.

It wasn't proper writing. Nobody else saw it, corrected her spelling or grammar, it was just notes. A letter. That's what it really was, a letter to her mother.

Because she missed her. She missed her so much sometimes that her chest burned with a dull pain she couldn't escape from. She wanted her so much, specially at times like this when she didn't know what she should be doing with her life and needed the help only a mother could give.

When Avril had lived with her dad and Lisa, she would

sit in her bedroom and stare at the wall, willing her mum, Ophelia – Phee – to appear and trying to imagine what she would look like now. What she would say. What she'd tell her she should do. Because she really didn't know. Her mother was a ghostly image who was frozen in the past. Avril had so few vivid memories of her, only faded family photos and hazy movies in her head.

And now she had a secret she really couldn't share. Phee had appeared. Not in her head because she'd been thinking about her, but because she'd actually seen her.

Avril had been leaving the house when she glanced up from her phone and there Phee was. On the other side of the road. The word 'Mum' had frozen on Avril's tongue. By the time her shocked body had come back to life, it had been too late. A lorry had obscured her vision for a moment, and when it had driven past, her mother had gone.

Had it been her mind playing tricks? Conjuring up an image of the person she was desperate to see? Because she couldn't have seen her. Phee was dead. Avril had been four years old when her mother had left her life – old enough to have some understanding of death, but not to know what it would mean to her.

Avril wasn't sure that she *could* miss her actual mother. How did you miss somebody you hardly knew? She missed the image she'd got in her head of what and who Phee would be now, if she was still alive. She missed the idea of having a mum, more than the actual person that Phee had been. Because she'd hardly known her at all. And it was the not knowing that hurt the most. Avril had no idea if, like she did, her mother loved pizza and hated anchovies. She didn't know if she loved the background hum of music, the warmth of the morning sun on her skin. She didn't know if Phee would have loved the woman she'd grown into or would have despaired of her choices.

Even the name Phee felt strange on her tongue.

It wasn't a name that was spoken in her dad's – or should that be Lisa's – house.

Avril wasn't going to call it 'home', because it never really had been, and moving into her own place had been a relief. She'd only stayed as long as she had at Lisa's because of her dad.

Ophelia, her mum's full name, tasted exotic, unusual, on her tongue when she whispered it out loud. Magical. It conjured up a flamboyant, unconventional image. Somebody who didn't care about who, or what, you were supposed to be. Which, Avril supposed, was why she'd decided she had to do things for herself. Be an individual, not sit in the slot that Lisa was trying to carve out for her.

But she was so sure she'd seen her mother. And she had nobody to tell.

———

Avril jumped at the strident ring of the doorbell. She was still in her pyjamas, sitting at the kitchen table, a piece of toast in one hand, while her other hand had been scrolling through 'job vacancy' pages on her laptop, until she'd been distracted by thoughts of Hattie.

Hattie had wanted to trade secrets. She was looking for somebody. Was it a lover from her past? The thought brought a smile to Avril's face. She could imagine Hattie with a spicy past, Harold had seemed far too strict and boring for her.

When she'd woken up on Friday morning, she'd had a strange urge to go back to the library, to ask Will what Hattie was up to, to find out more about the competition.

But she'd got there to discover it was Will's day off, and there was no sign of Hattie. The library felt strangely empty without them. In fact, it was very quiet. There was nobody using the computers, so she'd managed to book one. She'd sat for a while, looked at job vacancies that held no appeal at all, and stared at the competition poster.

She was just about to pack up and go to the café for some lunch when the bright spine of a book on the nearest shelf caught her eye. She wandered down the row of shelves, feeling slightly self-conscious, then gained confidence as she realised that nobody was interested. Her gaze flickered along the spines. How did you select one book from so many? Did you wait for one to grab your interest?

And then it happened. The emerald cover drew her back, demanded a second look. Is that what books did when you were a proper reader?

She didn't know. But this one caught her eye, and she slid it out. It was the book that she'd found the day before. The striking cover that drew her gaze, that compelled her to take it with her back to the table she'd been sitting at. She sat down again. Traced her finger over the gold lettering, and then she opened the cover, flipped the pages over to the prologue that she'd skimmed over the day before. Slowly started to read…

Before Avril knew it, she had read a whole chapter. She closed the book and made her way over to the front desk and the librarian.

'Can I borrow this?' she asked. She didn't quite know why, but she wanted to know what happened in the story.

'Of course.' The librarian smiled. 'I've just registered your details, haven't I? I'll just check it out for you.'

And then Avril had taken the book with her to the café and read. And for the first time in her life, she discovered that reading for pleasure was so, so different to doing it at school, where it was obligatory.

This morning she'd felt it again, the desire to head back to the library. But she hadn't, because that could have caused as many questions as *not* going into town on Friday would have done. Because Monday had always been her day off at the hairdressers. Monday was the day they expected her to be at home.

It was weird, though; Avril hadn't been able to get Hattie out of her head on the way home on Thursday. And despite not having picked up a book to read in as long as she could remember – she didn't own a single one – she felt pulled back to the library. Avril wanted to help Hattie, because it seemed that Hattie was starting over. And if a woman of Hattie's age could, why couldn't Avril?

The more she'd thought about the competition, and the further into her book that she'd got, the more the idea had hooked her. She wanted to do it. Even though Avril wasn't sure how good her contribution would be – after all, she couldn't decide what to do with her own life, let alone write a story about someone else's – perhaps it would be easier to put all her ideas into a character she invented?

The doorbell rang again, so popping what was left of her breakfast in her mouth, Avril went to answer the door.

'Dad!' She grinned as her father wrapped her in a bear hug. She wasn't usually a huggy person, she liked her space, but her father was different. 'What are you doing here?'

'Lisa's dropping something off at Chloe's for the new baby, so I thought I'd escape the cooing for a bit!' He grinned. When she'd been growing up, that grin had often been strained – being a single dad must have been hard work – so now she loved seeing him happy. People had always said she was her father's daughter, and now when she looked in a mirror, she could see it. They shared the same hazel eyes flecked with green, the high cheekbones, the slim, wiry frame, the look of impish mischief. But where her hair was shoulder length and streaked with colour, his was a mid-brown, short and neat. Where she loved a splash of colour, he stuck with traditional shades.

It had been just the two of them for a long time, but even back when she was younger, she could remember that sadness hanging around him. A weight, a weariness. When she was at school, she'd been aware that her home wasn't the same as everybody else's. There wasn't a mother, cakes and trendy clothes. Her dad was sad, and grieving for her mum, and it had felt wrong to giggle and enjoy silly jokes. She had never invited friends back after school.

She hadn't been bothered. Her dad was enough. But she'd wished she could have made him laugh more often.

Now that he was lighter, relaxed, happy, Avril was happy

for him. It was just a shame that the things that made his life better – Lisa, Chloe and Dawn – had made hers worse.

But at least she had this place now. Her bolthole. The savings fund that her mum had set up for her when she was little had made it possible.

For a long time, Avril felt that those savings were all she had left of her mother, and when they ran out, that would be that. The last link with Phee would be gone, too.

Because of that, Avril had been thrifty. Scared to dig too much into her savings. Until it had occurred to her that maybe buying a flat, investing in something solid, would mean she had something forever connected to her mum.

She'd loved her flat from the day she moved in. It was freedom, independence, the chance to be herself and not always feel judged. She bought bright cushions and colourful throws that clashed. She liked to think that the Phee in her had been released.

And then Chloe, her stepsister, had bought a house up the road. The twins might only be a couple of years older than her, but those two years felt like a gulf. They had steady jobs, husbands, babies – or in Dawn's case, baby plans.

All the things Lisa thought that Avril should aspire to.

Which was why admitting the only thing on that list she'd had – a steady job – was no more, was not something she had felt ready to do.

'Looking for a new job, are we?'

Shit, her dad had spotted her open laptop.

'I've left the salon.' There, she'd done it. Told him. She'd never lied to her dad. They had a pact. Honest, open, together. HOT. He'd said they were two hotties, made a joke of it. But there had been a seriousness behind his smile that she'd taken to heart, even though she was only ten years old when he'd first said it. Just before she went to high school. From then it had been their mantra. He'd been preparing for her transition to the new school and, she guessed, her teens. Her wild years.

Except, Avril hadn't really had wild years. She didn't want to rebel. She didn't want a boyfriend, or crazy nights out. She'd just wanted to know she had her dad. Because he was the only constant in her life.

'Can you, erm…' She stopped herself. She had been about to ask him not to tell Lisa yet, but that wasn't fair, she couldn't ask somebody else to lie for her. Specially not her dad.

'Keep schtum for a bit?' He hugged her to him. He'd guessed what was on her mind. Like he always did.

'Well maybe not offer the information if she doesn't ask?'

They shared a smile. 'I can do that,' he said, then glanced over at her computer again. 'So, have you got promotion in mind? I suppose you'd been there quite a while and it's small, not many opportunities.'

Not many opportunities to do anything but style hair.

'I want to do something else.'

He looked puzzled. 'But why? I thought you liked it? You did say that hairdressing was what you really wanted to do.'

It was true. She had said that. When she was still at school. When Lisa was pushing her to go and work for her uncle at his factory.

Seeing the advert for a junior at the salon when she was

seventeen had been a lifeline she'd grabbed without really thinking. Though she hadn't known what career she wanted, she was sure she didn't want to work in a factory. Even if, as Lisa said, there would have been 'lots of opportunity for progression, even for somebody who hasn't got many qualifications'. That was typical of Lisa, to point out Avril's shortcomings. 'And you are family,' Lisa had added.

But Avril hadn't wanted to progress somewhere because she 'was family', she wanted to tread her own path. Even back then she'd known that much. She liked her uncle, he was a nice guy, and she was sure his factory was a good place to work. If that was what you wanted. She didn't.

Avril wanted to reassure her father now. She knew he'd always been worried that at some point she'd go off the rails and she didn't want him to be worried. But what was she supposed to say? The truth, that she didn't know what she wanted to do, to be, that she'd never really wanted to work in the salon, it had just been a way out.

'When I was at school, I thought hairdressing was what I wanted, but I don't know now … I don't think it's really me, Dad.' She looked at him, willing him to understand. 'But I will find something, soon, I promise.'

He smiled, his gentle smile. 'I know you will, Avril. But if you're short of—'

'I'll be fine.' If he gave her money, Lisa really would go off on one. And Avril had enough money at the moment – enough put to one side to keep her going for a while, if she was careful. 'Cup of tea?' She leaned across and pushed the top of the laptop closed.

'Sounds good.' He reached out, took her hands in his.

'You take your time, Avril. I'm a bit jealous, if I'm honest.' His gaze was direct, but there was something sad, wistful in his voice.

'What do you mean, jealous?'

'I was never brave enough to take the plunge, do something I really wanted. Always played it safe. You do it while you're young enough, while you can.'

'You had to work, Dad. You couldn't just stop.' He'd had to look after her.

'It wasn't just the money, I couldn't pack it in because I'm not made that way, Av. That's why.' He kissed the top of her head. 'You didn't get those brave genes from me.'

His smile was gentle. It left an unspoken question. *Am I like Mum, would she have done the same?*

'Why don't you make a list, write down the things you love doing?' her dad suggested. 'Then you might hit on the right job for you. Sometimes you need to look at things from a different angle, you know, take the pressure off.'

'That's a brilliant idea. Thanks, Dad.'

'What was that about a cuppa? And a biscuit?'

He held a hand out and she moved in close letting him wrap her in his strong arms.

Now would be the perfect time to mention her mum. Tell him she thought she'd seen her. Tell him her heart ached to know more about the woman she'd shared such a short time with. But why stir up his feelings as well as her own?

'Sure!' she said. 'Actually, I might be entering a writing competition at the library…' She felt herself blush.

Her dad raised an eyebrow. 'Well, well, an author in the family! That's a turn-up.'

Avril laughed self-consciously. 'Not exactly, it's with a team of people, it's only a short story, not a proper novel or anything. But I thought I needed to do something while I was looking for a job.'

'Good for you. You get more like your mum every day you know.' He smiled at her, but it wasn't his normal cheeky, full-on smile, it was muted. Wistful. He was thinking about Phee. And it was making him sad. She didn't want him to be sad.

'Dad—'

'Chop-chop, kettle on, girl!' His forced good humour tugged at Avril's heart.

She turned to fill the kettle. She was glad she hadn't made him talk about her mum. It wasn't fair.

But she'd give anything to know *how* she was like her mum.

Chapter Nine

HATTIE

Stories and Secrets

She wouldn't say it out loud, but there were days when Hattie wished she had never sold her spacious house and bought the retirement apartment. At the time it had seemed like a good idea. After sixty years of being told what to do, she wanted to make a choice of her own – she'd needed to escape Harold and her suffocating past. But sometimes she wondered if she'd been too hasty, if she'd replaced one cage with another. She missed the space, the garden and – more than anything – the privacy. Yes, that was the crux of the matter.

She was hemmed in by *people*.

The place was quite pleasant in its own way, and easy to maintain. Cleaning had never been enjoyable exactly, more a necessary evil – as Harold insisted that there was never a speck of dust, he didn't want people to think they were slovenly. Not that he ever let anybody over the threshold to see how pristine she had kept their home. So from that point of view, she didn't regret scaling down. But the place was full of old people, interfering people. They tended to talk nonsense and they had a tendency to invade her privacy.

Hattie had always been happy with her own company.

The library people were okay, she had chosen to be with them. They were younger, interesting. They didn't talk about hip replacements and hearing aids.

Hattie slipped on her favourite shoes, the navy blue, smart but sensible ones, with the tiny heel. She'd always liked a heel, but at her age she wasn't going to risk a fall. A fall would mean a stick, or even worse one of those mobility scooter things, or home help, God forbid. She wasn't going down that route. It would make her feel old, which she wasn't. She checked her hair in the hall mirror.

Yes, the library people were fine. Especially young Avril.

'We liked Avril, didn't we?' she asked Nutmeg, before resting her bag against the chair so that he could jump in. 'Shall we go and see if she comes back? I have a feeling she might, you know. I do hope so.' The little long-haired dachshund wagged his tail, then jumped into the bag. 'Off we go, then.'

As Hattie walked out of the apartment-block lift, the first thing that caught her eye was the large poster on the noticeboard. She stopped dead.

'Hattie!' The shout, and wild gesture, jolted her back to the present, and she realised that the doors were just about to shut on her bag.

'Balderdash!' She swung it forward violently, nearly flooring her good Samaritan, but hardly noticing as her heart was going ten to the dozen. 'Oh, Nutmeg!' She peered into the bag, but the little dog just peered back, oblivious to the danger he'd been in. 'You could have been as flat as a pancake.' He huffed, and curled up again, like a tiny fox – nose to tail.

Reassured, Hattie took a couple of steps closer and stared at the poster intently. She couldn't believe her eyes! What was the poster about the writing competition doing on the noticeboard in the entrance hall of the apartment block?

That wasn't the main reason she was staring at it, though. The terrible twins, Mabel and Margaret, were heading her way. If she looked busy, they wouldn't bother her. She edged along slightly so that the poster about the latest coach trip was in front of her, instead. Looking busy was one thing, but she didn't want to draw attention to the competition.

If she spoke to the ladies, they'd want to know why she wasn't going to the coffee morning in the lounge. And she couldn't exactly tell them that she wasn't interested in their gossip (they loved to tittle-tattle, she'd never known such busybodies). She might be eighty-seven years old, but she wasn't ready to waste her days talking about toilet aids, and who was about to die next. She also didn't want to sit in the community lounge with a bunch of old people who had nothing better to do. She had a very good jar of coffee in her flat, thank you very much, and she liked to share her biscuits with Nutmeg, her dog. Not some nosy stranger. And she had the library. They did proper coffee and biscuits.

When she'd bought her luxury retirement apartment (it was a flat, but for some reason the estate agent insisted on calling it an apartment) she hadn't realised that so many of her new neighbours would be quite so old. Mabel was ninety next month. How could she not know that? The woman insisted on telling everybody – and Margaret, who wasn't actually Mabel's twin sister but the two of them acted as though they were glued together, was eighty-four. Hattie could have told them her own age, but it wasn't a competition, was it? And it was none of their business, they weren't her friends, and it was personal. My goodness, if you started to share your date of birth with all and sundry, where would it end? Hattie liked to keep herself to herself, like she and Harold had always done.

Hattie had been brought up to be polite, it was one of the things her mother had insisted on – 'If you've nothing nice to say, say nothing at all', she used to say – so Hattie bit her lip and stared at the noticeboard.

That was another thing she didn't like about this place. Noticeboards were for community centres, old people's homes, *residential* (she gave a little shudder) homes, not *luxury* private apartments that you'd paid good money for. They were also for libraries.

'Will you be coming for coffee, Harriet?' That made her bristle as well. Why couldn't Mabel call her Hattie? Harriet belonged in the past, with Harold. 'It is Thursday you know!'

'I am well aware of the day, thank you.' Did the woman think she'd lost her marbles? She glanced briefly at her. Mabel was the talker, Margaret just nodded. 'Sorry, I'm busy. I have things to do.' She would have quite liked to have read the notices properly, just in case there was something of interest, but she had no choice now. She had told them she was busy, so she would have to go. Immediately. 'I need to go to the library.'

Now why had she told them that?

'The lounge has a library, Harriet. You could select a book and have coffee with us. We don't bite you know, ha ha.'

Hattie tried not to grimace. Most of them didn't have their own teeth, so she had no fear of being eaten alive.

And, oh yes, the lounge did indeed have what the sales details for the apartment had listed as a 'library' – but it was just a bookcase and not a very big one at that. Harold would have told her it was satisfactory, sufficient for what he considered her needs. He hadn't just disliked proper libraries, he had disliked books. Her father had been the same. Thought they'd give a person fanciful ideas above their station and fill their head with rubbish. Had they both been scared that she'd learn something, that she'd have ideas of her own? Ideas above her station?

Maybe they'd been right. Discovering the library and all the wonderful murder mysteries had given her a new zest for life. In fact, if she'd read them earlier, she might have been plotting Harold's demise years ago. So he could have had a point.

'I don't want a coffee, thank you very much. I have research to do.'

Margaret raised an eyebrow but didn't speak. She'd make a good puppet, thought Hattie.

'And my name is Hattie.'

'Well, your loss,' Mabel paused, for what seemed to be a

very long time, then spoke very deliberately, '*Hattie*. Come on, Margaret.'

She turned abruptly and started to march towards the door of the lounge.

Margaret glanced at Hattie, winked, and mouthed, 'It's Peg, actually.'

Hattie turned back to the wall, trying to stifle the chuckle. Well, who would have thought Margaret had a sense of humour and a mind of her own?

Which reminded her, she had a mind of her own. She didn't have to live by anybody else's rules. Unless they were proper laws. She glanced around quickly to check there was nobody else around, and then she quickly reached up and ripped the library poster down off the wall. 'You don't mind, do you?' she whispered to Nutmeg, as she stuffed it into the bag next to him. 'You can rip it up if you like.'

She didn't want rivals; they had a team already. They didn't need anybody else.

She rubbed her hands together. And she hadn't been lying; she was busy, she had her research to do, but first she had a meeting with the rest of her team. The word made her smile. Team. She'd never been part of a team before.

Chapter Ten

WILL

The Notebook

'Well, good morning, Hattie. How are you this morning?'

'I am very well, thank you, Will.'

'Wonderful.' He was very tempted to ask about her dog, who, from the way her bag was rocking, was evidently feeling a bit restless this morning. 'Your team member has beaten you in!'

Will had come into the library this morning half hoping that Hattie or Avril would *not* appear, and the whole idea of entering the competition would die a quiet death. The other half of him was hoping that they would both be there. He liked the cantankerous Hattie, he'd have worried about her if she hadn't appeared, and he'd had to admit to himself when he'd opened up the library earlier that he would quite like to see Avril again.

His heart had given a little lurch when he'd logged onto

the system on Monday morning, to find out that she'd registered with the library, and had taken a book out. If she'd taken one, then she had to come back to return it, didn't she? Although he was rather disappointed that her last visit had been on Friday, his day off. He'd hoped that wasn't going to be her regular visiting day, so he was relieved when she strode up to his desk this morning.

If he was honest with himself, he'd much rather she was here and he had to endure the competition, than never see her again.

'Shall we all get a coffee before our meeting?' Hattie didn't wait for an answer but walked off towards her normal seat.

'We shall,' he said softly, following her over so that he could make the coffee. 'Would you like one, Avril?'

'I've already got one thanks, and'—she bent closer to Hattie, but he could hear the whispered words—'water for Nutmeg?'

'Here you go.' He put Hattie's drink down and looked her in the eye. 'I think you should let the poor dog out.'

She gave him what she obviously thought was an innocent look, but in fact looked anything but.

Will shook his head. 'I think you should let him out, Hattie. We all know what you've got in there.'

'You do?'

He nodded. 'I do. We shall call him…'

'An assistance dog?'

'I can order a yellow lead that says that?' Avril said, grinning. 'They do leads and coats, he'd look quite important!' She unzipped the bag and reached down to lift

Nutmeg out. 'Then it is official. Even if he does only work part-time.'

'Thank you, dear. I like things to be official.'

'Great.' Will put his mug of coffee down and pulled out a chair, thankful that they weren't going to be distracted by a fidgeting bag. 'Right, well, ladies, I did fill in the online entry, but there is a bit of a problem.'

'You can't do it? You're not allowed?' said Avril with a frown.

'Nope, not that.' Although he'd still rather not be involved, but what choice did he have? Hattie was more animated than he'd ever seen her, and he didn't want to smother that. And if they entered, then Avril would keep returning. For a while. Which would be nice. 'We really need four people, that's what it suggests in these guidelines – so that there's plenty of variety, and it doesn't become too big a task for anybody. They're trying to keep it fun, not intimidating or too time-consuming.' He laid a copy of the leaflet, which he'd photocopied so that it was twice the size of the original, on the table. 'We're writing a novella, which is much shorter than a full-length novel. It suggests between ten thousand and twenty thousand words, so, around twelve chapters of a thousand words each would work, but total word count is entirely up to us. As I mentioned,' he pointed to one of the paragraphs, 'it suggests that if there are at least four people in a team, then each member can contribute between three and five chapters.' He looked at Hattie, then Avril. 'It does seem sensible to me, there isn't too much work for any of us, but we do get a chance to influence the way the story goes. If there's only the three of us, then we might feel that we've only just finished our part and it's our turn again.'

'And we'll definitely have to write four or five each,' Avril said.

'But we could manage that,' Hattie said stubbornly.

'We could, but the more people we have then the more different ideas will be coming in, which will make a much more interesting story.'

'Hmm.' Hattie frowned.

'Ahem.' They all turned. The cough had come from behind the newspaper, which slowly lowered. 'I've reviewed the document you gave me, and would be delighted to join the team, if you will have me.'

'Fabulous! Of course we will have you.' Hattie spoke before Will had a chance. 'Come and sit next to me'—she paused for a moment, then finished—'Stuart!' triumphantly. 'So we're all set,' she said, looking at Will. 'Any more problems?' There was a note of challenge in her tone that made Will smile.

'Not at all.'

'Your teeth are gritted, dear. Is this personal?'

Will sighed. 'My teeth aren't gritted, Hattie.'

'Well, your jaw is locked. I think you need to tell your'— she paused—'team, what the issue is.'

Will looked around, all three of them – well, four, if you included the dog – were studying him intently.

'Well, it's not an issue exactly.' Their stares didn't falter. 'If you have to know, it just feels a bit awkward. I work for the library, and it's a library competition and—'

'But you're perfectly entitled, it says so in the rules!' Hattie tapped the leaflet that was on the table.

'Guidelines,' Avril said, her cheeky grin almost making Will feel better. But if he dropped out, they'd be back to three in the team, and he'd just told them it was better to have four!

'And I bet the other libraries do it.' Hattie's eyes narrowed; she'd seen him flinch. 'Ha! That's the problem, isn't it? One of the other libraries.'

'Okay, okay, Miss Marple! The organiser'—he took a deep breath—'Lucy Martin, is, was—'

'Ah! A lover! I knew it,' interrupted Hattie gleefully.

'Shh.' Avril nudged Hattie. 'Let Will tell us in his own time.'

'You think she'll try and scupper our chances?'

'No, I didn't say that, Hattie. I'm sure she wouldn't cheat.'

'This will make an excellent story! Hang on, let me write her name down.'

Stuart chuckled and Avril shook her head. 'You can't use Will's life as your story!' she reprimanded.

'Oh, we'll use some artistic licence, change the names.'

'And you wonder why I didn't want to do this,' Will said in a resigned tone.

'So, what is the real problem? Is there another man involved?' Hattie leaned forward.

'She has a boyfriend, Jake,' Will admitted. He'd never told anybody about Lucy and Jake, and his humiliation. Why on earth was he telling a group of strangers? Maybe this was how group therapy worked. 'Jake's an aspiring writer and he's bound to enter, with her help.'

'Ha! That's the important word.' Hattie nodded.

'What is?' asked Avril.

'Aspiring.' Stuart spoke for the first time.

'Exactly.' Hattie agreed. 'We're all aspiring writers, and I think we can be just as good as him, even if he is cheating and sleeping with the enemy!'

'Hattie!' Avril objected, but there was laughter lurking behind her eyes. Will found that he didn't mind. She was more than pretty when she smiled like that. She sparkled with fun. Her and Hattie were going to be difficult to keep in check.

'We shall kick them into touch! You will get your revenge.'

'Who said I wanted—'

'It is the things that people don't say that are more telling than the things that they do!' Hattie wagged a finger at him. 'Now are you going to start this meeting?'

'I thought you'd called it, Hattie.' He raised an eyebrow.

Hattie huffed. 'You can't expect me to be in charge, do you know how old I am?'

'Well, I'll lead this meeting, then, but you're in charge. Okay?'

Hattie nodded, looking quite satisfied.

'Okay, I entered our team online and they sent over a notebook.'

'A notebook?'

'Our entry has to be handwritten,' Will clarified.

There was a collective intake of breath.

'My handwriting is terrible,' muttered Avril. 'Nobody will be able to read it.'

'Nonsense,' declared Hattie, and Will shared a sideways smile with Avril. 'This is perfect.'

'It does sound rather nice.' Stuart was nodding. 'There's something more intimate when you write rather than type.'

Will had to agree, he liked a nice pen that sat comfortably in his hand. A pen he could twist in his fingers while he was thinking. There was something deliberate, connected about actually handwriting something. The process slowed, there was time to think, to imagine. And he liked a beautiful notebook, and this one was. It was, as Hattie said, perfect.

'I agree with Stuart,' said Hattie. 'I rather dislike using a computer; there is something impersonal about it…' She paused. 'Something detached.'

Avril's eyes widened at Hattie's speech, delivered as it was in a 'telephone' voice, as Will's mother would say.

'I suppose it's difficult if you're not used to typing,' Avril said gently, and Will warmed even more to her. She was instinctively kind; it wasn't forced, or to impress anybody. He liked kindness.

'Good heavens, no!' Hattie's tone had reverted to its normal brusqueness that he was used to. 'What do you take me for, girl? I was a touch-typist you know. I spent a lot of my youth typing things up for the type of person – type of man – who liked to show off his vocabulary, that's why I know so many long words! I find that those with the least accomplishments show off most, don't you?' She frowned.

'Computers are overcomplicated, though, you have to locate the "on" button for a start. How on earth are you supposed to work that out? Proper typewriters don't have that. Why do they have to hide the things? It's not clever, you know, I bet a man was responsible for the wretched switch, a woman would put it in plain sight, wouldn't she?'

Avril nodded. They were all stunned into silence.

'I'm sure it's the same as a mobile phone, isn't it?' Hattie went on. 'Harold never let me use the mobile, you know. That was his. He didn't like me being able to do things. But I soon sorted that after he went. I got my own mobile! I knew it couldn't be that hard, could it, if he managed to do it?'

'Definitely, er, not.' Will thought he needed to bring things back on track. He had work to do. At this rate it would be lunchtime before he got started.

'I'm getting distracted, aren't I? That's what happens at my age. Awful, awful.' Hattie shook her head.

'Not awful, at all.' Avril patted the back of her hand. 'I'm just the same.'

'Okay. Sorry to rush things, I've got a lot to do, though.' Will smiled apologetically. 'The book is to ensure that you can't change what somebody else has written—'

'Can't change?' Hattie interjected, looking aghast.

'—and that it's not the work of just one or two people. They're looking for something original, a story that's been written like an old-fashioned fireside tale, where one person starts and the next carries on the story.'

'Fireside stories are *told*.'

'Well, yes,' Will said. 'This one is written, but they're looking for the same kind of thing. Different voices, different ideas. A community effort. Which is why they're not expecting a full-length story. I think twelve thousand words is probably about right, now that we're a team of four.'

'Hmm. Is it a nice notebook?'

'A very nice notebook.' Will went over to the desk and returned with the book that had arrived on Tuesday morning. He held it out to Avril.

'Wow, this is beautiful,' she said.

Will nodded. The rich red, embossed cover was an invitation to touch, and Avril ran her finger over the gold lettering that lent an eye-catching contrast to the muted tone. Just as he himself had.

It really was gorgeous. The type of notebook that invited you to write in it. The type of book you noticed. The spine was designed to appear worn, as though it had been removed and reshelved by many hands, and Will liked that the book didn't look as though it was fresh from the printers or a stationery shop. It had been made to look like a treasured book that was crying out for a story to be written on its blank pages.

Avril reluctantly passed the book on to Stuart.

'*We Are All Storytellers*.' He read the title out, his smooth, deep tones making the title resonate. Grow.

'I like that.' Said Hattie.

'I've printed off a set of the guidelines for each of us.' Will carried on, trying to be businesslike. He was still worried that this project could be a mistake, and it was going to mess with his head as well as his heart, if he wasn't careful. And leave him working overtime.

'I'd already decided on the plot, though,' Hattie said, her disgruntled tone returning.

'You can only decide on the plot of your chapter,' Will said gently. 'Then you'll have to plot the next bit once you've seen what everybody else has written.'

Hattie frowned. Will got the feeling that she didn't want to be influenced by anybody else; she wanted to do things her own way.

'Your chapters should be exactly how you want them. This way everybody has complete freedom to turn the story in whatever direction they want,' he added.

'But we can decide the theme together, can't we?' asked Avril. 'Hang on.' She picked up the leaflet. 'It says love, loyalty or lies, any combination.'

'All three covers all the bases, doesn't it?' asked Stuart.

'Yes. I find you can't have one without the others,' agreed Hattie.

'I think you should write the first chapter.' Stuart's tone was serious as he looked at Hattie. 'You have inspired us to do this, so I suggest that you are the right person to start the story, and to cap it off at the end.'

Hattie gave a small smile, which Will was sure was hiding a much larger internal one. He nodded. 'I agree, Stuart. Any objections?'

'Not from me.' Avril shook her head vehemently, and her large hoop earrings trembled. 'I'll join in once it gets going.'

'You'll be wonderful.' Hattie smiled. 'Just remember, this isn't about spelling and the like. No grammar police here, this is about storytelling!' She paused. 'You couldn't take Nutmeg out, could you, dear? He's getting—'

'Bored?' Avril supplied, with a grin.

'Uncomfortable!' Hattie corrected. 'I would do it myself, but my computer slot has come up and I need to crack on. And I'll take this, shall I?' She picked up the notebook. 'I can write the first chapter at home and then bring the book back for whoever wants to add the next one.'

'I'll go second, if that's okay with everybody?' said Stuart, looking at each of them in turn.

Avril looked relieved. 'Can I be last?'

'Sure.' Will nodded. If Avril had something to read from all of them, he was sure it would give her ideas and the confidence to add to the story. 'I'll work out roughly how much time we've each got, so that we're not rushing too much to meet the closing date.'

'Fabulous.' Hattie slipped the notebook into her bag and, glancing towards Avril, motioned at Nutmeg.

Avril grinned. 'Okay, Hattie. I'll take him out, shall I?'

Will went back to his desk and pulled the pile of books in front of him. His gaze was drawn back to the competition information that had been delivered with the notebook, and the list of entries. One name jumped out.

Jake Trent.

Lucy's lover. Lucy's co-worker.

If he'd never moved back to Knutsford, Lucy would never have met the man. Will would never have had to see him again. She'd have been happy with the bright lights and buzz of Cambridge. They would have been happy.

Except Will wouldn't have been. He couldn't have lived with himself if he hadn't put his family first. His parents were the faces he'd seen as he'd taken his first breath, and they deserved the best. He wanted his smile to be the one they saw as they took their last breaths.

He didn't want to see Lucy again, and he definitely didn't want to enter into a rivalry with Jake. To be beaten by him again. For the third time.

But he didn't have to be beaten. He could win.

Chapter Eleven

AVRIL

The Plot Thickens

'What kind of dog is he?' Avril knew absolutely nothing about dogs, but she had instantly liked Nutmeg. She stooped down so that she could pat him on the head, before handing his lead back over to Hattie. He was a sweet little dog, and the sight of his little legs going ten to the dozen to keep up with her when she'd taken him outside had made her smile.

Hattie smiled at Nutmeg, too.

'He's a miniature long-haired dachshund, dear. I got him from the rescue, that's why I don't like leaving him on his own. He didn't have a nice start, so I'm making up for it.'

'That's nice.' Avril said quietly, she was beginning to think that Hattie probably hadn't had a nice start, either, as she seemed to be making up for lost time. She opened her mouth to ask Hattie who she was looking for, when Hattie spoke.

'Don't you like cutting hair?'

Avril shrugged her shoulders. If she had disliked working in the salon, she might have made the decision to leave earlier. But she hadn't, she just knew she wasn't particularly good at it. She never would be. She wasn't putting herself down, she was being realistic. To her, it had just been a job, not a dream, a passion – and something in her heart kept telling her it wasn't enough. She was twenty-eight years old and surely there should be more to life. If she didn't do something now, it would get more difficult.

'I didn't dislike it,' she said. 'I wasn't brilliant at it, though.'

'You were perfectly adequate,' Hattie said.

'Thanks,' Avril said ruefully.

'Oh, I didn't mean that as an insult, dear. I only meant that as far as I'm concerned, you were just as good as all the other stylists, and you listened to what I wanted. I swear, half of those hairdressers were completely deaf. "Keep it long" you'd say, and before you knew it you looked as bald as a coot.'

Avril grinned. 'Now that's an exaggeration!' The customers at the salon had been great, she liked chatting to them, and she did like finding out what they really wanted. She loved it when they were happy, pleased with what she'd done for them. Some of the other girls would grumble that a lot of the clients just went in for a good moan about their jobs, or homes, or families – to offload their problems on somebody else. But Avril didn't mind. Everybody had things in life that were difficult, didn't they? She couldn't really help most of the time, but she could listen. It didn't cost her anything, did it? She was there, putting in foils or cutting, so what was wrong with listening?

She'd miss the people – the clients, and the gossip and easy-going banter of the people she had worked with. But she wouldn't miss the smell of the chemicals, the noise of the dryers, or the feeling that she'd never be as good at cutting as some of the other stylists. Unlike some of her colleagues, she'd never *live* for work.

'I think I can find something I enjoy more, that I really want to do,' she said.

'Well, I think you've done the right thing, it's too easy to put up with things and waste your life.' There it was again: Hattie's regret. 'Anyway, I was asking,' said Hattie, 'because I'd quite like it if you'd cut mine. But obviously I wouldn't ask if you hated doing it. I stopped going in the salon because I didn't like the cut. It was Harold's cut, you see.'

'You could have gone somewhere else, or told them what you wanted?'

'I didn't know what I wanted, and I didn't like the way they looked at me when I went in before the funeral.'

'Looked?'

'They all had a face on. Pity! If I'd heard one more sympathetic "it'll get better", or seen that look in their eye, I would have exploded. I promise you, I would, I wouldn't have been responsible for my actions.' While Avril was trying to think of how to respond, Hattie carried on. 'Mourn, my foot. I wanted to finally enjoy myself, not wear black and sit looking at a flaming urn.'

'Well, yes.'

'So, I want a different haircut, and some colour added to

it. Not some old-fashioned blue rinse that they keep for old people.'

'Of course not.'

'But not as much colour as you've got in yours, because I'm no spring chicken.'

'Of course.'

'But I'd rather be more Judi Dench than Miss Marple, if you get my meaning. Harold was into plain and boring; conservative. But he's not here now, is he? I like your hair.' Hattie nodded. 'It suits you, mine never suited me. It wasn't my real personality.'

Avril was starting to feel a little bit scared of Hattie's true personality.

'I'll come to yours sometime, if you like, and do it there.'

'Next week would suit.'

'Well, I guess next week it is.'

'Wonderful. I'll pay you, of course.' Hattie sighed in satisfaction. 'Right. Enough of this chit-chat then, do you have time to help me with the computer?' She looked shrewdly at Avril now. 'Unless you're in a hurry to job hunt?'

'Not really. I don't know what I want to do, if I'm honest.'

'There's no rush, is there?'

'Well, there is, there's Lisa, Dad—'

'Tell your father and let him explain to Lisa,' said Hattie. 'She is his wife.'

'I suppose you're right; I don't want to cause any trouble, though.'

'Is that why you're hiding?'

'I'm not—'

'Oh, you are, dear. That's why you came in the library, isn't it? It's a secret!'

Avril sighed, 'I was planning on keeping it to myself for now. So, if that's my secret, what's yours? Who are you looking for?'

'Peter. And I'd be very grateful if you could help me.' Hattie sat down at the chair in front of the computer, and so Avril sat down next to her. She'd never heard Hattie talk so much, but she wondered now if it was nerves, or a distraction. Hattie was embarrassed, either to ask for help, or to explain what she was doing. 'I don't really know where to start. It's all very well being able to search for information, but there's just far too much of it and none of it seems to be what I'm looking for.' She sighed. 'I'm not getting anywhere.'

'It can be tricky to know how to ask questions in the right way.'

'And so many of these things want me to put bank card details in. Why would I give a perfect stranger information like that? And what if somebody else used the computer after me'—Hattie looked round suspiciously—'and somehow got hold of my money? I've heard all about these scams, and I'm not some stupid old woman. Oh, I'd love to be reckless, just to spite Harold, but the sensible part of me says no.' She gave a heavy sigh. 'I naively thought that computers knew everything, and if I put his name and a few details in, I'd find him. Just like that.'

'You will do,' Avril tried to reassure her. But now Hattie was in full flow there seemed to be no stopping her.

'Unfortunately, this particular computer has found a

million and one "Peters", and how am I to know which one to pursue? Do I try another computer?'

'It will tell you the same thing,' said Avril.

'Humph! Well, I don't like to bother Will. I want to manage on my own. For the first time in my life, I'm free to make my own choices and I'm flummoxed! I thought being free to do what I wanted would make my life better.'

Avril could hear the frustration, edged with disappointment, in Hattie's tone. 'I'm not sure if I can help you, but I'll try, Hattie. Let's start at the beginning, eh? My dad always tells me to write a list.'

'Has he told you to do that to help you find your new career?'

'Well, yes, actually he has.' Avril said. 'He told me to think about what I like, rather than just think about jobs. Maybe we need to do that with your search.'

'Write down what I like?' Hattie had raised her thin eyebrows so high they'd almost disappeared.

Avril laughed. 'No! Try and look at it from a different angle. What else do you know about this Peter, about what he liked, what job he might have done? Or about his family?'

She looked at Hattie, but found she was thinking about her mother and how little she knew about her. She wished she'd talked to her mum more, asked her more questions, when she was alive, when Avril was a child. But children didn't question, did they? They accepted things. And by the time she was old enough to wonder, her mother had gone.

'You've got another secret, haven't you, dear?'

'I write letters to my mum,' she blurted out.

'That's nice. Not many people write letters these days, it's all those e-message things.' Hattie waited. 'Don't you do those? I thought you said you didn't write?'

Avril's diary wasn't like proper writing. She would never in a million years have dreamed of writing an actual story, but she'd always written little notes. She'd left them for her dad, for her mum (just in case wherever she was in heaven she could see them), and for the friends she didn't have. Avril had spent a lot of time on her own as a child, and drawing, writing notes and playing games had filled her time as she'd sat in her bedroom. Not having a mother – and being dressed in tomboy clothes, playing football and computer games with her dad – had singled her out. She never had the chance to invite any friends round for tea, she had turned down party invites without mentioning them to her dad because she knew that she didn't have the right pretty clothes to wear, and wouldn't be able to buy the right present. It was easier to not join in. Easier to write notes.

So in a way, writing letters to her mother had come naturally.

'I don't write. But there's no point sending emails, she's dead.'

'Oh. Oh, well yes, there wouldn't be any point, I agree. And I'm sorry.'

'I don't tell people normally because I don't want to be defined by it. I don't want to be the poor motherless child.'

'Well, we have something in common then.' Hattie patted the back of her hand. 'I don't want to be the poor widow, either.'

'Do you ever think you see him – Harold?' The words

97

were out before Avril could stop them, and Hattie looked at her slightly aghast.

'Harold? Oh, heavens no, thank goodness.' She gave a little shudder.

'I think about Mum. I was sure I saw her the other day. Is that weird?'

'I don't want to see Harold, so I'd be horrified if I did. But if you really want to see your mother, then I don't think it's weird at all. People often think the ones they loved stick around, but as I didn't love Harold it's different. Quite different.'

'You didn't love him?'

'He was just there. And now he's not. So shall we get on with finding Peter?'

Avril nodded. Was everybody looking for someone? She knew she could never see her mother again, but she'd love to feel that she knew her better. She'd love to work out who she really was — which was almost the same as looking for a missing person. Like Hattie was.

And Hattie was lonely, Avril was sure of it. That was why she'd got Nutmeg — for company. Was that also why she was searching for Peter?

Maybe that was why she'd suggested to Hattie that their story had to be about looking for somebody — because even though she didn't read much at all, Avril thought that the best stories were the ones that you recognised. That touched on something that was important to you.

Chapter Twelve

HATTIE

The Beginning

Hattie had known, from the moment she'd decided to enter the writing competition, what the story should be about. The fact that everybody in the team had to write their own chapter had rather complicated things, but she would find a way round that, she was sure.

Chapter One

I've done a terrible thing. A wrong that cannot be easily righted, and it has been at the back of my mind, inescapable.

I am not the type of person to seek out professional help. To lie on a couch and talk about myself. My preference lies in reading other people's stories — not telling my own. But I have realised that I do not want to take this to my grave.

Hattie paused, then frowned. 'Hmm. This might be a mistake. I'm not sure it's a good idea writing it this way, what do you think, Nutmeg?' The little dog lifted his chin from his paws, and his head tilted to one side. 'It's all very well letting your personality shine through in your writing, but I think this is going a bit far, don't you? It's not supposed to be an autobiography.' He sighed and dropped his head back down. 'Ah, you want your tea before you're happy to comment?' This time he lifted his head higher and gave a little bark.

The moment Hattie got to her feet, so did Nutmeg. He spun round in a circle. 'Show off!' she chided him with a smile, then followed him through to the small kitchen.

She bent down awkwardly to give Nutmeg his bowl, then straightened up slowly, and made her way back to the lounge, picking up the notebook before sinking down grate-fully into the armchair, which still smelled new.

She liked the fact that most of the belongings in her apartment were new. She hadn't wanted to live with Harold's chair or Harold's grease-marked pillowcase or Harold's mother's tea service, or even Harold's ashes. She'd even known exactly how she wanted to get rid of those before she'd moved here. In her head, she would scatter them… Well, scatter was probably the wrong word – she'd upturn the lot as quickly as she could, before anybody could spot her, in the beer garden at The Ram's Bum, or whatever his flaming local was called. He could haunt them, rather than her.

There was a patter of feet on the kitchen lino, then Nutmeg barked to announce his arrival. She patted the chair at her side. She'd bought him a ramp, because his little dachshund legs weren't really designed for jumping and they did like to cuddle up together. Hattie had not cuddled up to anybody or anything for years. But now she had Nutmeg. His steady breathing, his warmth, was comforting.

Getting Nutmeg had initially been Hattie's revenge against Harold. He'd never let her have children, a dog or even a cat. So as soon as she got the chance, she'd been off to the rescue shelter. But as soon as she'd seen Nutmeg, she'd forgotten all about spiting her dead husband. She'd fallen in love with the little black dog with its tan eyebrows the second she'd seen him. He wasn't just a dog; Nutmeg was excellent company and seemed to be completely tuned in to her and how she felt.

Sometimes when she was sitting with him in the evenings, Hattie wondered what her life would have been like if she'd had a child to hug, to hold to her and feel another heartbeat. But what was the point in thinking about the past, about decisions that hadn't been hers to make? Except, maybe they should have been, she thought, maybe she should have been stronger.

She had tried at first, she was sure she had. But it hadn't done her any good. It was her generation: men made all the decisions. It was just how it was.

Hattie shook the thoughts away and picked up the piece of paper that she'd been jotting the opening of the story on. Avril had said she was going to write her bit out first then copy it into the notebook so that it was neat – which had seemed a good idea. Hattie was surprised that the young woman had left the hairdressing salon. What it must be like to have youth on your side and be brave, she thought.

She was a nice girl, Hattie remembered that much. She didn't talk as much as some of them did, she just listened. And she was good at just being quiet.

Being quiet was something a lot of people didn't understand these days.

Nutmeg did. She stroked his head absentmindedly, liking the feel of his hair beneath her fingertips.

She'd smuggled him into the library with her, because who was going to search an old woman? She didn't like to leave him at home on his own, because he pined. He'd been neglected by his previous owner and deserved better. She'd vowed he would never feel alone again – so he was in the big bag that she'd bought specially. Dogs weren't allowed in the library, except assistance dogs. So if anybody had asked her she would have told them that was what he was. Because it was the truth. Nutmeg kept her sane as well as keeping her company. She'd always told him, quite firmly, before they went in that he had to keep quiet. He stared at her with his big brown eyes as though he understood every word she was saying, then he'd rest his chin on his paws, close his eyes and sigh. He was a good boy. Patient. She always treated him to a bit of her fish when she got home. A nice bit of plaice it was.

But it was nice that Will had said he liked dogs, that Nutmeg was allowed in the library. Who would have thought it?

'You don't need to go in the bag anymore, Nutmeg,' she told him, and he gave one of his little barks that he often did in his sleep, when his paws were twitching, and she could imagine him chasing squirrels. 'I might leave it downstairs for somebody else. Only old people use those bags.'

Hattie turned back to her notes. She very carefully crossed out every 'I' and changed it to 'She'. She knew that the start of any story had to be good. It had to grab the readers' attention. It was a bit like when you met somebody for the very first time – those first few seconds left a lasting impression.

She was proud that Stuart had suggested she write the opening. He didn't see her as old and irrelevant; he saw her as useful. She'd never really looked at Stuart before, he had always been hidden behind his newspaper. All you could see were his eyebrows. 'I rather think I'm warming to him,' she told Nutmeg.

She smiled. Stuart hadn't written her off. And it was apt, because of course going into the library had been her attempt at a new beginning, not of entering a competition, but she was determined to embrace every new opportunity that came her way.

Hattie had felt outdated and forgotten for years, but the library didn't make her feel like that at all. People in libraries understood.

And writing this story by hand in a book was a wonderful idea, even though she was – as she said it herself – quite adept at typing.

And the library had been useful for finding out how to operate one of those computers, to get her stiff fingers back into the act of typing. Once, it had been instinctive, when she was a skilled touch-typist, when she'd typed so many words that it had never even occurred to her to look down to find the right letters, her fingers just knew the way. They had danced over the keys, but that had been a lifetime ago. Once she got married, her fingers had been expected to perform other tasks. Like peeling potatoes and chopping carrots. Her brain had been considered fit only for studying knitting patterns and cake recipes.

And now both her hands and her head were old, in danger of seizing up like an old bicycle chain. But she needed them. She wanted them to work again.

She flexed her fingers – even holding a pen was more difficult than it used to be – and sighed as she studied the page in front of her. This story was just a distraction, she realised that. Her real task was the one she thought about as she dropped off to sleep at night. The one she'd set her mind upon only a few days after Harold had taken his last breath. Find Peter. If she didn't do it, then she'd have regrets, and she didn't want to add any more of those.

She needed to proceed with her investigation. She liked the sound of that 'proceed with her investigation'. That was a job for tomorrow. But today she would let this fanciful tale stir up her brain cells.

Maybe that was what was needed, reading, writing. She used to enjoy a good book. Until Harold had spoiled her enjoyment by declaring the stories cheap trash.

Harold had even controlled the television remote control. How many times had she seen a glimpse of some interesting looking detective programme, before he'd denounced it rubbish, and switched to another channel?

Tomorrow, she'd write the notes about Peter that Avril had suggested. And maybe use that iPlayer thing on the television. She'd read through the instructions, it was good to have a new television rather than the old one that Harold had pre-programmed to frustrate her.

But she was tired tonight; she'd had a busy day.

She would finish writing the first chapter, though – they had to get cracking or they'd miss the competition deadline and she didn't want to be responsible for that – then she'd have an early night.

Hattie opened the notebook. The first page had been set up so that you could enter the title, and the names of the authors. She ignored that and turned to the first blank page. Then she slowly, deliberately, started to copy her opening words in. It was hard, painstaking work, but it had to be neat, legible, didn't it?

As she wrote, she found herself thinking about Avril again. She might not realise it herself, but Hattie was sure that she was searching for somebody. Just as Hattie herself was. Avril's suggestion of writing a story about finding a missing person was, Hattie was sure, significant. Not that she, Hattie, thought that should be the theme of their story. She might be looking for Peter, but he was not missing, or presumed dead, he had simply moved on with his life. He certainly did not know anybody was searching for him. There was no mystery, no disappearance.

But maybe everybody was searching for somebody or something, even if they didn't know it? The truth, the chances they'd never had?

Hattie would rather the story be more of a murder mystery. She liked a good murder. And she liked a mystery – hidden secrets, lies. That's what one of the themes was, wasn't it? Love, loyalty, lies. Did every life, every story, contain them? The power to uncover the truth.

So much had escaped her, but it wasn't truths. She knew what they were. It was opportunities. A life. That was what had escaped her.

Hattie stroked Nutmeg. 'If you have a good story, you've no need for a therapist, have you?'

As Hattie got to the end of her story opening, she felt a little shiver of excitement. This was all rather good. This was nearly as exciting as her project. She was a part of this, she was doing something new, leaving her mark. And Harold couldn't do a thing about it. After sixty years of being told what to do by him, he was now a pile of ash, and she could do whatever she wanted.

There was one flaw in this story, though: she rather thought she might have stepped too close to the truth. She might have to alter that – which she'd do straight after she'd rested her eyes for five minutes.

THE STORY

Chapter One

(Hattie)

Dear Eliza,

I have done a terrible thing. A wrong that can't be easily righted, and it has been at the back of my mind, inescapable.

I am not the type of person to seek out professional help. To lie on a couch and talk about myself. My preference lies in reading other people's stories – not telling my own. But I have realised that I do not want to take this to my grave.

I have always wanted to explain, but the right time never presented itself. It never does, does it? So, in my clumsy way, I have left you the clues so that you can make your own decision on whether to pursue my truth or not.

There are no villains in my story, however it may appear. Just normal people. People who have made mistakes, people who have been blind to the truth until it has been too late. People who have been so intent on a wild-goose chase that they have missed the real opportunities.

Forgive me, forgive them. Learn from my mistakes, wipe clean yesterday, enjoy today and look forward to tomorrow. Reach for the stars, but remember that chasing the rainbow may only lead to fool's gold.

I want you to lead the life that you deserve, my darling. Don't waste it. And please, forgive me. My actions have come from a place of love, not revenge.

Eliza carefully folded the letter, the paper starting to wear at the edges from the number of times it had been opened and read, and slipped it back into her pocket.

The thought of a grave was strangely apt she thought, as she stared across the pale golden sand. This spot on the headland was Eliza's favourite place. It was one of the good places she remembered from her childhood. One of the places she shared with her mother. The place her mother's diary had told her to revisit. On this day, at this time.

The first clue to who her mother was, to the terrible thing she had wanted to confess to.

She could not imagine her mother committing some awful sin. Eliza had always thought that they were close. That she knew her. But do you ever really know another person?

Eliza did, however, know every inch of this beach. She had always liked to be here when the tide turned, when the sea started to rush in to devour the debris of today and deposit the flotsam of the next. Except she didn't think it would carry this away.

The dark mound marred the vast expanse. It looked heavy, ugly. It could have been mistaken for a rock, but Eliza knew it was not. She stared dispassionately.

'That looks like a body!' The voice startled her. She hadn't noticed the man approaching; her senses had been too full of the crashing waves and the seagulls. Of memories. Of the knowledge that she could walk away now, or have her life changed forever.

She nodded. 'You could be right.' Her tone was strangely disconnected, even to her own ears. She felt no compassion, more a disdain. As though the body, if it was one, had no place in this glorious, beautiful, windblown cove.

'Do you think we should call the police or something?'

Or something, thought Eliza. But instead, she said, 'That's rather dramatic. It might be best to make sure it's not just a bag of old clothes somebody has dumped before you get into a panic.'

'True.' He nodded. 'Shall we go down?' The man's voice was hesitant. Nobody wanted to be alone if they stumbled across a corpse, did they?

Eliza didn't really want to go down onto the beach, she wanted to sit here with her thoughts a little bit longer. Make her own decisions. She didn't want to be a part of a 'we'.

'Of course.' She stood up and pointed. 'There's a path there, it's a bit of a scramble.' Far too much of a scramble to carry a shovel down that could be used to bury a body.

'Do you think they drowned?' The man's voice carried back up the steep incline, there was an edge to it that could have been a shortness of breath, or the wind catching it. But it was, thought Eliza, more likely nerves.

Nerves didn't bother her. She felt detached. She was used to seeing dead bodies, that was what working in an undertaker's did to you.

She wasn't, however, used to scrambling at this speed over sand that shifted dramatically with each step. Normally she would pick her way carefully. But the man's sense of urgency had stirred an unease in her.

Her mother was dead, her terrible secret could not have been to murder somebody. But she had directed Eliza here, to this beach, on this day. She had known what she would find.

Or maybe she hadn't. Maybe her mother's plan had been for her to meet somebody here who would give her the first clue as to what had happened.

And something had happened.

Eliza stared out at the sea. She loved its wild nature. The fact that this huge body of water could not be tamed. But it could be cruel. The tides were strong. The crashing waves that pounded this shore could end a life – accidentally – or assist with intention.

Had her mother sent this person here to perish? To help right the wrongs?

She felt a little shiver run down her spine.

'Here.' The soft tone drew her gaze back. The man had come back for her, was holding a helping hand out. For a moment Eliza hesitated, but what did she have to lose?

If she was to find answers to the questions that crowded her mind, she had no choice but to move forward. And to do that with a stranger was better than doing it alone. She'd been alone for too long.

Eliza was slightly out of breath. It was hard work keeping pace with the man, who was tall and had a much longer stride than she had. When the sand flattened out, he released her hand, and she slowed to a halt. She would let him cover the last few yards alone.

'Thank God for that!' His deep voice seemed to echo across the beach, then was picked up by the breeze and merged with the cries of the seagulls. 'It's not a body.'

'That's good.' She hadn't thought it was a body, but she had needed the push to come down here. Alone, she would have avoided it. Put off this moment.

'It's a pile of clothes, and'—he paused—'a suitcase of some kind.'

Eliza's curiosity got the better of her, and she covered the ground between them.

Her breath caught and she stared at the case. In a novel, it would have been old, leather, battered at the edges in an interesting manner. But it was not. To say so would be misleading and add unnecessary intrigue. The suitcase was very normal, nondescript. Apart from the fact that it was marked with sea salt and scattered with sand.

It was petrol-blue, dark, but not quite navy. The type of suitcase that you might see on a baggage conveyor in any airport of the world. But it wasn't in an airport, it had been abandoned on a beach that until that moment had been deserted.

Eliza realised that the man was studying her. Her friends had always said she had an expressive face, that she would never make it as a poker player. She didn't want to play poker, but she did sometimes wish her feelings weren't betrayed so easily.

'I've seen this case before,' she admitted. She had stumbled upon it by accident one day years ago, but at that moment it had felt like she had always known that it existed.

That it was significant.

'You've seen it before?' His tone was incredulous, but she didn't care if he believed her or not.

She had seen it in a photograph as a child, and then she had found it – hidden – and her imagination had been stirred. She had wanted to know what it contained.

Why it was so important to the person she'd loved and lost.

Chapter Thirteen

STUART

The Unexpected Twist

Stuart stared at the neat handwriting. It was a long time since he'd seen such beautiful script. Nobody took the trouble to write these days. It was yet another forgotten art. Nowadays it was all about computers, phones, keyboards. He smiled at the flamboyant flourishes at the end of some letters. The writing was unmistakeably Hattie, the neat precision, the flair that she couldn't quite hide.

The words were not what he'd expected from her at all, though. My goodness, talk about hidden depths! His mother's words from many, many years before jumped into his head, *It's the quiet ones you have to watch!* The thought brought a smile to his lips.

Eliza didn't really want to go down onto the beach, she wanted to sit here with her thoughts a little bit longer. Make her own decisions. She didn't want to be a part of a 'we'.

'Of course.' She stood up and pointed. 'There's a path there, it's a bit of a scramble.' Far too much of a scramble to carry a shovel down that could be used to bury a body.

'Well, now.'

'Everything okay?'

Will's voice made Stuart start. He hadn't realised he'd spoken out loud.

'I'm not sure, to tell you the truth. Have you read this first chapter?'

'I have.' Will smiled. 'Hattie dropped the notebook in yesterday, so that if you came in early, it would be here for you. She had a definite look of mischief in her eye.'

Stuart shook his head. He hadn't really planned on a murder mystery; he was more interested in the type of story that had a riddle at its heart.

'What's that about mischief?' Avril plonked herself down in the chair next to Stuart and glanced at the notebook. 'May I?'

'Of course.' Stuart handed it to her. 'This competition is certainly going to be a challenge. I know that it's against the rules to change what had been written, but there's nothing to stop me changing the direction of the story, is there?'

'Nothing at all. It's your chapter,' Will assured him.

Avril turned to the opening page and chuckled. 'Oh, my God! Trust Hattie! I knew she'd got some murderous intent in her!'

'Really?' Stuart felt a tremor of shock. 'She's always seemed perfectly innocuous to me.' He paused as a slightly blank look settled over Avril's features. He didn't want to assume she didn't understand, or insult her, but maybe slipping in a little explanation wouldn't do any harm. 'I mean, I couldn't imagine her causing offence, or harm to anybody.' He was surprised to see the grin on Avril's face broaden.

'You've not met the real Hattie yet, then! She could terrorise the juniors at the salon just by looking at them. But'—Avril paused—'this is a bit surprising. I suppose'—her words slowed as she was obviously thinking how to word her response—'we can change the direction, but I think we just have to be careful not to upset each other.'

'Oh yes, yes,' Stuart nodded, 'we have to respect each other's chapters, of course.' He'd not really thought about it, as he'd had his own idea about the direction the story would take, but they probably each had different ideas, preferences in their reading tastes. He nodded again. This wasn't like a work project where he could tell somebody they were wrong – there was no wrong in this competition. 'We have to be flexible,' he added thoughtfully.

'Exactly.' Avril smiled, reassured.

'We need to see each other's points of view, but we can use what is written to inspire us.'

'Hmm. Not sure I'd go that far.' Will took the notebook, and his gaze skimmed over the page. 'I'm not sure I want to be inspired by Hattie's imagination!'

'And what does that mean?' They all turned at Hattie's words.

'We think you've got an evil streak!' Avril said.

Stuart glanced between the two of them. They already seemed to have a comfortable relationship, and he was sure that only somebody Avril liked could make a comment like that. At any rate, Hattie looked very proud of herself.

'I really don't know how I'm going to follow an opening like this!' Stuart took the notebook back. He really didn't. He'd half expected to come into the library this morning, rattle off the next chapter and pass the notebook onto the next author – Will. But this was going to take some thinking about.

'I'm sure you'll cope.' Hattie sat down on the chair next to him and patted his hand. 'Don't let my wonderful story-telling intimidate you!'

They all laughed, and Nutmeg barked.

'You look like you're having fun!' The tinkling female voice brought a flush to Stuart's cheeks. He leaped to his feet, the chair feet screeching on the floor.

'Jo!'

'Sorry to interrupt.' She smiled, patted his arm. 'Hope you don't mind, but I came into town for some veg and I thought I'd pop in and see what you were up to.'

'Of course I don't mind, definitely not, no.' Stuart realised he was flapping, which was totally unlike him, but the last person he'd expected to see here was his wife.

'Hattie, Avril, Will – this is Jo, my wife.'

Had he finally found something she might think was interesting? She had encouraged him to join the team, but he hadn't been sure if that was because she'd like him to be out of the house more, or because she genuinely thought it was a good idea.

Maybe she liked the idea of being married to the author he could become. Although he was getting ahead of himself a bit. He needed to calm down and work out how to write the next chapter. Baby steps, baby steps.

'Hi, everybody! This competition sounds wonderful.' Jo smiled, then swung her shopping bag onto the table. 'I thought a bit of cake might help get the brain cells buzzing?' She reached in and took out a cake tin. 'Is that allowed, Will?'

'It certainly is! I'll get plates, shall I?'

'It's not much, just some carrot cake and a few slices of flapjack.'

'Splendid, I do like a slice of flapjack. Though I presume it's slightly sticky, not tooth-crackingly brittle? At my age I have to be careful.' Hattie tapped a front tooth for emphasis.

'Definitely sticky,' said Jo with a smile. 'But not too sticky!' she added quickly as Hattie frowned.

'Wow, that carrot cake looks amazing.' Stuart couldn't help but smile as Avril jumped in, no doubt to stop any more challenges from Hattie.

'It does.' He beamed at Jo. 'Jo is a fantastic cook.'

'Well, I'll leave you all to it,' said Jo. 'You look very busy. I can't wait to read your winning entry!'

Stuart grimaced. 'Let's not count our chickens!'

'Nonsense,' Hattie said, her tone brisk. 'We have to win, we're doing it to help mend Will's broken heart, and my opening chapter is gripping.'

'It certainly is. A hard act to follow.'

'I'm sure you'll come up with something.' Jo smiled at Stuart and he kissed her on the cheek. 'I'll see you later, darling.'

'Thanks for the cake, Jo.' Avril was already tucking into a big slice of carrot cake.

'You can bring that with you. You can't touch the notebook now you've got sticky fingers!' Hattie passed a tiny bit of cake to Nutmeg, then motioned to hurry Avril along. 'We have things to do, and Stuart needs some peace and quiet so that he can write something that is up to the standard I've set!'

Avril obligingly got to her feet, then glanced back over at Stuart and winked. 'Good luck!'

Stuart picked up his pen. He had an idea.

Chapter Two

(Stuart)

It was strange. From her viewpoint high above the beach, Eliza hadn't been able to distinguish what was down there, but she was not surprised to see the case here today. She'd recognised it instantly.

This, she felt, was why her mother had sent her here. This held the clue. The suitcase that could answer her questions, open up a life she had never known, or — she knew — it could dash her hopes. Disappoint, or simply add nothing. Which would be worse — shattered dreams, or never knowing?

Knowledge, she had learned, was not always power. Knowledge could be pain, truth could scar.

But ignorance was not always bliss. Ignorance could leave an unsettled mind, a life that sometimes felt it had no direction, no path to follow. Which was why she had followed the man down onto the beach.

Eliza did not consider herself a brave person, but she liked order. She liked answers, to base her decisions on facts. And so, at this point in her life, she had no option. She had to be brave.

She reached out to lift the suitcase, but the man's hand rested over hers. 'Hang on. Isn't this evidence? We shouldn't touch it. We should ring the police.'

'Evidence of what?' She surveyed him steadily. Originally, he had assumed he'd seen a body, so apparently, he'd decided that a crime had been committed. 'Maybe these are just lost belongings, abandoned.' She paused. 'Dumped down here.'

'On a beach? Would you really clamber down here just to dump

something?' He raised an eyebrow. 'Somebody must have had a reason to come all the way down here, and what about the clothes?' His gaze narrowed slightly, and Eliza shifted uneasily. She had a feeling she knew what he was going to say. 'And you've seen this case before. Are you worried about whoever owned it, is that why you're here?' His tone was gentle, but persistent. Whoever he was, he wasn't going to let this go.

'I saw it in my mother's wardrobe, and no, I'm not worried about her. She's dead.'

'Oh, I'm sorry, I…'

'It's why I'm here.' She didn't want his pity, pity brought back the pain. 'She told me to come here, in a letter she left for me. It was one of our favourite places.'

'So, she knew you'd find it?'

'I don't know.' She took a deep breath. 'And I don't think it was hers; I think she was looking after it for somebody. Maybe they came back, after she died. Maybe she left them a letter as well.' And wanted Eliza to meet them. She didn't say the last thought out loud. She kept it to herself.

'Well, whoever had it could have walked into the sea.'

'To drown, or for a swim?'

'I have no idea. Look, there's no footprints, is there another route down?'

Eliza pointed to the other side of bay. 'I've seen people walk down from that side, but you don't often see anybody here.'

'You're very calm about this.'

Eliza shrugged. Inside she did not feel calm. Why had she never asked more questions when her mum had been alive? Why hadn't she cared more? She sometimes felt now like she had not known her, that she'd in a way failed as she'd never found out why she was keeping secrets. *Eliza had always thought they had been close, but now she felt she had failed her. She hadn't even realised that her mother felt she had done something terribly wrong. That she was tormented. As Eliza had grown older, left home, she'd gone her own way. Been selfish. Not taken enough care of or paid enough attention to the person that meant the most to her in the whole world.*

They could have faced her mother's past together.

She should have listened. She should have asked more questions – before they had run out of time.

Now she had guilt. Was it too late to assuage that, were her actions now purely selfish?

'Did you expect to find the case?'

Eliza shook her head. Why should she share her secrets with a stranger? 'I come here every year, on this day, anyway.' She shrugged. 'It's my birthday.' It had been a birthday tradition, the place her mother had brought her to make a wish. But what was she wishing for this year? 'My mother probably thought I'd stop coming here after she'd gone, so that's why she put it in the letter. I didn't know what I'd find, or why she wanted me to come today.'

He frowned. 'So why didn't you come down and get it?'

'From up there,' she pointed back to the headland, 'I couldn't tell what it was. It didn't really occur to me that it could be the suitcase. I'd forgotten about it really, until now. It might have been a body, like you first thought. Messages come in different forms you know.' She couldn't help the small smile that crept onto her face.

'Who does it belong to?'

She sighed. 'I've got no idea. If we open it, we can find out.'

Chapter Fourteen

WILL

Lost Belongings

Will kicked his shoes off, put his bag down and then got a can of beer out of the fridge before returning to the lounge and picking up the notebook.

He had been reluctant to have anything to do with the competition, but now he couldn't wait to see what Stuart had done with the story.

He was well aware of the saying 'write what you know', but he'd always felt that applied more to emotions and feelings rather than actual experiences. All the thrillers, murder mysteries and even love stories couldn't be based on the authors' real lives, could they? Hattie might have murderous feelings, but he was sure she was no killer. What had made her feel that way, though? Avril had made a brief mention of a husband who had recently died; was it him who had made Hattie feel this way? Or was it connected to the man –

Peter, he thought she'd said his name was – who she was now searching for?

He wasn't sure that he wanted this story to reveal any of his true feelings to the rest of the team, but he was interested to see what Stuart's angle would be. Murder had not been on his agenda, Will had been sure from his shocked reaction when he read the first chapter, so he was sure he would have flipped the story in some way. Stuart, Will was sure, was a clever guy, and he'd said he'd done a creative writing course, so this could be interesting!

Will picked his mobile phone up, and ordered a pizza, then settled down on the spacious sofa, propping his feet on the table. He should just have time before the takeaway arrived to catch up on the story, and then he could plot his own chapter.

Eliza shrugged. Inside she did not feel calm. Why had she never asked more questions when her mum had been alive? Why hadn't she cared more? She sometimes felt now like she had not known her, that she'd in a way failed as she'd never found out why she was keeping secrets. Eliza had always thought they had been close, but now she felt she had failed her.

Will smiled. Stuart was clever. Eliza could be Hattie, he'd picked up on who she was, her voice in the first chapter, and had turned the story in a new direction. He frowned, the guilt bit, the lack of caring was interesting. It wasn't what he would have expected from Stuart. The man seemed perfectly at ease with himself, the type who'd had a very successful career and had now settled into comfortable retirement with his lovely wife. So why would he feel he didn't care enough?

He shook his head; he was probably reading too much into this. Stuart was probably just a good writer. They now had a mystery, and – Will tapped the pen against his teeth – possibly a romance. There was plenty of potential in the meeting between Eliza and the man – who had already held her hand. How could Stuart not have embellished? Have described her feelings at his touch? Will would have to try and address that, although the prime moment, that first touch, had been an opportunity missed. But this story could develop into much more, into a grand romance. The suitcase could belong to somebody who was fleeing an illicit love affair or returning to one – it could have been abandoned before the owner started a new life. The ideas were coming to Will so quickly, he couldn't believe it. He would have never thought a competition like this could be quite so inspiring! Maybe they did have the perfect team, even if it didn't look like it from the outside.

He took a swig from the bottle of beer he'd put on the side table, then pulled over a pad of paper and started to jot down his thoughts.

He already liked the Eliza character; in fact, she wasn't like a younger Hattie, at all. She was more like Avril. Strong, independent. Pretty.

The ping of his phone put everything on pause. Just when the words were about to flow, his pizza was due to arrive! He glanced down, to check what time they were saying it would arrive and realised it was not a message, it was an email.

He tapped on the notification and the email opened, and just as swiftly his good mood faded.

It was from Lucy.

He hated himself for the involuntary reaction it caused in his body.

The clench in his gut, the dryness in his mouth.

He should be over her; he was over her. He had his own life. But he couldn't escape this feeling, this jealousy – or whatever it was – that rose up however much he willed it not to.

When he thought of Lucy, he thought of Jake. When he thought of Jake the past was raked up.

Some things were better forgotten, and Jake was one of them.

His concentration returned to the email.

Dear Will,

Welcome to the Inter-Library Competition – we are delighted that your library has registered an interest.

His grip relaxed. It was a standard email. Probably automated.

He scanned over the following paragraphs.

I look forward to meeting your team on my visit in the coming weeks.

Kindest Regards,
Lucy Martin

How was he going to avoid seeing her? He could ask one of the others to cover him and have a day off? But that wouldn't be fair. He sighed inwardly. They were a team.

Will's phone pinged again, and another notification popped up. This time it was his pizza, which was three stops away. Good. He always thought best on a full stomach.

After he eaten, he'd write. And then he'd decide how to deal with Lucy. Maybe it was time to move on from what Jake had done to him. To accept that Lucy was all grown up and it was her choice, not his fault, if she wanted to date the man he could never trust or like.

Chapter Three

(Will)

The catch was broken, which was lucky as Eliza's hands were shaking far too much to turn the tiny numbers of the combination lock. It finally snapped open, and she struggled to draw the zip back. She took a deep breath, her hands trembling, her forehead clammy, the sand grating against her knees.

'Are you okay? You don't have to do this now, here, you know.' His tone had softened.

'I do.' It felt right to do it here. This was the setting her mother had chosen.

On an intake of breath, she lifted the lid. Closing her eyes as she did so.

She didn't know what she was expecting. But the case obviously meant something to her mother, who had kept it for years — and hidden it. Maybe she had just been taking care of it for a friend, but Eliza had always felt it was more significant. That it held secrets. Answers. And now she was sure she had been right. Why else had her mother told her to come here today?

Eliza had not expected to find the case. She had thought, hoped, that she was here to meet a person. A person who held the answers she was looking for. But instead, they had left the case for her. Had that been her mother's plan, or the stranger's decision?

She opened her eyes. There was surprisingly little in the case. But it still told a story.

The owner had not been preparing for a journey, unless it was the kind of final one that did not require a change of clothes. For a moment she stared at the contents. The framed photograph, the small plastic bag filled with what appeared to be shells, and the diary. The diary drew her attention because who could resist reading the secret words of another?

She opened it, her fingers stiffening as her gaze came to rest on the name at the top of the first page. And she knew with a certainty she'd not felt before that she'd done the right thing, opening this suitcase.

Harold Gold.

'Are you okay?'

Until he spoke, she had forgotten she wasn't alone. All she had been aware of was that name. A name that had meant nothing to her until recently.

She glanced up, and found that the man was studying her, concern etched into his features.

He stooped down beside her on the sand, his shoulder close to hers.

'I'm fine,' she said shakily. Not sure if it was the shock of seeing the diary that was familiar, or seeing that name that had made her feel this way. Or the proximity of a man her body seemed unable to ignore. He wasn't tall for a man, not much taller than she was, but there was no doubt that he was attractive. He had a presence that made you want to look at him. Made her want to look at him.

Her gaze met his. His eyes were a startling shade of blue that she hadn't noticed before. They reminded her of the sea on a clear day. Intense. Beautiful.

He reached out, rested his hand on her arm. Its warmth drifted through her body. Comforting and yet stirring something else within her. Something that made her heart beat faster, something that made her want to move closer to him.

For a second it felt like nothing else existed. That there was only him and her. Nothing else mattered.

'Who's Harold Gold?' His words broke the spell.

'He's…' She hesitated for a moment. Was this a betrayal of her mother? 'He's the man I've been hoping I'd find.'

'You know him.' It wasn't a question.

'No. Not really, well not at all. I've seen his name before. My mother, Sally, knew him. I, well…'

'And any other family, your father, does he know him?'

She shook her head, her throat dry. 'My father hasn't been part of my life. It was just me and Mum.'

Just me and Mum. Out there somewhere was the man who had fathered her. Somebody else that Sally had loved, however briefly.

Had there been a time when her mother had felt the same feeling that she had just a moment ago? A feeling that nobody else existed. That it was just this moment, this person.

But why had it ended? Was it love that her mother had written about? The type of love that had led her to do something terrible?

Was that why this suitcase had been hidden away? Or was she fantasising?

'I don't want you to think I'm interrogating you with all these questions.' His smile was gentle, the corners of his mouth lifted into a gentle bow. 'But maybe I can help, or we can help each other. Two heads are sometimes better than one.'

The warmth of the man's hand tingled along the skin of her arm, bringing her back to the present. And a certainty flooded through her. She could trust him.

She had been alone for long enough.

Chapter Fifteen

AVRIL

Love Is...

'What tosh! What on earth does he mean? That was most definitely not a pile of clothing, it was a body!'

'Your Eliza did say that it could be clothes,' Avril pointed out. She'd arrived at the library, to be confronted by a cross Hattie who was waving the notebook in her face indignantly. She must have been queueing for Will to arrive and open the door, thought Avril – excited to see what Stuart and Will had written. Avril was excited, too, but she also had a stomach full of butterflies, because this meant that it was her turn to write next. She had no idea what she was going to write about, and what if the others had written about things she knew nothing about? She'd gone to sleep last night imagining that there would now be a body laid out in the morgue with a forensic pathologist at the ready, and she had absolutely no idea of the lingo involved in an autopsy apart from odd snippets she'd heard on TV dramas – which might not be accurate, and she wasn't sure she could remember the full details anyway.

At Hattie's words, though, her pulse rate slowed a notch closer to normal. No body meant no autopsy.

'Eliza might have said it, but she didn't mean it.' Hattie's tone was sharp. 'Why didn't Stuart realise?'

'I think it's quite clever, actually.' Avril had managed to pull the book from Hattie's hand and read Chapter Two. She was relieved to see that the story wasn't going to open with a dead body on a beach. 'Anyway, I thought you liked my missing-person idea?'

'You can be missing if you're dead.'

Hattie's disgruntled tone made Avril laugh. 'I mean, it's a real mystery now, isn't it? The person might have gone into the sea to drown, or they could have just disappeared. He's left it so that Will can take it either way.'

'Harumph.' Hattie was still determined to show her displeasure, but Avril wondered whether it was more about saving face, because she had reclaimed the book and was reading on.

'So, what's Will written?'

'You can read it for yourself, it's a bit soppy for my taste.'

'Shh, he'll hear!' Avril giggled. 'That's mean saying that.'

'I'm just saying, I wouldn't have written that.'

'But we all have to be sympathetic to each other, don't we?' The deep voice made them both look up.

Avril had not heard Stuart join them. 'We do! I love your

chapter; I can't wait to read what Will has put in the suitcase!'

'Not a body,' Hattie muttered. 'He had the perfect opportunity there.'

'Hattie, you're terrible! How would you feel if he'd put a dog's body in there?'

'That is different! A lot different.' Hattie glared at her. 'Nobody would murder a poor defenceless animal in a story. I'd have had to claim the chapter was a dream and it never happened!'

'But murdering a human being is fine?'

'Of course it is! I think I am going to go and open a new packet of biscuits; I spotted some Jammie Dodgers.'

Avril and Stuart shared a smile. He was, Avril had decided, a nice man. And with Hattie's dark side coming out, they definitely needed a steadying influence, or they'd end up with a bloodbath, or at the very least a dismembered corpse.

Stuart walked over to his normal seat, and picked up his newspaper, so Avril turned her attention back to Will's chapter.

She shook her head, her throat dry. 'My father hasn't been part of my life. It was just me and Mum.'

Just me and Mum. Out there somewhere was the man who had fathered her. Somebody else that Sally had loved, however briefly.

The corner of her mouth lifted. Did Will understand how she felt about not knowing her mother, and he'd cleverly mirrored it in the story? Whether he'd intended it or not, she liked his chapter. She liked the fact that it was about the characters, the way they felt. She read on.

'Who's Harold Gold?' His words broke the spell.

'He's…' She hesitated for a moment. Was this a betrayal of her mother? 'He's the man I've been hoping I'd find.'

The warmth of the man's hand tingled along the skin of her arm, bringing her back to the present. And a certainty flooded through her. She could trust him.

'And who on earth is Harold? I can't have a Harold in the story.' Hattie was back, a packet of biscuits in one hand. She tapped Avril's arm with the other; to hurry her up and Avril closed the book with a sigh.

'May I?' Stuart stood up and held his hand out, so she passed it over.

'Well,' said Avril mildly, 'there's another potential dead body for you. No,' she added hastily at the look on Hattie's face. 'I didn't mean it. You can't keep killing people off!'

'I haven't had a chance yet as you lot keep bringing them back to life! But I'll find a way to kill Harold, if he's not already dead!' exclaimed Hattie, and Avril fought the shocked look which she was sure had appeared on her face.

'But…' Avril stared at Hattie, the grim thin line of her pursed lips, the tiny lines that radiated out from her mouth and were more pronounced than ever, and the piercing glare. Then something else hit her and sent a tiny somersault in her stomach. Hattie's eyes were glistening. She wasn't angry, she was upset. She didn't want a Harold back in her life. Not even a fictional one. She glanced over at the desk by the entrance, but Will was busy talking to somebody. She'd mention it to him later. She was sure it was perfectly within the rules for him to go back and change the name, it wasn't like somebody else was altering what he'd written. And how was he to know that it would upset Hattie? That one Harold in her life had been one too many.

'I suppose you've got the mystery you wanted,' Hattie continued, grudgingly. 'The missing person.'

'Ahh, and it's turning into a love story, I see!' Stuart's voice broke the silence. 'How lovely. Who would have thought Will was a romantic?'

'A love story?' Avril frowned.

'Of course!' Hattie still sounded cross but seemed to be mellowing. 'Eliza and this man. There is tingling going on! Have you never had tingling?'

Avril smiled at the huff of Hattie's tone. 'I might have done, what about you?'

'That's my business!'

'Well, that's fine. And I think it's cute!' Avril took back the book and smiled. 'It's nice that Will's a secret romantic.'

'There's nothing secret about it,' said Hattie, 'I've seen the way he looks at you.'

'Nonsense.' Avril picked up the notebook and slipped it into her bag.

'What are you going to write?'

'I don't know, I need to think about it.' She did need to think about it, to write down some ideas, but as she'd read the chapters that had already been written she had realised she wasn't worried about doing this any longer. Okay, her spelling and grammar were rubbish, but her biggest worry had been knowing what to write about. But now she knew. There was a mystery. Who was this Harold, and where was he now? The items in the suitcase had to be important, they were clues. And Eliza wasn't on her own any longer, she had this mystery man to help her. That was good. After she'd mentioned her mum to Hattie, she had realised that it had made her feel so much better. She had often been on the verge of asking her dad about Phee, but that wouldn't be fair. And telling him that she'd thought she'd seen her would only make him worry. Worry that she was losing the plot.

She grinned. That was strangely appropriate under the circumstances!

'You look like you're planning mischief, young lady!'

'Something like that. Would you like me to get you a drink, Hattie?'

'I thought you'd never ask. That would be lovely. And then I'll show you my list, the one you asked for.'

Avril frowned. 'I asked you for a list?'

'And I thought I was the oldie with the bad memory. You did, about Peter. You said write down what he was like.'

'Ah, right. Well, it was more of a suggestion, really.'

'A good one. I think I might have hit on something!'

Hattie reached into her large handbag and drew out a sheet of paper. She looked so happy, quite a transformation from her disgruntled attitude when she'd seen how Stuart and Will had 'butchered' her story, that Avril felt she had no choice but to sit down with her and see what she'd come up with.

'Peter wrote poems.'

'Ah.'

'I don't know why I didn't think about it before, what with the competition and everything. He was always scribbling and saying romantic things. A bit like Will.'

'I've never seen Will scribbling, or'—Avril paused—'saying romantic things.'

'But he's thinking them. And he's always got a book at hand, even if he's not scribbling.'

'He works in a library.'

'Whatever.' Hattie waved a dismissive hand.

Avril studied Hattie who was now cuddling Nutmeg on her knee, the fierceness that had shone in her eyes before was now more of a dreaminess. 'Did you love him?' she asked softly. 'Peter.'

Hattie nodded slowly. 'He was the man who gave me the tingles.' Her voice was barely audible, but the words and their meaning carried clearly.

'What happened, Hattie?'

'Harold happened.' A tiny edge of hardness crept into her tone, but not much. Peter was still obviously in her thoughts. 'Harold barged in, declaring love and offering me all kinds. He'd already been to see my father, and I couldn't disobey my father.' The pain in Hattie's voice spoke of years of being repressed, of words she'd never been able to voice.

'Why?'

'It wasn't the done thing in those days. Harold had asked him if we could be wed and my father had said yes.'

'But, if you didn't—'

'What I wanted wasn't relevant, Avril. It was a different time. I knew better than to say anything. I had learned that lesson, and unfortunately it was a style of love that Harold had also bought into.'

Avril blinked. 'What do you mean, you "knew better"?'

'Let's just say I learned to pick my battles carefully; very carefully.' Hattie sighed, fondling Nutmeg's ears gently. 'Peter just walked away. He didn't stand up for me, for us – we both knew it would be useless. And he liked Harold. For a short time, I hated him, Peter that is, because it was the easy thing to do. Easier than loving him. But I couldn't blame him. And he cut ties with me completely because it was for the best.'

Best for whom? thought Avril, but she didn't say.

'But now… After all these years, I'd quite like to find him, to say hello'—Hattie paused—'and goodbye, if he's still around. We never said goodbye.' She put Nutmeg on the floor and struggled to her feet. 'I thought the poems would be a good place to start; he may have published some, or something.'

'True, we can look. It's a good start.' Avril tried to sound encouraging, but how many people were poets, authors or artists but had never actually had anything published? Loads. 'Did he not have any family?'

'Not that he knew of. He was living in the children's home up the road when I met him. I think he was an orphan.'

'Well, that might help, too, if we can work out when he might have been orphaned we might be able to find some family.'

'And how will that help?'

'I'm not sure.' Avril frowned. 'But I think any little thing we can find out could be useful. Like, how did you meet him?'

'He was Harold's friend. We were all friends when we were at school. We weren't allowed to mix much with the opposite sex, but we could look.' She smiled. 'I've written it all down, and the name of the school.'

Avril hesitated. She didn't want to, but the question had to be asked. 'Could he have kept in touch with Harold?'

'No,' Hattie said firmly. 'I'm sure he didn't.'

'Or could he have kept in touch with any of Harold's family, if he knew them?'

'Harold had no family that he spoke of. He said he was better off alone. He wasn't a very sociable man, you know. There was just the two of us.' Hattie glared at Avril, as though challenging her to criticise.

'Everybody is different, it was just me and Dad for ages.' Avril shrugged. 'I liked it.' She had. She had felt safe when there was just the two of them. But she couldn't be sad when he had met somebody else. What kind of a life was it for somebody like her dad, to just be with a little girl? People needed other people, someone else to talk to. She'd realised that more than ever when she'd worked in the hairdressers. The problems poured out, because to some of their clients the person doing their hair wasn't a real person. They were just a sounding board and, like a doctor, wouldn't repeat things. Well, not often, Avril couldn't help but smile, because there were plenty of gossips at Summers salon.

Avril had enjoyed going out with the girls from the salon. It didn't happen often, but she'd been able to relax with them. They were a mixed bunch, different ages, different styles – but with work in common. And none of them knew her past. She wasn't seen as different.

She hadn't really realised it at the time, but she'd needed to offload sometimes in the same way a lot of the clients did. Maybe she should make more effort. Go out with the girls again. Maybe if she talked to people more, she'd feel the need to talk to ghosts less.

'What are you looking happy about?' Hattie interrupted her thoughts.

'I was just thinking about the salon. It was fun sometimes.'

'I'm sure it was, which reminds me, you are still coming to do my hair tomorrow, aren't you?'

'I am.' Avril nodded. 'I hadn't forgotten; it's in my diary.'

'Good. Well enough of this chatter, we've got work to do.'

Avril watched as Hattie made her way over to the particular computer she liked to use and felt sad. She ached for her mother, but Hattie had had a far worse time. She was so sociable, so enthusiastic here in the library, but she'd never been allowed to be like this, to be herself, while her husband had been alive. No wonder Hattie imagined killing him off in a story after he'd made her feel so unloved and cut off. Avril hoped that they could find Peter. Although if he'd loved her, why had he left her so easily?

'Hurry along dear, I've only booked the computer for an hour you know. Oh'—Hattie paused, then smiled—'I've just had a thought, that man in the story could be the murderer. He could just be pretending to be a friend; Eliza could be dead by morning!'

There was a funny strangled noise from behind Stuart's newspaper, and the sheets trembled.

'And you can stop laughing, young man!' Hattie shook a reproving finger. 'I'm being serious!'

'That's what we're afraid of,' Avril said and made her way over to the waiting Hattie.

Chapter Four

(Avril)

Eliza glanced up at the man, and then back down at the diary. Admitting she knew Gerald Old to somebody else, that she was looking for him, had been something she didn't think she could have done. But there was something calm, accepting about this man, and the fact he was a stranger helped.

It still felt like she was betraying her mother, though. This was her secret, and Eliza should have kept it.

She'd never done anything but love her mother with all her heart. Her mother had been her everything. She'd looked after her, protected her, made sure she had everything she needed. It had always been just the two of them, for as long as she could remember. They hadn't needed anybody else. But now Eliza had discovered that the woman she thought she knew had kept secrets from her.

Her mother would have known this moment would arrive, that Eliza would look for the truth. She had planned this, and she'd left Eliza to make her own decisions. She'd left the suitcase with its clues, and it was up to Eliza to work out what had happened and where this man had gone. Who he was.

Eliza missed her mum. She didn't feel self-pity. She had a good life. A busy life. But that didn't stop her missing her. She still talked to her. There were times when she was sure she'd seen her. But she knew that wasn't possible.

But that was why Eliza still came here, because it had been their place. Hers and her mother's, She would sit on the headland as they had done so many times before. But now when Eliza asked her questions, there were never any answers.

The suitcase was one of the questions. Her mum had pushed this suitcase right to the back of the wardrobe, where she thought Eliza wouldn't see it. But she had. And she had looked for it after the funeral, and it had gone.

'I think Mum knew him,' she said softly. 'Gerald. She left me a diary that looks just like this one,' she admitted, sitting back on the sand. 'That can't be a coincidence, can it? She gave it to a friend to pass on to me a couple of weeks ago. The final entry in the diary was made the day before she died and told me to come here, today. Mum mentioned him in the diary. Gerald.' Eliza stared out at the sea, which was tossing and turning, as agitated as she felt inside. 'I never even knew she kept a diary.'

'But she didn't mention him to you when she was alive?' The man's hand dropped away from her arm, leaving it cold. He was studying his hands, deep in thought.

She couldn't help herself; she kept looking at him. He had broad shoulders, strong forearms that were resting on his knees.

'No.'

'People have their reasons sometimes. She was probably protecting you.'

'Or herself.'

And the terrible wrong.

Was this missing man something to do with her? The answer to the questions she'd never dared ask, about the other half of her. The man who might make her feel whole – understand the little parts of her that she'd never understood.

146

Was she going to find him too late?

She reached for the photograph, as a distraction from the turmoil inside, from thinking about the way his touch had made her stomach flip, the way the diary was making her head spin. She needed something to ground herself. She needed something real, different.

'I'm Sam by the way.' The man's voice broke into her thoughts. 'If you want to be alone…'

'No.' She shook her head. There was something comforting about his presence. 'It's fine. I'm Eliza.' She turned the frame over almost absentmindedly and the skittering he'd created inside her froze abruptly.

It was a photograph of a young woman. A woman who might be her mother but wasn't. A woman who was strangely familiar, but a stranger.

She clutched the frame more strongly to try and still the faint tremble in her fingers.

Sam gently took the picture from her and placed his hand over hers. Waiting until the shaking had stopped.

'Eliza?'

When she turned to look at him, he was staring at the photograph, a faint frown creasing his brow.

'Do you know this woman?'

She nodded, unable to find words for a moment. Gulping for air, for time, and when she did try and speak the words were scratchy and broken.

'I think I've seen her, or somebody who looks just like her.'

He turned, and his gaze met hers.

'For a second I thought it was my mother, how daft is that?' She gave a self-conscious laugh. But the photo drew her gaze back.

'She reminds you of your mother?'

Eliza nodded, wordlessly. She searched his face looking for some ulterior motive that she couldn't find. She had to take a chance. She had to tell him.

'Mum didn't just leave the diary, she left a letter. I think it might have something to do with all this. And,' she paused, looking him in the eye, 'Gerald's disappearance.'

Chapter Sixteen

HATTIE

Chasing Dreams

Hattie opened the notebook and flicked through the pages. The crossing out caught her eye too late, and she had to turn back.

The name 'Harold Gold' had been altered, now it said, 'Gerald Old'. It was definitely the same – Will's – handwriting, so somebody must have said something to him.

She stroked Nutmeg's head. 'I think we know who is responsible, don't you?' He turned his head to gently lick her hand. She moved on to the next chapter – the one which would lead on to what she wrote next.

Avril's handwriting was large and looped, very different to the script of the preceding pages, but easy to read. It did, thought Hattie, suit Avril. Open and generous. She liked that – the fact that a person's writing could reflect their personality. Except she had a feeling that Avril's life was more complicated than she let on. She had mentioned, very briefly, that she thought she had seen her mother who had passed away. Hattie wished sometimes that she could see Peter, he'd feel more real, then. She wouldn't feel like she was chasing a dream. For so long she'd locked him away, but since deciding to open that door, the need to find him had mushroomed. Oh yes, she'd decided to concentrate on the competition, she'd told herself, everybody, that it was more important. But it wasn't. Not in her heart, in her heart she couldn't stop hoping. Wishing.

But it was different for Avril. Thinking she had seen her mother had upset her, which Hattie supposed was a normal reaction. At her age, things changed, seeing the dead, forgetting the living, dismissing yesterday, but remembering decades ago as though they had just happened – well that was normal.

But that was why Eliza still came here, because it had been their place. Hers and her mother's. She would sit on the headland as they had done so many times before. But now when Eliza asked her questions, there were never any answers.

Hattie took a sip of her tea. Poor Avril, she obviously missed her mother very much. It was hard when somebody left before you had chance to ask them all the questions you wanted to. There was no way the young girl could have known she would have run out of time. Hattie at least had seen her loss coming, she had just been too much of a coward to do anything about it.

But this was very good, very good indeed, she would have to make sure she told Avril when she saw her – she checked her watch – which would be shortly.

The buzz of the intercom broke the silence, and Hattie closed the notebook and put it on the side table. She would write her chapter this evening.

'Yes?'

'It's Avril.'

'Wonderful, I am opening the door. I'm sure you'll find the flat without any trouble, it is well signed.'

Five minutes later, she was sitting on a chair in the centre of her kitchen, and Avril was studying her. 'You said you wanted it like Judy who?'

'I do like the fact that you listen and take things in, even if your knowledge is a bit sketchy.'

'We know about different things, Hattie,' she said, laughter in her tone.

'I'm sure. Judi Dench, dear. You must have heard of James Bond.'

'Yep, he's a man. Unlike Dr Who, who—'

'He is, but M isn't always. Judi Dench was Daniel Craig's M.'

'Oh.'

'I really don't think you know what I'm talking about. Look on your phone. You can find her.' She waved a hand towards Avril's mobile phone.

With a raised eyebrow she started to tap it.

'Ah, yes, I know who you mean. She's been in lots of stuff, and an advert. She's pretty kick-ass for her age.'

'Exactly.' Hattie agreed. 'I want to look kick-ass. Not old.'

Avril stared at her again, then glanced down at her phone, and back up. 'I think it'll suit you, you've got the same kind of bone structure. You're definitely not a Miss Marple, Hattie, she looks much older than you, and really fuddy-duddy.'

Something lifted inside of Hattie. Her life really was taking a turn for the better. She was part of a writing club, had actually made some progress with finding Peter (they'd narrowed the search down considerably since looking at poets and the school), and was now going to look like M.

'I'll have to do a blue rinse, though.'

'I don't—'

'Not an old-fashioned perm-and-set type, it just lifts the colour.' Avril paused, as though trying to remember something, 'Dame Helen Mirren did it, though she went really blue and I'm not going to do that.'

'Did she? The queen?'

'Helen Mirren, not the queen.'

'She played the queen, in the film.' Hattie tutted. 'I think you need to get out more, dear. Even I seem to have watched more films than you.'

'I'm sure I've watched lots that you've never even heard of, Hattie. But I think you're right. She was in *The Queen*. But like I was trying to say, a blue rinse will make the grey colour look brighter. I promise, you won't look old-fashioned, it won't even *look* blue. I'm sure Judi has hers done like that, or it would look a bit yellow.'

'Nonsense, her hair doesn't look yellow at all.'

'No, it looks white, because of the blue. Believe me, I know what I'm talking about. Now.' Avril's voice was firm. Hattie liked that. It was good when she was assertive. She was a nice, capable young woman. 'Are we going for a similar cut and style to Judi, as well?'

'We are.' Hattie nodded. 'And while you're doing it, we can chat about Peter, and'—she paused, glanced at Avril who was collecting her scissors and combs from her bag— 'your mother.'

———

Avril was combing out Hattie's damp hair when she finally mentioned what was obviously on her mind. 'I've seen her again.'

It was about time. Hattie was beginning to think she'd have to bring up the subject herself.

'Your mother? That's good, isn't it?'

'I don't know.' Avril's hand stilled for a moment. 'It's not like she's some ghost or something, she's a real person. In the street. She was carrying a bunch of flowers.'

'What kind of flowers?'

'White roses. She always liked roses, Dad told me. He takes them to the cemetery.'

'Do you? Take flowers?'

'No.' She sensed the shake of Avril's head. 'I don't go there. I don't want to, it won't change anything, will it? She's dead.'

'I suppose not. But remembrance isn't for the dead, it's for the living. You can remember them…' She paused, but it had to be said. 'It's about acceptance. That they're dead,' she added, in case she wasn't being clear.

'I know she's dead, Hattie. Honestly, that's why this is so weird, spooky, because it feels so real.'

Oh dear, now Avril would be thinking she shouldn't have told her about seeing her mum. 'I'm sure you do. Maybe she's coming to you in the street because you're not going to the graveyard, though?'

'I didn't think ghosts were like that. I thought they drifted around, you know, they could be anywhere.'

'I'm not sure, ghosts and witchery aren't my thing. I had Harold cremated, you know. It was what he wanted, it said in his will that he didn't want to be an inconvenience or cause me any extra work. Which is a bit odd, because he could be very inconvenient when he was still breathing. It didn't bother him one iota then.'

'Oh Hattie.' Avril laughed, but she didn't contradict Hattie like a lot of people did. 'Oh, you don't mean it' was the normal response when something controversial came out of Hattie's mouth.

'I scattered him in the beer garden of the pub he went to. If he's going to haunt anybody, then they're the ones that deserve it.'

'Did he like the pub then?'

'Oh, he liked the beer, but he wasn't keen on the other people. He didn't really like anybody, apart from Peter.'

'And you.'

'Oh, I'm not sure he really liked me.' Hattie shook her head, she felt like they were digressing. 'So, this woman. Was she how you remembered her?'

'No, that's the strange thing. She's like I think she'd be now. But recognisable. Do you think I'm going a bit crazy?'

'Not at all. I don't want to disappoint you, but maybe she's one of those, double, dop, er, doppelgangers. Just somebody that looks like her.'

'Maybe.' Avril sounded doubtful. 'But it's just her hair, her clothes and the flowers, they all seemed so—'

'Her?'

'Yes, her. I've written it all down in my diary, the letters to her, so I remember where I saw her and what she was wearing.'

'A diary is very useful.' Hattie confirmed. 'I wished I'd written one, then I'd remember things.'

Avril looked at her. 'What was he like, Peter? Did you date?'

'He was nice, but no, we never courted. It was always the three of us, Peter, Harold and me. But Peter and I used to look at each other, and we knew. Well'—she shook her head—'I thought we knew. We never had the opportunities like you do now. Maybe if we had, things would have been different.'

The looks she'd exchanged with Peter had made Hattie warm up inside, and his hand as it briefly touched her arm, her back, even her waist one day for the briefest of times, had made her skin tingle in a way that it never had before. Harold had never made her tingle. Now she thought about it, he had rarely touched her in a good way, only in anger.

'So, what happened? I know you said Harold asked if he could marry you, but was that it?'

'It was. It sounds so silly now.' It was easier to talk when

Avril was behind her, busy doing her hair. Hattie had never talked about the past to anybody. 'I was friends with both of them, but mainly Peter. Harold didn't say much. He was a quiet one, but I knew he watched me. Then they both went away on National Service and it was Harold who came back first. He called on me, and we carried on where we took off. I didn't think anything of it, I was just waiting for Peter to come back.' Hattie paused, remembering. It had been a long wait, a wait in which she'd fantasised about what it would be like when he came home.

'Harold told me that he'd been planning to talk to my father all the time he was away. He said he'd told Peter, and Peter had said he'd be honoured to be our best man. Harold had secrets, but I don't think he ever lied, so I believed him. And my father thought he would make a good husband – "solid", he said. To be honest I think he just wanted rid of me, he wanted somebody else to take responsibility. I never had a chance to talk to Peter properly, we never got any time alone as he only came back a few days before the wedding. It was a bit of a rushed affair, they often were in those days because you never knew what might happen. We had a few days away for a honeymoon and that was that. Peter had gone by the time we came home, and we moved into lodgings that Harold had arranged. He arranged everything.' The weariness, that hadn't crept up on Hattie for a while, was back. It was draining, life had been draining. When somebody arranged everything for you, it should make life easy. But it hadn't. 'I told everybody that I got Nutmeg for company, and he is wonderful company, but the real reason was because I could. Harold would never let me have a dog, he was selfish, he didn't want to share my attention, which is why we never had children, I think. Nutmeg was my first act of defiance. I didn't dare when Harold was alive, because what if he left me?'

'He's cute.'

'He's one of the best things that ever happened to me.'

'Apart from Peter?'

'Peter never really happened, dear.'

'But maybe he will.' Avril's voice was soft. 'Here, what do you think?' She passed Hattie a mirror.

'Well, now.' Hattie stared at the image in front of her, and her eyes misted over. She could see her cheekbones in a way she hadn't for years. True, there were plenty of wrinkles around her eyes, but the eyes themselves now looked bigger. She swallowed down the lump in her throat. This was how she used to be, used to feel, when she'd first known Harold and Peter, when they'd been young and carefree. When she'd thought she was in love.

'Is it okay?' Avril sounded concerned.

Hattie nodded, then found her voice. 'It's perfect.'

'Have you got a larger mirror, then I can show you the back?'

Hattie didn't need to see the back, she knew it would be wonderful, but she led the way through to the hallway because that was what Avril wanted. Avril wanted to know her opinion, to know what she thought.

They stood side by side looking into the mirror. If she'd had children, she might have had a granddaughter standing beside her like this now.

'Thank you, dear.'

'You're ready to kick ass now,' Avril said softly, then they turned and looked at each other.

'And so are you.' Hattie patted Avril's hand. 'It's perfect. And you'll find her, your mother, you'll find your answers, just like I hope I will.' She smiled. 'You've just got longer left to do it than I have.'

'You've got years left in you, Hattie!' Avril slipped her phone from her jeans' pocket and looked at it. 'I suppose I'd better get off,' she said. 'I've just got time to get the next train if I go now.'

'Off you go, then. I will see you at the library?'

'You certainly will, I can't wait to read your chapter!'

'You've set me quite a challenge, writing a follow-on chapter worthy of yours!'

Avril beamed and Hattie suddenly found she was close to tears again. It was strange, this kindness thing, it really did make you feel better.

Would she have been different, kinder, if she'd married Peter, not Harold? There was no answer to that question. But maybe she could be nicer without either of them.

Chapter Five

(Hattie)

Detective Inspector Sam Ford could not believe his luck. He may not have found the body of the missing Gerald Old – yet – but not only had he found his belongings, he'd also found a woman who was looking for him. A very beautiful woman, who had stirred his interest in a way that he had to admit wasn't entirely professional.

That, he supposed, was the reason for not immediately introducing himself and producing his identification. He suspected that if he had done so at the start, she wouldn't have come down to the beach with him. And she wouldn't have admitted to an interest of her own.

She also wouldn't have told him her name.

She would have set up a barrier and left as soon as she could.

He met her gaze. Not just because it was something that in his line of business you were always advised to do, but because he rather liked to look into her hazel eyes.

'I have something I need to tell you, too.' He wasn't some shady PI, he had to be open, honest. And he wanted to be, he didn't want to deceive her. She had shared things with him, which he was sure hadn't come easily. 'I'm with the police.' He searched her face for a reaction, but she calmly looked back at him as though she had expected the news. Or maybe she was in shock from the events of the past hour. 'We've been looking for him, too.'

'For whom?' Eliza frowned. 'Gerald? Why?'

He nodded. 'He was reported missing by his daughter quite some time ago.'

'Daughter?' she echoed, her tone hollow.

'Yes. We've not been able to find any trace of him up until now and my suspicion has been that he vanished on purpose. He left his family.'

Eliza was obviously shocked to learn that the mysterious Gerald had family. So who was she? What was her link to him?

'And then this'—he motioned towards the suitcase—'turned up. Shall we go back up to the headland? I've got a flask of coffee, and I'll explain.'

'And I expect you'll want me to explain as well.' She'd changed. Her tone was guarded, wary now, she'd pulled away from him and the gap was more than physical. A strange feeling of loss lodged in his stomach. 'I've got nothing to do with him disappearing. I didn't even know him, so you can't blame me for his abandoning his family!' There was a defensive edge to her tone now. 'And I've not driven him into the sea, if that's your next line of questioning.'

'I know that. I'm not accusing you of anything, I'm just trying to find out what happened,' he said softly, wanting to reassure her. Wanting her to trust him. He needed to know more about her, what she knew about Gerald, because it was becoming clear that this was another case where the missing person appeared to have a hidden side to their life. But it was more than that. Plain and simple, he didn't want her to go. 'But what about your mother, you said she left you a letter?'

'You think he's dead?' Eliza ignored his reference to the letter.

'I don't know.' He shrugged. 'I go on facts, not guesswork. Come on, let's take the suitcase with us.'

'I thought you needed to fingerprint it or something?' She was wary, and he couldn't blame her. He looked her straight in the eye, wanting her to believe him.

'We'd already been down and seen it. I was waiting to see if anybody else came looking.'

'And they did.' She sighed. 'Oh lord, this is getting so complicated. When Mum said she'd done something terrible, I thought it was just robbing a bank or something!' She gave a wry smile. 'I just can't believe that she's involved in some man disappearing, or in'—she paused, toying with the word before voicing it—'adultery. Do you think this all means that I've got a sister?'

'I really don't know what to think at the moment.' He narrowed his eyes and studied her. 'I can't see a huge family resemblance. But you said the woman in the photo is familiar?'

Eliza nodded.

'I'll have to let Marie, his daughter, see it. See all of this.'

'Secrets never end well. Don't they say most murders are committed by people close to the victim?'

He smiled. She was interesting, smart, as well as pretty. 'Missing doesn't always mean murdered.'

'So why are you here? I thought the police didn't have the resources to chase grown adults who had just decided to leave their homes.'

'We don't. But this is different, don't you agree? There are the belongings, and'—he paused—'you.'

'And my mother.' Eliza stared out to sea, and he was sure there was something else, something that she wanted to share with him.

'And your mother,' he repeated softly. Giving her time to make her decision.

She turned back to him, studying his face wordlessly for several long minutes.

'Her letter said she'd done something terrible and this'—her gesture took in the bay, the abandoned belongings—'was her way of explaining. The first clue that I could follow, if I wanted to.' She paused, and conflict flickered in her expression. 'She said she didn't want to take her guilt to the grave, but she's dead. I think I was supposed to be sent all this stuff while she was still alive.'

'How did she die?' He resisted the urge to reach out to her, to try to chase away the look of distress. He had to be professional. Especially now.

'They said it was an accident. But she never normally went along that road, she had no reason to drive out there. I've no idea where she was going.'

'I'm sorry.' This time he did reach out, touched her arm gently. 'I need to look into this, you understand?' She was motionless. 'I need to, Eliza. I need to make sure nobody else gets hurt.'

'Unless they already have been.' Her voice was flat, as she once more turned away and stared into the sea as though she was expecting it to tell her its secrets.

Chapter Seventeen

STUART

Write What You Know

'What are you smiling about?' Jo put her hand on Stuart's shoulder and leaned forward so that she could see what he was reading.

'It's Hattie's chapter, she's quite a card! The crafty thing has managed to put us back on a murderous track.'

'Sounds like she's set in her ways,' Jo said softly, and he glanced up. There was no judgement in her tone, but he knew what she meant. He'd been set in his ways for too long. Oblivious of Jo's life and what was going on around him.

'I think it's something she needs to get out of her system, but I think she's softening. Avril is good for her.'

He nodded. 'He was reported missing by his daughter a while ago. It was a cold case, and then this turned up.'

'Daughter?' she echoed, her tone hollow.

Eliza was obviously shocked to learn that the mysterious Gerald had family, so who was she? What was her link to him?

'Well at least the body hasn't washed up on the beach,' Jo pointed out.

'Yet!' Stuart smiled and put the notebook down. 'I'm not quite sure if she wants to murder this fella Gerald, or find him!'

'Maybe a bit of both! Didn't you say that it sounded like she'd had a difficult relationship with her husband, and was looking for some other man?'

'Fiction reflecting fact.' Said Stuart.

'Write what you know! She's very intriguing.' Jo paused, then pointed at the sentence. 'You don't think she's worried that this man she's searching for will have moved on, have a family?'

Stuart nodded. 'You could be right. She must have thought of that.'

'I'm so glad they're coming round to the house later; it'll be so interesting to find out what everybody's angle is on the story.'

'Oh, we can't really talk about it, the chapters have to be written quite independently.'

'Really? What a shame, but it will still be so interesting to get them all together. You didn't mind me suggesting it, did you? I was just feeling a bit left out; you chat about these people, and I don't know them! And you all seem so invested in this story, it's lovely.'

'Left out?' Stuart raised an eyebrow. Now this was a development. Not only was she interested in the competition, and his fellow writers, she actually wanted to know more. 'I never meant to leave you out. I didn't think you'd be interested, to be honest, and we have only just started.'

'I guess I did feel a bit cut off from you when you were so busy at work, which is why I started painting, but I suppose I thought we'd see more of each other once you retired.'

'But I didn't want to interfere.' He felt slightly confused now. 'You're so busy with your painting and everything.'

'I suppose I am.' She sat down next to him. 'But it's habit, filling my own time. But we should do more together, don't you think?'

'I'd love to.' He wasn't sure he wanted to get involved in painting random naked butchers, but there had to be something they could enjoy together. 'And I think it's a wonderful idea to ask everybody round for lunch. Ah, I think the first of them may have arrived!' He made a move to stand up, but Jo put a staying hand on his arm.

'What are you going to write next?'

'I'm not sure, but I think the story needs moving on, don't you? Maybe a bit of romance?'

'Talking of which.' Jo inclined her head towards the window, and he glanced through to see Will and Avril waiting on the doorstep, deep in conversation.

'Young love.'

'You think so?'

'I do. Right, you get the door, and I'll get the vol-au-vents! Isn't that Hattie as well at the bottom of the driveway? I think it's the first time I've seen her without her big trolley bag.'

'I think she just takes it to the library, to hide Nutmeg.'

'Oh no, I've seen her in the town with it. Bouncing off the kerbs as though there is nothing in it. I think it's her comfort blanket.'

'Instead of a hand to hold?' Stuart smiled.

'That husband of hers might not have made her happy, but he was always there with his hand on the small of her back, or with an elbow out for her to slip her hand through.' Jo sighed. 'I wonder if she misses him, or at least his company, much?'

'I miss you when you're not around,' Stuart said on impulse. Then bustled about pushing his chair in to cover his confusion. He loved Jo, but had he ever told her before that the hours of the day were empty when she wasn't there.

'I'm glad that you're around more these days.' She kissed his cheek lightly, as though she knew, then headed off towards the kitchen. He paused for a moment, watching her retreating back. Did she know more than he credited her for? Did she know about his feelings of guilt, of letting people down?

'These are fun!' Avril was looking at the vol-au-vent on her plate with a strange mix of interest and suspicion that made Stuart smile. Any minute now he expected her to poke at it, to see if it moved.

'The trouble with youngsters today, is that it is all about sharing boards with fancy meats and cheese that tastes like it is going off. You've not lived until you've had proper party food! These look wonderful, Jo.' Hattie reached out and placed a second vol-au-vent on her plate. 'It won't kill you Avril, it's just like a sausage roll without the sausage.'

'And round? So not like a sausage roll at all?'

'Those have a mushroom and parmesan filling, and these are prawn with a tiny bit of smoked salmon.' Jo pointed to each plate in turn. 'I suppose they're more like crostini, but in a pastry case rather than on toast.'

'Or a slice of sausage roll, without sausage,' muttered Hattie. 'Oh, my goodness, devils on horseback!'

'Now you've lost me completely.' Avril shook her head in disbelief.

'Me too.' Will chuckled.

'Prunes wrapped in bacon,' Stuart explained.

'I'm not sure…' Avril's face had gone a shade paler.

'Just eat what you fancy.' Jo smiled. 'There's a bit of everything; I wasn't sure if anybody had any preferences, so I thought I'd go for variety.'

'Er, yes.' Will scanned the array of plates.

Stuart tried not to grin. Jo did like to cater for every eventuality, but she'd excelled herself today. There was enough food to feed an army, not a small writing club. Hattie, though, was doing her best to take her fair share. They'd have to send her home with a doggie bag. Which reminded him.

'No Nutmeg today?'

'Oh no, he's not much of a social butterfly so I left him at home with Classic FM on the radio. He likes that, or a bit of jazz. Do you mind if I take one of these for him? He's rather fond of smoked salmon.'

'Of course you can! I'll pop some in a container before you go, Hattie. Maybe he'd like a selection?'

'I'm sure he would. Though neither of us is keen on cucumber.'

'I'll remember that,' promised Jo. 'I meant to say, Hattie, you look stunning today. Not that you don't always look lovely, but that new haircut suits you so much! It brings out your cheekbones and wonderful eyes.'

'That is Avril's doing,' said Hattie, and they glanced across to Avril, who was grinning – but at Will, not Hattie's comment. 'She's rather clever, isn't she?'

'She is, but she had some good raw material to work with!' added Jo. Then she tilted her head to one side and Stuart held his breath. When Jo did that, she was coming up with a plan. Her plans were often quite scary, she was far more adventurous than him. 'I'd love to paint your portrait, you have so much—'

'Wonderful pâté, darling!' he interjected, before she could carry on. Oh, my goodness, she wasn't going to start doing life portraits of his writing group, was she?

'—character,' Jo finished seamlessly, ignoring the interruption. 'And I don't mean that in a derogatory way. You're stunning, and so vibrant!'

'I've never been painted before.' Hattie frowned. 'You can paint I presume?'

'Oh yes, she's very good.' Stuart nodded.

'I'm part of an art group, we're exhibiting in the library, actually. I've painted—' Oh please don't mention the butcher, thought Stuart. And then he looked his wife in the eye and saw the laughter.

'You're teasing me!'

She smiled gently. 'I am, darling.' Jo turned back to Hattie. 'We do life studies, but also—'

'Death?' Hattie interjected.

'I was going to say still life.' Jo laughed. 'I'll show you the ones in the study, if you're interested.'

'Oh, I am!' said Avril, reentering the conversation. 'I'd love to see what you've done. Why didn't you tell us you had such a talented wife?' she rebuked Stuart gently.

'Because of this!' declared Jo, pushing the door closed so that they could see the painting that hung in the crevice by the door.

Avril burst out laughing and pointed. 'It's the butcher!'

'He's not very well muscled for a man who wields a cleaver for a living, is he,' remarked Hattie.

'Quite toned, though.' Avril studied the painting a bit more closely. 'Don't you think so, Will?'

'I think I like that one. Great pose, Stuart!' Will gestured towards Stuart, who spun round. He certainly had not posed for Jo, with or without clothing. His shoulders dropped with relief when he saw that Will had in fact spotted the photograph of him playing golf.

Hattie was chuckling, Will was grinning, and Avril and Jo were laughing.

'Very funny! Anybody like a cup of coffee or tea?'

'A cup of tea would be lovely.' Hattie nodded. 'And you're very talented, Jo. Are you sure you want to paint an old codger like me?'

'You're a long way from that!' Jo tutted. 'And a long way

from the Miss Marple you seem to be – I hear you're doing some detective work?'

'My search for Peter? Ah, yes, I am, but the clues are few and far between.'

Stuart stopped at the dining room door. Hattie was deep in conversation with Jo, and Will and Avril had their heads together, studying something on her mobile phone.

He smiled to himself before announcing his return, and clumsily putting the tray down. He might feel more at home running a boardroom meeting than serving refreshments, but maybe Jo was right. If you did things together, it didn't really matter what it was. Did he need to share what was in his heart and his head more?

After Jo had packed a box full of goodies for Hattie, she insisted that she would walk her home, and Stuart could stay and wash up. She led the way down the path, and Stuart watched as they turned right, and then Will and Avril turned left.

The younger couple walked in step, their shoulders occasionally bumping. Maybe Jo was right, there was love in the air.

He remembered when it was like that between Jo and himself. When his mother joked that you couldn't slide a sheet of paper between them. They'd never go back to those days, too much water under the bridge, but they could learn to do things together again.

Stuart reached down and picked up the notebook, then

tapped the cover thoughtfully. It wasn't exactly romance that was needed, it was understanding. The detective had to begin to understand the case, to understand who Gerald was, who the young woman searching for him was.

They needed each other to fit all the pieces of the puzzle together.

Just like the writing group did.

Chapter Eighteen

AVRIL

Unravelling the Clues

'Oh wow, look at this! I think I've found something!'

Avril's heart was pounding, she couldn't quite believe it. When she'd been sitting with Hattie the other day, they'd started to put some of the details that Hattie had written down about Peter into the search engines and they had thrown up some tentative leads. Today she had come in early, keen to make a start before Hattie arrived. It was lovely doing it together, and it was *for* Hattie, but explaining what she was doing and why raised all kinds of questions that Avril didn't really have answers to. Her searches were more instinctive than anything else so it was impossible to answer Hattie's questions – 'Why put his age and art next to each other, that doesn't make any sense?' 'What on earth does trainspotting have to do with anything? I'm sure he doesn't do that now, and if he did it's not going to be on the web thing is it?' Explaining took so much time, especially when there wasn't a simple answer. So Avril thought maybe she could shorten the process a bit, and find out which bits of information were red herrings and which might lead somewhere – before she shared her findings with Hattie.

And now one of her weird combinations of search words seem to have led straight to Peter.

Trainspotting, it seemed, did have something to do with their search. And present-day Peter.

'Found what?' Will asked, getting up from his desk and walking over.

'Look!' Her hand was shaking as she pointed at the screen 'I think this could be Hattie's Peter, don't you?'

Will pulled up the next chair closer to her. His arm brushed against her and for a second she felt like she should move away, but when her gaze met his, a smile flitted over his lips, and it felt so natural she realised that she didn't want to. She'd not dated anybody for ages, she'd not even thought about it. But something about Will felt right. She dragged her gaze away and looked back at the monitor, aware of him doing the same.

'He looks a bit younger than— Hang on, this article is how many … nine years old,' he said. 'You're right, it probably is him.'

'I don't want to raise Hattie's hopes, but do you really think it could be?'

'Oh yes, I do. You're a genius!'

She turned, glancing at him again at exactly the moment he turned to share a smile with her. 'Do you fancy going for a coffee at lunchtime?' Avril blurted the words out before she could stop them, and the heat rushed to her face as his gaze stayed steady for what seemed ages before he replied.

'Sounds like a plan—'

'Good morning, both.' They both jumped as Stuart's voice boomed across the quiet library, before he remembered where he was and coughed nervously. 'Sorry.' He lowered his tone to a whisper that made Avril smile. 'I have the notebook, though I'm not sure Hannibal Hattie will be pleased with what I've written.'

Avril took the book from his outstretched hand. 'Lucky for you Hattie said she'd probably not make it in today,' she said. 'Something about a doctor's appointment, or'—she tried to mimic Hattie's tone—'"a date with the vampire! What they do with all this blood they've taken out of my poor body in the name of tests is anybody's guess. Ridiculous! I'm quite fine, thank you very much, and if there's anything wrong with my blood then an extra tablet or two isn't going to make any difference now. If you shook me, I'm sure I'd rattle."'

Stuart and Will both laughed, and Avril handed the notebook over to Will. 'You're next up!'

'Well.' He glanced at his watch. 'As it's just about time for my lunchbreak, we could take it with us to the café and catch up?'

'Sounds like a plan!' Avril repeated his words back at him and they smiled at each other again.

They walked down to the nearest café in companionable silence. It was busy, but there was one free table at the very back, squeezed into a corner. The same café she had come to on her first day of freedom. The same table she had chosen the last time she had come here – when she'd wanted to hide.

'This is where I found that library book.' Avril pointed to the empty seat at the next table. 'It seems ages ago!'

'The lucky book.' Will grinned. 'You'd have never come into the library if you hadn't seen it.'

Avril laughed. 'Got me in one!' It was strange what could lead you along a new path.

'We'll have to give it pride of place when you bring it back. Have you finished reading it yet?'

'I'm about halfway through, I'm a slow reader,' Avril apologised.

'It's not to do with how quickly you read, it's what the story means to you.' He was studying her intently. But this time, Avril found she wasn't blushing. She smiled back.

There was nothing forced about Will, she felt like she could trust him, that when he said something, he was always genuine.

And when she looked in his eyes, there was something else. That flutter inside her that she felt when his arm brushed hers, when he briefly laid his hand over hers. Will would be easy to fall for, too easy. But would he also be easy to lose? He didn't even live here anymore. He was passing through.

'It was the lost bit in the title that got me, lots of people feel a bit lost, don't they?'

Will nodded, thoughtfully. 'I think we're all searching for something, one way or another,' he said, and his tone softened. 'What have you lost, Avril?'

'My mum,' she answered simply. 'I mean, she died years ago, but I guess I've realised lately that I really do feel like I've lost her now. A huge part of her. It might sound daft, but I feel like I'm missing a part of me. I want to know who she was, which bits of me are from her. I feel'—she took a breath, but Will's gaze never faltered. Neither did he rush her—'that I might have a better idea of who I really am, and what I want from life, if I could get to know her a bit.' She hesitated. 'You know how I said I've never come to the library, how I don't read?'

'Yes?'

'Well, I've got this vague memory of her sitting with me, reading. I think she might have liked books. Maybe, well, I know this might sound crazy, but maybe that's why the library kind of felt a safe place to hide?'

'It doesn't sound crazy. Maybe because you've been thinking about your mum more lately, then a place like the library, with memories of her, has drawn you? And the bit about knowing who you are, well, that figures, too.' He nodded. 'It's that "did she hate anchovies too" thing, isn't it?'

It was Avril's turn to nod. 'And I keep thinking I've seen her, which is totally crazy but maybe it's just my mind's way of saying that it's important. I feel like it's a—'

'—turning point?' Will finished for her. 'I had one of those when I decided to move back up here from Cambridge. It felt like it was something I had to do.'

'Why did you move back?'

'Family.' Will stirred his coffee slowly. 'My dad wasn't well, and I felt that if I didn't come back, it would be something I'd regret.'

'And are you glad you did?' There was something about his tone, the way his shoulders had tensed that made Avril ask. It was weird how so in-tune she felt with him after such a short time. They'd seen each other for a matter of hours since she had first visited the library, but his mannerisms, his tone, had seeped into her unconscious. She could tell when he wasn't happy.

'I am, and I'm not.' He glanced up and smiled at her, his gaze steady. 'Sometimes life isn't as straightforward as you expect, is it?'

Avril thought about her ghosts, about Hattie's lost lover, about her old job, and shook her head. 'Is your dad okay?'

'He is. He needed a heart bypass, but touch wood'—he tapped the table—'all is good.'

'Good, it's great you could come back for him, though. I'd hate to be away from my dad if he was ill.'

'Yeah, you only get one dad,' Will said, his tone soft. 'I couldn't have not been here. And the job fits in well.'

'I bet the library in Cambridge was a bit posher than this one.' Avril couldn't imagine moving from a big, historic place like that back to a small town.

He shook his head. 'I didn't work in a library. This is new.' He shrugged. 'I had a bookshop; it was my uncle's. I used to love it when I was a kid, so when he decided to take early retirement, he asked me if I was interested.'

'Wow.'

'It was like a dream come true!' Will went on. Avril

hadn't heard this much enthusiasm in his tone before. His eyes shone.

She frowned. 'But you gave it up?'

'My uncle said he'd look after it for me for a year, give me some time. He's a bit of a nomad these days, he'd just come back from a stint in Italy, and I think he quite fancied a break from the high life.'

'And you got a job here, in the library.' Avril smiled.

'A year's a long time. I need some income, and I'd get bored just hanging around. It suits me. I'd miss my books otherwise!'

'But you'll be going back soon?' Avril had had to ask the question, but she realised she was holding her breath now. She didn't want him to go. Not yet. She might have only known him for a short while – in fact she hardly knew him at all – but something inside her was telling her that she wanted to get to know him better.

'At some point. But I've not been here long, and I want to be sure Dad is back on his feet before I disappear again. I don't get to see enough of them when I'm in Cambridge and it's nice to catch up with mates that are still here. Though most of them scattered after uni.'

Mates. Avril couldn't help herself; the thought was in her head. Did that include Lucy? Avril didn't want Will to think she was grilling him, but had he come back for her, as well as his parents?

'And old flames?' she asked jokingly.

'There aren't any of them, I'm a late developer!' He matched her tone.

'Apart from Lucy?' She couldn't help herself, though she

saw him frown. 'You told us the competition organiser was an ex?'

'Did I?'

Avril felt flustered, but she really wanted to know. 'Hattie was asking about why you didn't want to do the competition?'

He sighed. 'I know. I do remember. But Lucy wasn't an old flame from school, I met her in Cambridge.'

'Oh.' So that was why this was so raw with him. Lucy wasn't old news; she was the present not the past. It was no wonder he didn't want anything to do with the competition if they'd only just split up.

'I met her down there, and she loved Cambridge. She was a city girl.'

Avril glanced up to see he was studying her. Met her gaze.

'She wasn't happy when I said I needed to come back up here for a while, and at first I thought she'd stay in Cambridge. But then she fell out with her boss at work and suddenly decided it was a great idea – a career break. We came up a couple of times looking for somewhere to live … and she met'—he paused—'she met somebody.' He looked down and stirred his coffee slowly, even though there was very little left in the bottom of the cup. 'In the end, she moved up here before me.'

Will met Avril's gaze again and his eyes seemed hard, not sad. He must have taken it really badly, she thought.

'It was odd,' he went on. 'She was here in my home-town, somewhere she'd never been, with somebody else. I still can't believe she did it.'

'Met somebody?' What was his name? Avril wondered. She could remember Will telling them that Lucy had a new boyfriend. Jack? No, Jake. Will didn't even seem to want to say his name, though, as if he was angrier about him, than Lucy.

'No.' Will's laugh was dry, when he added, 'If I'm honest, it wasn't the meeting somebody that knocked me sideways, it was the fact that she moved here, well a few miles up the road, when she knew that I'd be here, that I had no choice. You'd have thought she'd have wanted to be further away from me, wouldn't you?'

'Did you … do you know this guy – Jake, isn't it?' Avril took an intake of breath at the look that settled on his features.

'Oh yes, I know him.'

Will shook his head in what looked like disgust, then took a breath and put his spoon down and sat up straight, putting a smile on his face.

'Do you fancy doing this again sometime?' he said, changing the subject. 'Or maybe a drink one evening before you head home?'

Avril blinked at the sudden turn around. 'I do.' She did, she couldn't believe how easy she had found it to chat to Will. To say yes. They were so different. He was a book lover, a bookshop owner, a librarian and – she was sure of it – a romantic who was looking for love. And she was a girl who'd not read a book since she left school, until the one she'd found in this café. And a girl who couldn't imagine falling in love. She didn't want to promise to love somebody forever, because that was a promise that was too easily broken – wasn't it?

But she had a feeling that Will would be a good friend. That would be all he wanted, too. She probably wasn't his type anyway. He probably dated girls who read books, wore sensible shoes. Didn't have pink hair.

'Here.' On impulse, Avril unlocked her phone, and held it out to him. 'Send your phone a message from mine, then we've got each other's numbers.'

They paid, and as they left the café, Will held the door open for her.

'Hattie's going to be so pleased that you've made some progress finding Peter,' he said.

'I know. I just hope it's not a dead end.' Outside on the pavement, Avril waited for Will to fall in step with her. 'At least it's straightforward, though, there's information out there. But it's not so easy to find out about Mum. I don't like to ask Dad, it upsets him, and my stepmother would not be happy if she found out.'

'Oh?'

Avril sighed. 'She'd find life easier if I'd moved away like you did!'

'Maybe she just finds it difficult, dealing with your dad's past.'

'Yeah, I've thought about that, which is another reason I don't dig. But'—she shrugged—'he does have a past and she knew that when she married him, didn't she?'

'She did, but falling in love doesn't always take stuff like that into account, does it?'

'I wouldn't know.' Avril sighed.

They'd reached the top of the path that led down to the library doors, and Will stopped.

'Avril. You can't research your mum on a computer, you need to talk to people.'

'Talk?'

'Well, you said you can't talk to your dad about her, but there must be other people. I mean, there are parent and toddler groups here, did she go to one where you live? She must have had friends, places she went to, hobbies?'

Avril nodded slowly. 'That's true. Yep, that's a good idea. Thanks.' She smiled at Will. 'Oh, we never read Stuart's chapter!'

'True! Here, you read it and let me have it back before you leave the library today.' He held out the notebook.

'Long time no see.'

Will froze, his arm still outstretched, as the softly spoken words reached them.

Framed in the doorway was a woman who had obviously been waiting for him. She was the type of stylish woman that Avril sometimes wished she could be, then decided was far too much effort.

Blonde, bobbed hair that looked like she'd just walked out of the hairdressers. Immaculate make-up, as far as Avril could tell from this distance. Slim, and wearing what had to be, from the way it hung gracefully from her slender shoulders, a silk top and the type of full, floaty trousers that would have made Avril look, and feel, like a hippo.

'Lucy.' Will's tone was flat and Avril snuck a sideways glance at him.

So, this was her. Lucy.

'I'll leave you to it,' she said, slipping past Lucy and into the library. But she wasn't sure that Will even heard her.

'It's so lovely to see you.' Out of the corner of her eye she saw Lucy close the distance and fling her arms round Will.

Inside, Avril put the notebook on the desk as she passed it.

She didn't want to see him in a clinch with the woman who, good or bad, still had the power to touch him. And anyway, he'd be back off down to his bookshop soon, wouldn't he.

Was it even worthwhile being friends?

Chapter Six

(Stuart)

Sam sat down at his desk and picked up the diary. He'd already read through it several times, but the answer had to lie between its pages. Or at least a clue or two must be there. The missing-person's report had been pretty run of the mill, but since starting his search for the missing man, Sam had begun to wonder exactly who he was.

The diary was doing little to help. The trouble was, the entries were scant. In fact, apart from his name there was very little in here that could say it ever belonged to him — let alone give a clue as to his whereabouts.

His daughter had seemed down to earth, but worried, as she said Gerald was a man of routine. She had moved away from home but kept in touch with him, and he was always there when she expected him to be. He would normally go to his allotment each evening and shut the hens in before stopping off at his local for a pint.

He'd done neither for ages, according to the neighbours. He had, it seemed, disappeared into thin air.

She'd insisted he was reliable. Ordinary. That his divorce a few years ago had not affected his day-to-day life. He had expected it. Her parents, she'd said, had not been close, not for years, but had stayed together for the sake of their child. Her mother had gone travelling — which had come as no surprise — and was occasionally in touch, but often in locations where she was unable — or unwilling — to contact her daughter. If she had not been able to contact her mother, she would have thought nothing of it, she said. But her father was different.

Now, though, it seemed he was neither reliable nor ordinary. The mysterious Eliza had said she suspected that she was his daughter. That he had a second, secret, life.

How did all the pieces of this jigsaw fit together?

Sam had a feeling that he needed to understand this man and his life, or he had no chance of finding him.

Eliza's mother was, he was sure, one part of the puzzle. But she was dead. Which was why Eliza was looking for answers. She'd uncovered lies, deception, and now she didn't trust her mother, nor this missing man. Sam was sure that she had a deep distrust of him as well. But she had at least given him her contact details and promised to bring him her mother's diary and the letter.

It seemed that she wanted to move on, and she couldn't until she had the answers she was looking for.

He was sure Eliza wasn't seeking revenge; she'd shown very little interest in finding out more about the daughter – had just passed comment that she might not be the only child that she believed herself to be.

Two very different people worried about where Gerald was.

Was that because the deception ran deeper? A deception that his daughter was unconsciously aware of. Could he have been in danger?

Was there somebody else involved? Somebody other than the two women, somebody out for revenge?

Was that why the two women were so worried about finding him?

He turned the pages, barely seeing the writing on the page as he mulled over the possibilities in his mind.

And there was of course the mystery over Eliza's mother's death. It had been an accident – but now Eliza seemed to be questioning that. He needed to see the report, to find out what happened.

He jotted another note on the pad. It was all question marks, no answers. But that was what his job was often like. The truth could be hard to dig out, because situations like this were always mired in lies and distrust; personal agendas and prejudices were a smoke screen, and often people didn't realise that the little things they had forgotten were the clues needed to solve the bigger puzzle.

Sam needed to see how this all fitted together — otherwise he had no direction, no way of knowing which were facts, and which were assumptions. He needed to identify the lies.

Sam wasn't really a loner; he liked being part of a team — and he wanted more than anything to be able to have Eliza on board. For them to work together. But before he could do that he needed to eliminate her as a suspect.

He pulled out a new sheet of paper and wrote the names down.

Gerald Old.

Marie (daughter).

He hesitated for a moment then added another name.

Fiona Old (wife, and Marie's mother).

He'd had trouble tracking her down. Marie had said she could be elusive, that she was often in places without internet access or phone connections, which was very convenient — for her.

He picked up the photograph that had been in the suitcase. Eliza had referred to it as Gerald's, but Sam wasn't sure. There was no proof of that. The case had been in her mother, Sally's, wardrobe. If he could prove it did belong to Gerald, then he had a definite link between the two families. But it could have belonged to Sally, or somebody else — even though the belongings were Gerald's.

He'd shown Marie the contents of the case, and she had told him that the photograph was of her mother. Fiona.

But why would Sally have a case with such personal belongings —

a photograph of his wife. A diary. It didn't exactly suggest that they were in a relationship, did it?

He frowned as he underlined Fiona's name and added a question mark.

The diary bothered him. Eliza had said that her mother had left a matching one. He really needed to see it. To compare the two.

And then there was the letter. Admitting to some terrible wrong.

But he knew full well that one person's 'terrible' was another's barely noticed mishap.

But Sally had not wanted it to rest. She hadn't wanted to bury her truth. Maybe if somebody else had paid more attention to it when she was alive, they would have been able to help – persuade her that no problem was insurmountable. That people loved her. She didn't have to die.

He wiped his palm over his eyes, suddenly feeling tired. Was he really suspecting that she had committed suicide? He must not make assumptions. Whatever guilt she had clearly been living with (according to her daughter), he must not jump to conclusions.

He carefully added to the list of names.

Eliza Marsh (daughter?).

Sally Marsh – accidental death?

Sam was sure that Eliza felt guilt: guilt that her mother had secrets she knew nothing about – guilt that she had never pushed for answers. Had never tried to help. But sometimes it doesn't matter how much you help, sometimes things are just meant to be. He knew that from experience. Sometimes parents keep things from their family to protect them, to stop them worrying. For a million different reasons.

He wanted to help Eliza move on, and to do that he needed to close this case. He picked up his phone. It was clear what he needed to do next. Find Fiona Old, examine the report on Sally Marsh's death, and look at the second diary and letter.

His colleagues could help with the first two. Tomorrow, he was meeting Eliza to gather the rest of the information.

He felt the corners of his mouth lift, along with his heart.

It would be good to see Eliza again – and not just to solve this case. Although he was sure she held the key to it, a solution she wasn't aware she knew.

They could work together; he wanted to work together.

He turned to the photograph again, and felt goosebumps rise along his arms. This was important. He didn't know why, but his gut was telling him, and past experience told him to go with his instincts.

Fiona Old. Why had she disappeared? Was she responsible for her husband's disappearance, and possibly his death? Was that what Sally was trying to tell Eliza? Or, and he paused, was Gerald actually with Fiona? Had they done a moonlight flit together? And was that in some way connected with Sally's death?

He shook his head. He might be getting carried away. But he had to investigate every possibility. Every angle. He had to be thorough. It was his job.

Chapter Nineteen

WILL

Turning the Page

'Oh, my God, it's been so long.' Lucy's breathless tone filled Will's head – which wasn't surprising seeing as her mouth was inches from his ear. He felt suffocated in Lucy's grasp and had to fight the urge to push her away. Instead, he took a firm hold of her forearms so that he could extricate himself as politely as possible. Just in time to see Avril disappear into the library.

A weird sense of loss lurched in his stomach.

He'd enjoyed spending time with Avril. He'd not enjoyed talking about Lucy, about the move, but it had probably done him good. He'd not talked about it to anybody, and things gnawed away at you if you didn't let them out, didn't they?

'That's what happens when people move on with their lives.' His tone was stiff, even to his own ears. 'I thought you were coming next week? The team aren't all here today.'

'Well, I was in town, just a social call really.' She smiled, the old beguiling smile that he used to fall for. 'I can't believe you're still here! You must be due to go back to Cambridge soon?'

'I don't—' Will didn't know when – or if – he'd be going back. And it was none of Lucy's business. But before he could finish what he was saying, she butted in. She'd always done it, and he'd not really noticed. But he did now.

'Well, I'll be back again next week for our meeting, I guess you'll still be here!' She laughed.

Great.

'Was that one of your team, or…' The question hung in the air, so Will chose to ignore it. 'Are you going to introduce me?'

Will made a move towards the library doors, and Lucy followed. 'How's Jake?'

'Oh, he's fine, you know Jake, ha ha.'

He did, oh yes, he knew Jake all too well.

'I see you've made a start.' Lucy pointed at the notebook, which Avril had left for him.

'We have.' Will looked down at the notebook, then back up at Lucy.

He'd known this moment would come, and he'd been dreading it. But now, when he should feel wrong-footed, instead he felt relief.

When Lucy had hugged him, he'd felt smothered. Not even a hint of the excitement or longing that he'd half expected to feel. He'd wanted to shake her off. To go after Avril.

He didn't care about Lucy anymore, if he was honest,

not in that way. And Lucy hadn't even bothered to ask about his parents. The reason they'd come back to Cheshire, the move that had led to her meeting Jake, the move that had led to their split when he'd found them together. That feeling of déjà vu that had hit him in the gut.

The only problem he had was Jake.

'Does he ever mention—'

'You? School?' She laughed. 'Oh Will, not everybody is stuck in the past you know. It doesn't matter what happened between you back then.' She shook her head, still smiling. 'We've all moved on.'

'Does he ever mention Sarah?' This time he managed to finish his sentence, even though saying her name made him flinch.

'Sarah?' Lucy was wearing a puzzled frown. Of course Jake hadn't mentioned Sarah, Will's sister. Jake had moved on. 'Look, Will, I don't know why you're trying to cause trouble between me and Jake. We both knew our relationship wasn't working out, didn't we?'

He nodded. They did. They'd been treading water for a long time, not even really enjoying each other's company. Just being there. Too comfortable to do anything about it.

'I'm not trying to cause trouble,' he said wearily, 'it's just…'

'I don't want to hear it, Will. Okay? I'm sure Jake went out with this, Sarah, and lots of other people. So what?'

So what indeed. 'Well, if that's all, I've got a lot of work to do, Lucy. I'll see you next week.'

'You will.' Her smile was just a little bit too bright.

'And don't forget to say goodbye before you go back to Cambridge.'

'I won't. You'll be the first to know'—he paused—'as you'll see my letter of resignation.'

'If you're still working here. It is only maternity leave you know.'

'I know.' Will glanced down at the notebook. Waited for her to turn away. To walk out.

If she didn't want to hear about Jake, if she wouldn't ask him herself, then who was he to interfere? She'd made it clear that it was none of his business.

But it still made him uneasy.

He felt sorry for her.

He took a deep breath, to ground himself and then glanced around, to check that nobody had been watching their tense exchange.

It was quiet in the library. Avril and Hattie were sitting at one of the computers, totally engrossed – presumably in their search for Peter – and Stuart had already left.

He was pleased for Hattie, hopefully Avril's search would come to something. It was good to have something to work towards, as long as disappointment didn't lie at the end of it.

He wanted to help Avril in the same way that she was helping Hattie. If she wouldn't talk to her father, then hopefully they could find somebody else who knew Ophelia. And sometimes a friend knew a person better than their family did. Sometimes there were things that you'd share with a friend, somebody who you felt wouldn't judge, that you felt unable to share with those closest.

He'd look later. See what he could find. Altrincham

wasn't that far away, and the library might be a good place to start. After all, didn't Avril say she had vague memories of reading books with her mother?

Will reached for the notebook.

He felt the corners of his mouth lift, along with his heart.

It would be good to see Eliza again – and not just to solve this case. Although he was sure she held the key to it, a solution she wasn't aware she knew.

They could work together; he wanted to work together.

Will realised that he was smiling. Did you have to understand the lies before you could move on? Stuart was analytical, he liked answers. He wanted loose end to be tied up neatly. But was that how life really was?

He shook his head. This Sam and Eliza deserved some happiness, there was a clear attraction there that had developed in the story, even if the others in the group hadn't really intended it. He'd push that on. A romance could be kindled before they found the answers – surely two people working together stood more chance of solving a riddle, than one on their own?

He sat back in his chair. Stuart had written that Eliza was mistrustful but wasn't seeking revenge.

Will thought of his own life. He probably had to be more Stuart, more Eliza.

He didn't like Jake; he didn't trust him.

His gaze scanned back up the page. One paragraph drew him back. Why had Stuart suspected Sally of committing suicide? He frowned. It was an odd addition, one that didn't seem to fit with Stuart's open, matter-of-fact approach.

He wiped his palm over his eyes, suddenly feeling tired. Was he really suspecting that she had committed suicide? He must not make assumptions. Whatever guilt she had clearly been living with (according to her daughter), he must not jump to conclusions.

Will flicked back through the pages to Stuart's previous chapter. He'd mentioned about not caring enough. There was definitely, Will felt, something on Stuart's mind. Emotions that were easier to write about than talk about. Did Stuart feel some guilt about not understanding somebody? If he did, Will was sure it wasn't Jo. They seemed so content together. But then again, on the outside, he and Lucy had looked like a good match.

Maybe he needed to try and understand Lucy better, and then he might find a way of talking to her about Jake. But was it any of his business any longer?

Life was nearly always more complicated than it appeared. It was true that you shouldn't assume that the people who appear together on the outside are okay on the inside.

He closed the book slowly. Maybe this project was going to be therapeutic for all of them.

Chapter Twenty

HATTIE

Reading Between the Lines

'He won't go back, dear.'

'Sorry?'

'Don't give me that! You know what I mean.' Hattie had been watching Avril, the poor girl hadn't been able to keep her eyes off Will and the dolled-up young woman who was trying to keep his attention. It was, to Hattie, blatantly obvious that Will was struggling to stay polite. Another man, like Harold, would have given the woman short shrift and shown her the door.

But it was, she supposed, a library. One had to be polite. And Will was a nice man.

'I assume that is the woman he was talking about, the one in charge? The one who upset him?'

Avril shrugged her shoulders.

'And what's—' Hattie copied her shrug, which brought on a coughing fit. They both waited for it to subside.

'Well, if he wasn't still bothered about her he wouldn't have minded doing the competition would he?' said Avril.

'But he is doing the competition,' Hattie pointed out.

'And now who's pretending not to know what I mean! You know he didn't want to; you bullied him into it.'

'I did not bully him!' Hattie paused. Maybe, on reflection, one could call it bullying. 'It was for his own good. I just pushed him in the right direction. We need him.'

'Hmm.'

'And he doesn't need her. He's curling his lip.'

'No, he isn't!'

'He might as well be. He's not the type to make the same mistake twice.'

'Everybody is when it comes to…' Avril paused, and Hattie fought the smile that was twitching at the corners of her mouth.

'Love?'

'Something like that.'

'And have you made the same mistake twice, then?' Hattie was intrigued, she knew nothing at all about the Avril's love life. But such an attractive young woman must have, or have had, one.

'No, Hattie. I have not. I've no interest in love.'

Or maybe not. 'I think you'll find you will if the right person happens along. You can't fight it, Avril, it's hormonal.'

'Really?' Avril raised an eyebrow, and Hattie suspected she was going to overstep the mark and mention Peter. So she was going to get in there first.

'Really. That is why Peter had to run away, or he

wouldn't have been able to help himself. He couldn't have stayed close by and watched me and Harold.' The words came out rather more forcibly than Hattie had intended. Sometimes she hoped that they were true, but often she knew that they probably were not. Avril's gaze met hers and she knew what she was thinking. If Peter had cared that much, why hadn't he stayed and fought for her? Except, they would have had to flee – nobody would have fought her father and hoped to win. She looked at Avril. It was hard being young. It was all well and good saying that whatever didn't kill you made you stronger, but she sometimes thought it just hardened you, made you put self-protective barriers up. Loss, suffering, unkindness could make you more alone. Alone wasn't good. She'd never wanted to be with Harold really, not after those first few honeymoon years – but being without him had left a yawning gap. People weren't, she'd realised, meant to be alone. To suffer in silence.

Sometimes Hattie didn't want to be strong. She wanted to be loved.

Just like Avril wanted to be. By a mother.

'Your mother wouldn't have left you if she'd had any choice,' Hattie said softly. 'I'm sure she would have wanted to see you grow up, she'd have wanted to know who you were, just as you want to know who she was.'

Avril tapped on the computer keyboard. 'I don't want to lose anybody else.' Her voice was low.

Hattie patted her hand. 'But you miss out on so much if you don't decide to take a risk sometimes.' But she did understand what Avril meant. Commitment could mean loss. 'And Will is a very nice young man, and he fancies you!'

'So you say! Anyway, I'm not bothered whether he still likes her or not. We're just friends, he's helping me. He helped me find this guy for you.' Avril pointed at the screen.

Hattie studied her. She wasn't quite sure if Avril was kidding herself, but her normal open face had that shut-down look that told Hattie not to push things. She'd bide her time and try and be patient. Losing her mother must have been hard for Avril. And now, just as she'd got chatty with Will, that other woman had shown up and draped herself over him like a wet flannel. Not that he'd responded. Even from where she had been sitting, Hattie could see Will's body language. He had tensed up. He most definitely was not a man in love, or even lust.

'Is there anything you think we need to put in this email, Avril?' she asked.

She looked at the screen. The moment Avril had shown her the article – and the photo, of the man – she'd known it was Peter.

Her heart had given that tiny skip it had always done when she'd seen him.

But now that he was here, in front of her again, it was slightly frightening. To do this, to get in touch, was risking destroying the dream Hattie had held onto for all these years.

He could be dead. He could be ill. He could be married, have a family he loved. He might not even remember her.

But hadn't she told Avril to be brave, that taking a risk was worth it?

'To be honest,' said Avril, 'if it was me, I'd keep it pretty short and to the point. You know, just say who you are, ask if he's the Peter you used to know, tell him you hope he's well, and that it would be nice to get in touch. That kind of thing.'

'That sounds perfect, Avril, I will go with whatever you think as you know best about these things.'

'Well, I don't—'

'About this emailing thing, I mean, not about finding people.' Hattie frowned. 'But how will he get in touch with me? I've not got a computer, you know, and is it wise to put my address, in case he isn't Peter?' Though she was sure it was. 'Or somebody else gets hold of this?'

'I'll put my email address if you like, unless you'd prefer to keep it private between the two of you?' Avril offered. 'We could say I'm a friend and if he's happy to chat he can give a phone number or something, then it's up to him? Just in case it's, er'—she paused— 'awkward?'

'Whatever you think.'

'Actually, I think we should set up a new email address, I'll do it, and you can write the password down. That way you can check for new messages yourself.'

'Do you think we should say that Harold has passed away?'

'Hmm.' Avril frowned, thinking. 'Maybe, I mean you've got a kind of opening, then, haven't you? I'll put that in. Here, what do you think?'

Hattie looked at the short message.

All those years of heartache and hope bundled up into a few short words. Words that might hold promise, or disappointment.

Dear Peter,

I am getting in touch with you as I am hopeful that you are somebody that I knew many years ago. If you knew a Harold and a Harriet at school, then you might well be the Peter I am looking for. If you are, I hope you do not mind me getting in touch.

I have sad news to convey, Harold died a short while ago, and I have thought much about the three of us and our childhood, since. It would be so nice to talk to you again, if you were so inclined, though I know that you have probably moved on, and it may be difficult.

I am writing this from the town library with the help of a friend, and you can contact me at this email address if you so wish.

I have recently moved to a new apartment, but still have the house that we lived in. It would be so lovely to talk to you again, but please do not worry if it is not convenient.

I hope you are well.

Hattie

'Perfect.' Hattie leaned past Avril and tapped the 'send' button, before the doubts had time to raise their heads. She might not know that much about computers yet, but she knew that much. 'Well, now that's done we need to think about this competition. We need to win this, for Will! We're going to show that woman that she can't dilly-dally with his emotions.'

'What about Peter?'

'Well, we've written to him now, there's not much else we

can do, is there? All we can do is wait and see if he responds and I'm not going to just sit here and stew.'

'Of course you're not,' said Avril with a small smile.

Hattie smiled back. Success! Avril was smiling again.

'And Will needs us.'

'I think he can look after himself, and he's busy enough without this competition.'

'He's busy doing the competition,' Hattie said with satisfaction. 'Look, he's reading Stuart's chapter. Now, there's a man who doesn't have a problem with commitment. Stuart's doing this competition to impress that lovely wife of his!'

'Do you think so?'

'I certainly do. I think, despite the lack of hair, he's like a swan. He's committed for life, she's his future.'

Avril giggled. 'Lack of hair! You can't say that!'

'Follicly challenged, then? Well, however politely you put it, he's not much of a swan now, is he?'

'I thought it was elephants that commit for life?'

'I'm sure it is swans, but he's definitely more of an elephant. Now, is that a box of homemade flapjacks I can see by the kettle?'

'I'll get you some, shall I? Do you mind if I use the computer for a bit, or did you want to look at something else?'

'Of course you can. What use is it to me now?'

'Will gave me an idea.'

'Oh, did he?' Hattie smiled as Avril blushed.

'About finding out more about Mum.'

'That sounds like a plan. What was the idea?'

'To look at groups she might have been involved with,

like the library, or parents and toddler stuff. See if I can find anybody that she might have been friends with.'

Hattie fought to get the key in the lock of her front door. She was tired, and when she was tired her body didn't work properly. And she was, as her mother would have said, 'mithered'. She might have told Avril that they'd done all they could as far as finding Peter went, and it was now just a waiting game, but as the steps took them closer to him the doubts swirled around more furiously in her head.

It felt like a betrayal of Harold, even if he was dead. They'd not had an easy relationship, but he had still been her husband.

The key finally found the lock, despite her trembling hands, and relief flooded through her as the door opened. These days, small things could seem like insurmountable problems.

If Harold had been here, he might have tutted at her ineptitude and pushed her aside. But he would have been there.

She'd wanted to be alone, wanted her own life back to do with as she wanted. But now that she had it, she missed his presence. Two was easier than one, even if he had been a grumpy, and occasionally cruel, bugger.

At one time it had felt like a relief that he hadn't let her have the baby she'd wanted – because if he'd not been kind to a child, she wouldn't have stood for it. But there had been so many times when she had wondered if fatherhood would have mellowed him, brought back the old Harold. Because when they had first met, when they'd been mere children themselves, he had seemed happier, freer. He'd always been the silent type, the watcher rather than the talker – which had been Peter's role. And he had never been showy or flamboyant. He didn't seem to care about impressing anybody else. But he'd drop in remarks that would make her laugh, and he'd remember comments she'd make about her favourite colour or flower, and he would shyly sneak gifts to her.

The memory brought a smile to Hattie's lips. She'd not thought about those gifts for years; about Harold's kindness – that had been lost.

At the time she'd not paid that much attention to Harold's gifts because Peter had won her heart. But she had kept the trinkets, the beautiful butterfly brooch, the pressed four-leaf clover, the pretty shell.

Peter had never given her gifts; she hadn't really thought about that before. At the time, his company was all that she had wanted. But when he'd left, it meant she had nothing to remind her of him.

When Harold had gone, though, she had been surrounded by memories of him, and their past, good and bad. Until now, it had been the bad that had preyed on her mind.

She sighed as she sank down into the armchair. What had happened to that old box of bits and pieces. Souvenirs of the young Harold, of the couple they'd once been?

No doubt it would turn up when she emptied their house – once the contract with the buyer had finally gone through. The box had sat in the bottom drawer of her bedside cabinet for years, until she'd pushed it onto the top shelf of the wardrobe one day when he'd been particularly cruel. The day he'd told her he'd made sure they couldn't have children.

But that box was Harold's youth. The nice bits, before he became her controlling husband.

Chapter Seven

(Will)

Eliza caught her breath as Sam handed over the diary they had found in the suitcase. She laid it next to the other one that she had brought with her.

They matched, just as she knew they would.

'When I saw the diary in the suitcase I didn't expect to see Gerald's name in it, that was a shock. But'—*she paused*—*'it was more of a shock that it was just like Mum's.'*

'They're identical.' DI Sam Ford nodded.

'Which means—*'*

'Your mum and this man have to be connected.'

There was no escaping that fact. The books were identical and distinct – not the kind you bought from a local supermarket. This wasn't some coincidence.

'You've read your mother's?'

'Of course. That's why Gerald's name was familiar, why I knew that's who she wanted me to look for. Gerald Old.'

'She mentions him?'

Eliza nodded.

'Were…' Sam hesitated, as though looking for a delicate way of putting what he was about to say, so she finished the sentence for him.

'Were they lovers?'

He nodded.

'Well, the way she talks about him suggests that they could have

been — that's why I wondered if this daughter of his is my half-sister. But I think Mum had put a stop to it.'

'She wasn't in love with him?'

'I think she had been.' Eliza was glad that he had left his pen on the table, that he wasn't taking notes. It was easier to explain when he felt like a friend, not a detective solving a case. He'd make a good friend, she was sure of it. 'But then the entries changed. She talked about love, regrets and wasting time instead of moving on.'

'She ended it?'

'She vowed to finish what had been going on. She said she had fallen out of love with love. Here, look.' She flipped the diary open at a page she'd marked.

Sam moved closer, his forearm brushing against hers, the smell of his hair reaching her nostrils as he bent his head over the book.

He read aloud.

'"I've not just decided I need to move on, my heart has actually already done so. I've realised that it wasn't love, it was an infatuation, it was deliciously wrong, it only grew so big because it was illicit. When I saw you the other day, at a distance, I realised that I felt nothing. That delicious thrill had disappeared, and I didn't even want to know what you were doing, who you were with. All I could think of was how wrong it had been. I came back to reality, and I found somebody that I actually did love for who they were. I realised what love really is."'

'She wrote this quite a while ago. Her final words about him in the diary were written many years before she died. After this one, the entries are about other things,' Eliza explained.

But Eliza still needed to know who he was. Was Gerald her father? Was he just a lover? Was he the reason they moved house so *often, that she had to move schools, was it this man who was responsible for the hours her mother had spent crying, then the hours she laughed?*

Eliza could tie in the date the last entry had been written to the change in their life.

She was only young, a child. But she remembered. They had moved home for the final time, and it was as though her mother had been freed from some cage. She was happy again.

But if Gerald really was her father, was that why her mother had carried on the relationship for so long? she wondered.

'It looks like she loved him for years.' She paused, then looked up from the diary, at Sam. 'If he was my father, maybe that's why Mum didn't move on earlier, because she hoped I'd get to know him?'

'But you didn't know him?'

'I don't remember ever meeting him. But maybe I did, as a baby. Was I to blame for my mother's tears and heartache?'

'You can't be to blame for her actions, Eliza. They were her decisions, and you were a child.'

She'd been desperate to find out who this man was. But suddenly Eliza felt fear. Her mother had walked away — maybe it would be better for her to do the same thing.

He silently pushed the other diary closer to her, his finger resting on it to stop her opening the cover.

'I don't think you're going to find your answers yet, Eliza. I'm really sorry.' She could hear the concern in his voice. It built the anticipation in her, but also the need to touch him, to lay her hand over his. But she couldn't. She mustn't.

'There's very little in this diary,' Sam said. 'It's not like your mum's. It hasn't told me anything about him, or where he might be. But you might spot something I've missed.' He lifted his hand off the book.

The moment had gone, and she felt strangely sad. 'I don't know how he felt about your mother. But whatever it was, he's not put any explanation, or written about his feelings, in here.'

Eliza stared at the cover of the diary. 'Maybe that was the point.' Her voice sounded hollow to her own ears. 'Maybe he didn't have any.'

She reached forward, lifted the first page. She had to know.

Chapter Twenty-One

AVRIL

Research

'That was good!' Avril's dad grinned and pushed his plate away.

'Can't beat fish and chips.' She smiled back at him, then pointed at the chips that were left on her plate. 'Want more? No way can I finish that lot.'

'Waste not, want not, as your gran used to say.' He tipped some of the chips onto his own plate and tucked in.

Her phone beeped with a notification.

'Get that if you want.' He waved a finger. Avril shrugged. She'd never been one to spend a lot of time on her phone. Sure, when she was waiting around, she might scroll through it, but a lot of the time she'd hear a beep and ignore it until she'd finished what she was doing. Apart from her dad, and her job – which she didn't have now – nothing was ever that important. And her dad was here. It was their regular treat – he'd pop in with a takeaway on the day that

Lisa met up with the twins. It was a fortnightly thing, something they'd started a long time ago. It had not really occurred to her before, but it was something she remembered her dad had been quite insistent about. He'd told Lisa that they each needed some time with their own kids. Fenced time.

'Go on, I know you want to. Don't mind me.'

She glanced down at the screen and was surprised to see Will's name in the notifications. She'd not forgotten that they'd swapped numbers in the café, but after seeing him with Lucy, she'd pushed the thought out of her head.

For a brief moment in the café, it had felt that there was something more between them, and she'd been surprised that she hadn't wanted to push it away because that was what she normally did. Maybe unconsciously she'd realised that it may have felt that way to her, but to him it was just friendship.

He'd be moving on soon. Even if he wasn't interested in Lucy, he was interested in Cambridge and his bookshop. She'd overheard Lucy ask him about that.

Avril opened the message he'd sent her.

'I found this, any help?'

She clinked on the link. A link to a local newspaper. Why would he be sending her that? Then the photograph caught her eye, and her throat dried.

The picture wasn't clear, but that was probably because her hand was trembling.

She put her phone down on the table and stared at the image.

He'd have come across it by accident. Except he hadn't,

because it was from an archive she realised. He'd been looking.

Her vision blurred with tears. Will had been searching. For her.

'*That's really kind of you. Thanks!*'

'*No probs. There might be more, I'll keep on looking.*'

It was a group of people sitting on chairs. Her mother was one of them, and with her, Avril was holding a large picture book.

So, Mum had read with her. They must have been to a library. The memory hadn't been false. Avril swallowed down the lump in her throat.

Her mother had an arm around her but her head was turned away and she was grinning at the woman sitting next to her.

A friend?

Will had said she needed to talk to people if she wanted to learn about who her mother really was. And if she couldn't talk to her dad, then she needed to find her friends.

Nobody had ever spoken about Phee having friends. But she must have done. Friends like this woman sitting beside her. Friends that you made at different times in your life, who could support you. This woman had a child sitting in front of her that looked the same age as Avril.

She studied the text at the side of the photo. And yes, her mother's name was there – but it was hard to match the other names to the faces. They didn't seem to be in any particular order. So, she would have to do a little detective work of her own. She had to find some of these people. Talk.

'Everything okay, love?'

She'd forgotten her dad was there, and she jumped guiltily, reaching to grab her phone and put it out of sight before he could see what she was looking at. But his hand was over hers, stilling her.

She looked up, and his steady gaze met hers.

'It's okay, Avril. I don't mind you—'

'I need to know.' She blurted out.

'I know.' He sighed. Leaned back in his chair. 'I know, love. I'm sorry.'

'I want to know who she was,' she said softly.

'She was my everything.' The gentle words cut through her. There was such a certainty behind them, a note in her father's voice she'd never heard before. 'Every day I wish she was still here, but that's not fair on Lisa, is it? I shouldn't think thoughts like that. I don't want to hurt Lisa, so I feel bad if I bring Phee up. But I wish she was here for you, Avril.'

Avril's eyes filled with unexpected tears. 'I know she's not here,' she said, 'I do accept that, but I feel like a part of me is missing.'

'So do I.' He paused, then leaned forward to pick up her mobile. 'What's all this about, then?'

'I thought maybe if I could find out what she used to do, find people she knew.'

'You could ask me.' There was a hurt edge to his voice.

'I didn't want to upset you, Dad.'

He sighed. 'But you might be right about her friends. They might show you a different side to her.' He nodded, as though for his own benefit. 'It does upset me, thinking about her, but it's not fair on you. I guess I've run away from my own feelings and forgotten about how it's been affecting you. She wouldn't be happy if she knew.'

'I'm sure she'd be happy with everything you've done for me, Dad.'

'There's a box of her stuff in the loft. I should have given it to you before, but I didn't want to let go of it.'

Avril moved to his side and wrapped her arms round him. She knew exactly how he felt. She'd not wanted to let go of anything that had been her mum's. She'd hung on to the money, the few possessions that her mother had always said were for her, the things that used to hold her scent.

'You don't have to.'

'I know I don't. But if I keep it then it's locked away. You'll let it breathe,' he said. 'You'll look at it. There's not much, mind,' he warned. Then he pointed at her phone. A small smile crept across his features as he studied the photograph. 'Ahh, now there's a face from the past.'

'Who?' Avril looked at the photo. 'Was one of those girls a friend of Mum's?'

He pointed at the woman her mother was grinning with. 'Oh yes, they were friends. Like that they were'—he crossed his fingers over—'like twins. They even looked alike. But I've not seen her for years. After your mother died, I didn't mix with that group anymore. I couldn't bear going where she had with you, or keep in touch with her friends, it was too difficult.'

'What was her name?'

He tapped on the article. 'Mandy. That was her, Mandy.'

'You don't mind if I see if I can find her?'

'Of course I don't, love. If there's anything else you want to know, though, ask. Okay?'

'Okay.'

'I've got better photos of the two of them than that one. You can hardly see her in this, but people thought they were sisters. I'll dig them out when I get home and send you copies if you like?'

'Please.' Avril smiled, trying to lift the mood. 'Did she hate olives?'

'Nope, you've got that from me, I'm afraid, girl! She loved them.' He chuckled. 'So, who's this fella, Will, then? New one?' He winked.

Avril felt the heat rush to her cheeks. 'He works at the library; he's helping with the competition.'

'Is that right?' Her dad was studying her intently. He knew that she didn't talk about her feelings – a side of her that also came from him, not Phee.

'He's kind,' she said simply. 'And not at all like me. He reads books, and he's'—she paused—'well, a bit of a romantic.'

Her dad chuckled. 'Ah, well, not at all like you, then.'

But the way he said it was strange. Teasing.

She stared at him, slightly puzzled.

'Are you going to show me this story of yours, then?' He pointed to the notebook, ignoring the look she was giving him.

She pulled it over. Opened it at the latest chapter. Will's.

She'd been desperate to find out who this man was. But suddenly Eliza felt fear. Her mother had walked away – maybe it would be better for her to do the same thing.

Avril had almost forgotten that this wasn't a real book, she had turned the page eagerly until she'd reached the end, then turned it again, but the next was blank. Will had finished his chapter, and now it was her turn.

'Where there's love there's heartbreak.' Her dad's words broke the silence. 'A bit like that farmers' saying about where there's livestock there's deadstock.'

'Hattie would love you,' Avril said drily. 'With the "deadstock" bit. She keeps trying to put dead bodies into the story!'

But Avril's mind was thinking about the first part of her dad's sentence. Love and heartbreak. Was there a message in Will's chapter? Was he trying to tell her that she had to move on. Like Eliza's mum had, like Eliza was trying to. Would her search really make her feel better or was she asking questions that could never be answered?

Chapter Eight

(Avril)

The room that Sam had taken her to was quiet. Eliza lifted the lid of the suitcase.

He had been apologetic when he explained that she couldn't take it away with her, and she understood that. But she'd needed some time to look at the contents, to search for a clue as to why her mother had told her to go the beach on the day she had.

Sam was no nearer to being able to tell her whether it was Gerald, or the case, that her mum had wanted her to find. But for now, she had the suitcase, and that had to be good enough. She had given Sam the letter, as well as the diary her mum had left her, reluctantly, but what choice did she have when it was a missing-person enquiry?

In her heart, Eliza didn't believe that Gerald was dead. She was beginning to think that he felt as much, or probably even more, guilt than her mother did. He had to be the man her mum had loved, because why else would they have matching diaries? Why else would his suitcase have been at their home? Had he known that Sally had wanted them to meet and been a coward? Fled the scene leaving the case for her to find?

Was he a man she didn't really want to know, after all? If she found him, would she be disappointed?

She'd never really thought about her father much at all growing up and a part of her wished that her mother hadn't done this. Hadn't stirred this unrest. But she must have wanted her to know for a reason. Wanted Eliza to know exactly who her mother had been. And so it was Eliza's duty to find out.

She opened the bag of shells and tipped them out onto the table.

They were just like the ones she and her mother used to collect on the very beach where she had found the suitcase. Eliza's throat tightened and she blinked away the tears that were building up. They'd raced to see who could find the best one, the biggest, the most colourful, the one that the sea hadn't managed to damage. Whatever her mother had done wrong, she didn't care. She loved her. Her mother had given her everything, including laughter and happy times.

Did Gerald love the sea, too? Had she collected shells with him once upon a time – a time that was too long ago for her to remember?

She wiped the dampness on her face away with the back of her arm and with a shaking hand picked up the photograph.

Sam had told her that it was Gerald's wife.

Had Sally known her? Was this what she was trying to tell Eliza – that she'd hurt this woman? That she'd tried to take Gerald away from her and their child?

The mainly blank pages of the diary told her nothing. Unless the point was that they told her that Gerald had not cared. For Sally, or Eliza. She'd said as much to Sam, but had hoped she'd read something that would change her mind.

Had he collected these shells with somebody else, his other daughter?

Eliza walked home from the police station, to give her time and space to think. She had to find Fiona, the woman in the picture. As far as she could see there were two possibilities here.

Her mother had told her to go to the beach on her birthday, so she must have intended for her to find something, and surely that had to be Gerald – as who else could have left the suitcase for her? She must have sent Gerald a letter in the same way she had sent Eliza one. And if Gerald had left the suitcase, then he'd left the photograph so must have wanted her to look for Fiona.

Or Gerald knew nothing about this, and her mum had arranged for the suitcase to be left for her to find. And it was her mother who wanted Eliza to search for Fiona.

In Eliza's mind, there was no other explanation. If she was to discover the truth about her mother, set her free of guilt, then she had to find Gerald's wife. She had no choice. Fiona was the clue that Sally had left for her.

And there was only one person she could talk to who might lead her to Fiona. Her daughter, Marie.

She would ask Sam if it was possible for her to meet Marie, but meanwhile she could actually get on with this in her own way.

She walked into the park and sat down on a bench then slipped her mobile phone from her pocket.

And then she typed 'Marie Old' into the search bar.

Dead or alive, everybody left a trace, didn't they? Fiona and Gerald were out there somewhere. A person could be anywhere in the world, could be uncontactable, or simply lost, but somewhere on the internet there would be something about them. They would have friends, job, relatives.

And if you could find even one little thing it meant you had the start of the chain. Something to follow.

So she would start with Marie.

Chapter Twenty-Two

HATTIE

Closing the Chapter

Hattie's morning had not started well. The postman had brought a letter from the estate agent. They had, they said, tried to reach her on the phone but been unable to contact her. That, she knew, was because she seldom answered her telephone. Sometimes she didn't hear it, but more often than not, she did, but didn't answer because she didn't recognise the number on the display.

She didn't like the telephone's intrusion into her life. The only reason she had one was so that she could contact people when she needed to, and not vice versa. She had no family, and if somebody else wanted to reach her they could write. Reading a letter gave her time to think and prepare a response. She always felt befuddled, wrong-footed when she talked to people she didn't know on the phone. She worried about saying the wrong thing. About committing to something she didn't mean to.

When she opened this letter, she was glad that she hadn't answered the telephone because she wouldn't have known what to say. It left a hollow feeling in the base of her stomach, and her hands shaking.

It would appear that things had finally progressed with the offer she'd accepted some time ago on her house. Surveys had been done and mortgages arranged and the young couple with their family wanted to agree a date for exchange and completion of contracts. They would appreciate her immediate attention to the matter.

Hattie carefully refolded the letter and pushed it back into the envelope.

Since the day of Harold's funeral, she had wanted nothing more than to escape the house, as she'd been unable to do when he was living. But moving out had been one thing – the reality of actually selling it and leaving it forever, left her feeling quite poorly.

She would never set foot in there again once it was sold. She would never have a chance to stand in her kitchen and remember making blackberry and apple pies, Harold's favourite. To look out on their garden and watch the squirrels digging holes in the immaculate lawn. Watch the fledglings line up on the fence before they finally left for good.

But for her, it was harder than just flitting the nest. She would have to tidy it out.

Moving out and leaving everything had been a relief – but that was, she now realised, because it would still be there to return to. Maybe.

The thought of going back and having to decide what to

keep and what to discard permanently left her feeling quite shaken.

Nutmeg seemed to sense her unrest and nestled up against her feet.

'I think we need to go to the library, that might make us feel better. Don't you agree?' She slipped the letter into her handbag. Maybe Avril would be able to help?

———————

The notebook was waiting for Hattie when she walked into the library, along with a note. Avril's familiar looped writing informed her that the young woman was not going to be at the library this morning, and a twinge of disappointment hit Hattie. But Avril had written her chapter – very quickly it would seem – so that she didn't hold anybody up.

Hattie was pleased – about the chapter at least. Avril had been very reticent at first, and convinced that she didn't have a story to tell. But Hattie knew that everybody did. And telling a story could help you unravel your own. Stories were about life, beliefs, morals and fears. You could unburden your soul; you could tell secrets that you didn't even know you were keeping.

As a storyteller you could be anybody you wanted, or you could be you.

She made herself a drink, and sat down in her usual seat, before opening the book so that she could catch up on the story.

She smiled as she came to the end of Will's chapter – now if that wasn't a message to Avril that his love affair was over, what was? Was it also a message for her? A warning that Peter might have shut her out of his heart the day he left.

She turned the next page, ready to read Avril's chapter, but something stopped her. She needed to check if Peter had responded to her, their, email message.

Very slowly and deliberately she typed in the details that Avril had made her write down into the computer.

There was nothing there. No response. She hadn't really expected one, but the disappointment still hit her. Except now it was worse than it had been before.

Now she couldn't spend her time searching for him. They'd found him. It was the end of the line, a dead end.

Now that she was on the verge of clearing away her old life with Harold for good, knowing that Peter was there would have made her feel so much better about it.

'What am I going to do now?' she asked Nutmeg.

'You could write the next chapter!' a deep voice boomed out from behind the newspaper, which Stuart lowered as he smiled at her. 'Everything okay, Hattie?' He looked quite concerned.

'Do you believe in love?' Hattie asked him on impulse. Stroking Nutmeg's head. She loved the little dog, but she wasn't sure she had ever loved a person.

'I do.' He nodded then folded the newspaper carefully and placed it down on the table. 'But romantic love is just the start, isn't it?' He spoke slowly, deliberately, as though he was thinking as he spoke. 'It's one tiny element, isn't it? A lump of coal on its own can't make a fire, can it?'

Hattie smiled. 'You sound like my mother!'

'I think it was my mother who told me that,' he said with a chuckle. 'But it's true, isn't it? You need a pile of coal, or logs, or it only takes one *pfft* of a breeze and it's gone.'

'I did think I might have had that lump of coal once upon a time, but maybe there was nothing around to help keep it going,' mused Hattie.

She thought about Harold, their lives. Why had the fun stopped, making her feel alone and empty not long after they had married? He hadn't liked friends; they'd not gone out. It was after Peter had disappeared, she realised. When that happened, the trips to the pub, and the dancing, had stopped. It was as though Harold lost his anchor when Peter had left their lives. She'd felt a poor substitute. She hadn't been able to encourage him to do things, motivate him, like Peter had done. So it had been easier to go along with what Harold wanted – if she'd disagreed with him it would always turn into an argument. He'd never change his mind or admit he might be wrong. And the more she tried, the angrier he had got.

'I was a big lump of coal for a long time,' Stuart said. 'But Jo deserves better.'

'I think you're doing just fine,' Hattie said.

'I was used to ruling the roost at work and at home I just made myself comfortable. I'm surprised Jo put up with me. I was more of a guest than a husband. Do you know, I never made the supper once, not until I retired. I had no idea where we even kept the serving spoons.'

'My Harold was the opposite. He liked things his way at home, and he didn't mind throwing his weight around. He didn't even like libraries you know!'

'Well, I'm glad that you do,' said Stuart. 'We'd never have entered this competition without you, and it's been wonderful. I didn't realise quite the effect it's had on me until recently. It's helped me get my thoughts in order, so thank you.'

'You're welcome.' Hattie could hear the slightest quaver in her voice. Nobody had thanked her for anything for a long time. Although she supposed you had to do things for people, if you wanted to be thanked and she'd never been very good at that until recently.

'No Avril today?'

Hattie held the note up. 'She said she was going to Altrincham, to talk to people about her mother.' She paused. 'It was such a long time ago, though; I hope she's not going to be disappointed.'

'Well, all she can do is try I suppose.'

'I suppose so.' Hattie logged out of the computer. 'Well, I have done my best to find Peter, and now it is up to him, or the gods, or whichever part of the universe is in charge of these things!'

'I like to believe that the right people will come along when we need them.' Stuart looked more thoughtful than she'd ever seen him. 'Like you came along for me.'

Hattie nodded. She'd needed Nutmeg, and then she'd needed Avril. Now she needed to close the chapter of her life that still hadn't had a satisfactory ending.

'And if they don't come, we don't need them?'

Stuart shook his head slowly. 'Maybe,' he said softly, 'it means we can manage without. We're strong enough to find the answers on our own.'

'You could be correct. Now, if you'll excuse me there is something I need to do. I'll take the notebook with me; I've not even had chance to read Avril's chapter yet, but I'm not sure I'm in the right frame of mind. I have other things that are bothering me.'

She slipped the notebook into her bag, her fingertips fluttering against the letter from the estate agent.

'You know I'm always here, or Jo is, if you need a chat about anything. You don't need to cope on your own,' Stuart told her.

'I may take you up on that. My house sale is mithering me. And a chat, or a hand, may be just what I need.'

'I think you need Avril and Will for the heavy lifting, I'm more brain power.' Stuart winked and Hattie found herself smiling back at him. 'But any help with the legals, then I'm your man.'

'Thank you, Stuart. You are very kind. I'm a very lucky old lady.'

'Less of the old! But I think the four of us make quite a good team, don't you?'

'I do. Yes, I certainly do.'

'Don't struggle on your own, Hattie.' His voice had lost its jovial edge, and the look in his eye reminded her of Peter. She hesitated, then spoke before she had time to overthink and change her mind.

'If you're not busy now, I'd really welcome some company. I have to go and look at my old house. It's been sold, you see, and I need to work out what to keep and how to discard the rest.'

'House clearance,' Stuart said decisively. 'I had to do it

for my parents. I know just the man who might be able to help. Come on.' He picked up the newspaper again, and tidied it away on the rack, then held out his arm so that she could slip her hand into the crook of his elbow. 'Let's go and look together, shall we? We could go for coffee and cake afterwards. I always think cake helps after you've had difficult decisions to make.'

'Well, if you're sure you have time.'

'I have plenty of time. We need to pop into the estate agent's, as well, they mustn't bully you into rushing. These things take time.'

'They certainly do at my age.' Hattie was conscious of her slow speed, but Stuart didn't seem to mind.

'Things will happen when they're meant to,' he said, guiding her towards the door. 'Lead the way.'

'We're going out,' Hattie said, as they approached the desk, where Will was sitting – concentrating very hard on his mobile phone. He jumped guiltily and pushed it to the back of the desk.

'Stuart and me. We are going out,' she repeated, in case he hadn't heard.

She watched his gaze flicker to the large clock above the door, and he frowned. She knew why. It was only eleven o'clock. Normally Stuart stayed until 11:45am, and she would be here until at least 2pm. Along with Avril of course.

'Is it something I said?' he asked, trying to keep his tone light.

Hattie tipped her head on one side. 'Avril had things to do. She has gone to Altrincham today; I'm surprised she didn't tell you.' She narrowed her gaze. 'Oh dear, that woman isn't causing trouble between you, is she?'

'Which woman?' he asked, which made Hattie smile. Who was he trying to kid?

'The one with the bosom,' she replied, and she heard Stuart splutter with a stifled laugh.

'Oh. You mean Lucy. She was here on library business. She's coming back again for our meeting, next week.' His tone lacked its usual lightness, and Hattie felt a sudden pang of guilt at what he could have called harassment. But it was Avril she was mostly concerned about.

'Well don't you go letting anybody upset Avril. She's a nice girl.'

'She's a lovely girl,' he agreed. 'And I will do my best.' His gaze flickered back to his phone.

'I'm sure you will!' Hattie said, as his obsession with it suddenly became clear. She tried not to smile. 'If Avril should return from her mission – from wherever she's gone – tell her we are going to my old house, should she want to come there, too.' Hattie got a pen out of her bag. It was kind of Stuart to offer her company and help, but Hattie had to admit to herself that right now she wanted Avril. She could never remember wanting, needing, anybody. But she'd started to realise that maybe she had needed Harold, and not known it. And now she would like Avril's help, and she wasn't going to make the mistake of denying it for a second time in her life. 'Here you are.' She wrote the address carefully on the piece of paper Will handed over.

'I will tell her if she comes in.'

'A telephone message is quicker!' Hattie retorted,

embarrassed about her sudden neediness and wanting to move on from Will's concerned look. 'But if she doesn't come that is fine. We're fine, aren't we?' She smiled up at Stuart, who nodded. 'Are you ready, Stuart?'

As they reached the door, she was sure she heard Will's phone buzz with a notification.

Hattie adjusted her handbag on her arm and glanced up at Stuart, satisfied that whatever complications Will had in his life, he had in hand. Or was at least trying. As Stuart had remarked, that was all they could do, wasn't it? Try. 'I've not walked out with a handsome young man for years!'

Stuart chuckled. 'I've not been called young for years!' He paused. 'Or handsome.'

'Well make the most of it! I might not be around much longer.' But as the words came out, Hattie realised that for the first time, she didn't really mean them. She wanted to be around, she had so much that she wanted to do.

She wasn't afraid of dying, just of not living the time she had left properly.

Had Harold been afraid of life? Was that why he had lashed out at it? Life – not her. But she had just got in the way?

Chapter Twenty-Three

AVRIL

Old Haunts

Avril sat at the bus stop and watched the café opposite. It felt like she was about to take a massive leap – but she wasn't sure whether it would turn out to be a forward one, or one that took her deep into a hole.

After her father had gone home, she'd written her chapter of the story then gone back to the link that Will had sent.

It had actually been much more straightforward than she imagined to find an address for Mandy. Her full name was in the article – Amanda Cox. Her daughter's name was also there, Sadie. Avril had googled both of them, and it was Sadie who was on all the social networks. There weren't many girls with that name, around her age, in the area, so she'd soon found all the information she needed. And now she was here. Sitting outside the café where Sadie worked, plucking up courage to go in.

Avril didn't normally balk at talking to a stranger – she'd never had a problem talking to people – but it was finding the courage to face the possibilities that was daunting.

She knew now how Hattie must have felt. She had to follow the leads, had to know – but the truth could be scary. She hoped Hattie had found her Peter. Her happy ever after. She deserved it.

Her phone vibrated with a notification as she hesitated.

Will. A small smile lifted the corners of her mouth. Despite what she'd said to Hattie, seeing Will and that woman wrapped in each other's arms *had* spoiled her mood the last time she'd been in the library. She'd not enjoyed the rest of the afternoon in the way she normally did.

She'd felt uncomfortable, as though she'd stumbled on some secret.

And when she'd left the library, on her way out Will had been deep in conversation with somebody else, so she'd sneaked past without even speaking to him. She wished now that she'd waited. Said goodbye. It had felt strange not swapping jokey comments as she left. It had thrown a dampener on the rest of her day. Until, of course, her dad had arrived with their fish and chips.

Will had sent her the article and the photo of her mum of course, but it had felt like a formal message, not like their normal relaxed chats.

It could have been her fault, she knew that. She distanced herself; she knew she did. But she didn't want to with Will. In the café she'd felt like she'd known him for years. That she'd be happy if she did.

And then it had hit her, like a bucket of cold water in the

face, when Lucy had thrown herself at him, that she didn't know him at all.

She looked again at the text that he'd just sent.

'*Looks like you used to enjoy a book!*'

'*Big ones with pictures!*' she typed back, a slight tremor in her fingers, her pulse. Relief that he was joking with her again. That they could still be friends.

'*Have you gone to find your mum's friend?*'

She nodded. Then typed. '*It's a bit scary actually. I don't know which is worse – finding her friends, or not finding them.*'

'*You need to find them. You will.*'

She was glad at least one of them could be positive. On impulse she dialled his number.

'Hey.' He answered straight away. The sound of his voice, even that one syllable made her feel better.

'Not busy, then?' She laughed as the tight band around her chest eased. What had her dad always said, two heads are better than one? And Dad had always been there, the second, sensible head. But she couldn't ask him to be this time.

'I've been abandoned!' said Will. 'Hattie went off with Stuart, something about needing to clear her old house?'

'Oh.' Avril frowned. 'Is she okay?'

'She seemed it.'

'I think it's a big deal for her,' she said softly. 'Letting go of her house. I wish I'd been there to help.' Leaving the house, the memories of her life with Harold, was something Hattie told everybody she wanted to do, but Avril was sure it was more complicated than that. They'd been married for so long. They *were* each other's lives – even if Hattie hadn't always been happy. They must have been close once, maybe even in love, but something had gone wrong. Something had caused a rift. Hattie had been frightened of him, but Avril was sure that she would never have befriended him in the first place if she'd thought he was cruel.

'I could come back.' Hattie, today, was more important than looking for somebody who may have once known her mum. That had waited for over twenty years, what was a few more days, weeks, even?

'She's fine, honestly. She went out arm in arm with Stuart, she did leave her address in case you got back early but I'm sure he'll look after her,' said Will.

'Oh, that's good. She's not alone, then.' Avril sighed. 'Do you think I'm doing the wrong thing, Will?' The words that had been turning in her head since she'd left her home, tumbled out of her mouth.

'What do you mean? With Hattie?'

'No. Coming here, trying to find out about Mum.'

'No, of course I don't! You need to do it, Avril.'

'But'—she paused, he'd said it, he'd more or less spelled out his thoughts—'in your chapter you said, you, well you wrote that Eliza's mum had let go of him, Gerald. It made her feel better.'

The line was silent.

'Do I need to let go?' Her voice was small, the words reluctant but she had to say them.

She'd begun to wonder if Will had hung up. Then he broke the silence. 'It's just a story, it's not about you.'

'But…'

'Okay, if it's about anything that chapter is about me,

not you. Honestly, I really think you should find out about your mum if you can.'

'Oh.'

'It's complicated. But I was thinking about me.' He gave a self-conscious laugh. 'Me, me, me, eh?'

'You're not like that at all,' she said softly.

'Maybe we could meet up, talk properly? I can't do this phone thing, and, well I'd like to explain, tell you stuff about me and Lucy.'

Her heart gave a tiny lurch, her mouth was dry.

'I moved on from Lucy ages ago, but there's some other stuff.' He sighed. 'It wasn't how it looked when she came.'

'Well, normally if people hug you like that…' She could hear the defensive note in her voice. If he'd been here now, she'd be challenging him, chasing him away.

'You hug them back, and I didn't. You just thought I did. Honestly, I let Lucy go a long time ago, but there are other things I need to let go of as well.' There was a long pause. 'Things like Jake. But I can't explain over the phone.'

Avril let the words sink in but stayed silent. She'd been so shocked at Lucy's behaviour, at the idea that Will had some-body else in his life, she'd not really seen his reaction.

Because it had hurt.

And she didn't like feeling hurt, because it meant she had let herself like him more than she'd realised. Apart from her dad, everybody she had cared for had left. And even her dad wasn't hers any longer.

'I wondered where you were this morning, I thought I might have upset you. Hattie told me where you were.'

'I'm sorry, I should have told you.'

'No, I'm sorry, I didn't mean it to sound like that.'

'No, no, I should have told you I wasn't going to be in.' She realised she meant it. She'd just dismissed him, written his friendship off and set off on her own. Like she always did. He deserved respect, if nothing else. He'd been kind, he'd pointed her in the right direction, so she'd been able to find Mandy.

'It's just, you've not missed a Thursday since we decided to enter the competition. It feels strange without you here.' He laughed self-consciously.

'And without Stuart and Hattie!' she said softly, trying to distance herself. Then regretted it. 'It feels strange not being there,' she finally admitted.

'Where are you?'

'I'm outside this café where I think my mum's friend, Mandy's, daughter works. It was Mandy in the photo that Mum knew. Dad said they were pretty close.'

'I can go in with you, if you hang on?'

'By the time you've finished work and got over here, they'll be shut. But thanks.' She meant it, it was nice of him to offer. 'I'd better go in.'

'You'll let me know what happens?'

'Sure. Speak later.' She ended the call and cradled her phone for a moment in her hands. Maybe Will *was* there for her. Maybe she should trust a little bit more.

She glanced up at the café. Then stood up and slipped the phone in her pocket before she had chance to change her mind.

The café was quiet, the lunchtime clients had long since

gone, and most of the people who'd popped in for afternoon coffee were leaving or about to.

Avril picked a table near the window, scanned the QR code and ordered a drink. Should she go to the counter and ask? Or ask whoever brought her coffee? Or just sit here and wait?

'Coffee?'

She glanced up and knew. 'Sadie?'

The girl put the cup on the table and frowned. 'Yes?'

'My name's Avril. My mum knew yours – and, well, I guess you and I knew each other, too – years ago.' The words tumbled out, because there was no other way to say this.

'Phee,' Sadie said. There wasn't even a question in her voice. She half smiled. 'Hang on, don't go away. I'll get rid of this tray and be right back.'

Waiting for Sadie to return, Avril could feel her heart pounding, see the faint tremble in her fingers as she fought to act normally, stir her drink.

'Avril?' She looked up at the softly spoken question, and all hope of behaving normally deserted her. It wasn't Sadie, but an older woman standing there.

Avril's hand flew to cover her mouth, and she burst into tears.

'Oh, I'm sorry.' The woman sank onto the chair opposite, tears welling up in her own eyes. 'I didn't mean to shock you; I thought seeing as you were here you…' Her words drifted off.

As Avril stared at the woman a sudden realisation hit her.

'It was you,' she said, wiping her tears away with the back of her hand. Then taking the paper napkin that the woman held out, she blew her nose, took a deep breath. 'It was you that I saw watching me…' Her dad had said that Phee and Mandy had been close, that they looked like twins. They liked the same things, spent hours together. Knew each other. 'With the white roses.'

'She loved white roses,' Mandy said softly. 'They were her favourite; she said everybody should have roses.'

'I thought…' Avril swallowed the lump in her throat down, feeling silly, wishing she could stop shaking. 'I thought you were her, my mum.' Mandy didn't laugh, as she'd been afraid she would. She reached out, squeezed Avril's hand.

'You saw me? Oh God, I'm sorry. I'm so, so sorry, Avril. I didn't mean to scare you. People used to think we were sisters, I should have thought… I shouldn't have…'

'It's fine. Really. I knew she was dead; I thought I must be imagining it because I wanted to see her so much.'

'I want to see her again so much too.' Mandy's smile was gentle, understanding. 'That's why I came to find you. I wanted to see what you were like, if you were like her, like Phee. I'm sorry, I didn't think for one minute that you'd see me and think I was…'

'Am I?' Avril asked. 'Am I like her?'

'You are.' Mandy smiled.

'So are you,' Avril said softly. Her gaze searched Mandy's face, the features that should be familiar, but weren't quite right. Close up, she could see that Mandy wasn't Phee. They were similar physically, or at least Mandy was similar to how she imagined her mother would look now, but her nose, her eyes, weren't the features she remembered gazing down at her.

'How's Joey?'

'He's good.' Avril smiled, and Mandy raised a questioning eyebrow. 'It's funny, hearing you call Dad Joey. Lisa, his wife, she always calls him Joe.'

'Ah, she would.'

It was Avril's turn to wonder.

'It's hard being the second wife,' Mandy said softly. 'Especially when a man can't forget his first one.'

'I suppose.' Avril agreed. It made sense. 'Lisa does her best to do everything differently, to act like that part of his life never existed.' She shrugged her shoulders. 'Except she can't do that with me. She can't escape me. She must wish she'd met him first, before Mum.'

'She did.' Mandy took the cup of coffee that her daughter had brought over for her. 'She did meet him first. She's known your dad for years,' she said slowly, watching Avril's face for a reaction but Avril tried not to react; afraid that if she did, then Mandy would stop. And she needed to hear whatever she had to say. She needed to hear anything and everything about her mother that Mandy knew. 'Your mum, Joey and Lisa were all at the same school, apparently. I mean this is just what Phee told me, I didn't live here then.' Avril waited quietly, willing her to continue. 'Lisa had a thing about Joey, your dad, but he had a thing about Phee.' Mandy smiled, a small smile, and Avril was sure she was remembering Phee. The chats. The secrets they shared. 'And Phee had a thing about him. Lisa didn't stand a chance, they were proper childhood sweethearts, no eyes for anybody else.

Phee was a real romantic.' Mandy shook her head and laughed softly. 'And so was your dad. They were both besotted. The only time I saw her look at anybody in the way she looked at him was after you were born.'

'I never knew, he never talks about her … them.' Avril felt the warmth flood to her cheeks. It was strange imagining her parents being madly in love. Yes, she'd known they loved each other, but Mandy was describing something that seemed passionate. It explained so much, how heartbroken her dad had been, how hard he'd found it to rebuild a life without her.

It also explained why Lisa didn't want to hear Phee's name. See her face echoed in Avril's. Lisa had always felt second best, been second choice.

'He was devastated when he lost her. I couldn't blame him when he shied away from me and her other friends, he just couldn't cope with any reminders about her, what he'd lost. He didn't want to see me doing the things that Phee never had a chance to.'

'I wish he hadn't.' Avril knew that Mandy would have helped him, if she'd been able to. That she would have kept Phee's memory alive for her.

'We do what we need to do to survive,' Mandy said simply. 'Does he know you're here?'

Avril nodded.

'Good. I'm pleased.'

'I didn't want to tell him I'd seen Mum; I thought he'd think I was going crazy.'

'He'd never have thought that. I'm sure he sees her.'

Avril had never thought about it like that, but Mandy

was probably right. Lisa could try and banish Phee from their lives, but she would always be there.

'Maybe we could meet up one evening? I'm sure you've got lots of questions and I'm happy to try and answer them if I can.' She grinned. 'It's me being selfish, really; seeing you is wonderful. I feel like a little bit of Phee has come back for me.'

'I'd love it. If you're sure?'

'Of course I am! Why do you think I've been stalking you? They're trying to close up the café now, but we can fix a day? I'd love to hear about your life, and what you're up to.'

'I'd like that.'

'Here.' Mandy scribbled something on a napkin. 'My number. How about we meet at this pizza place down the road. Me and your mum used to go there, and amazingly enough it's still going! How about this time next week? Or is that too much of a rush?'

Avril smiled, thinking of the photo of Mandy and her mum and her. She couldn't remember ever going into that library – and it had since relocated anyway, she'd checked – and she felt a twinge of regret in her heart that she'd never be able to go back to that space she'd shared with Ophelia. To see if it awoke memories that she wasn't aware she had.

But it would be good to meet Mandy at another of their old haunts. Very good.

'That would be great.'

'Around 7pm?'

Avril grinned. 'Great! I can message you if anything changes. Thank you.'

Mandy stood up then reached out, leaving it up to Avril whether she leaned in for a hug or not, but Avril didn't think twice.

The hug was good. Short, but warm. The type of hug her mother would have given her.

———

Two minutes later, Avril sat down at the bus shelter looking across the road at the bus stop she'd arrived at only a couple of hours earlier, plucking up the courage to walk across to the café. It was such a short time ago, but now she felt completely different.

Her eyes still prickled with the emotion of the hug with Mandy, but they were happy tears, not sad.

She stared at the photograph that Mandy had just messaged over.

The two young women were both holding glasses of lager, their heads close together, matching wide smiles.

Avril needed to share how she felt right now, and she wasn't sure why but there was only one person she wanted to share it with.

Chapter Twenty-Four

STUART

Every Picture Tells a Story

Stuart gazed around the living room. He wasn't quite sure what he had expected, but it wasn't this. It was crammed full of furniture; dark, heavy furniture, but good quality pieces.

'You have some lovely things,' he couldn't help but say, wondering why Hattie hadn't moved more to her new apartment.

'Harold had some lovely things,' she corrected. 'I didn't have much say in the matter.' She sounded tetchy, even by Hattie standards. But when he looked at her, he was sure that she was actually quite upset. He couldn't imagine being left by Jo, left all alone, especially at Hattie's age. She was, he realised, coping extremely well.

'It must be difficult,' he said softly.

Hattie stepped properly into the room and sank down on one of the armchairs.

'I thought I'd be better off without him. I thought that for years.'

Stuart sat down on the chair next to her and waited. If he'd been at home he'd have offered to make them both a cup of tea, but he couldn't do that for her.

'I miss him,' she said, staring at the piano – on which there was still a photograph of her and Harold. They had a slightly stilted pose. Not quite touching. Dressed in Sunday best with smiles that looked like they had been produced on cue, not out of happiness. 'Harold. There, I've said it. I never thought I would. I really did think I'd be better off without him, free. But it's not that easy.'

She gazed into the middle distance, then, became uncharacteristically quiet.

'It's a lot to cope with on your own,' Stuart said when the silence had extended beyond what he thought of as comfortable. He'd thought she was expecting him to speak, but her look told him he was wrong. She'd just been thinking.

'It's not the day-to-day practical things, it's the thoughts. The knowing what to do with yourself. Being able to do whatever you like is harder than you think.' She paused. 'Than I thought.'

'It is.' He nodded in agreement. 'You've hit the nail on the head there, Hattie. The knowing what to do with yourself,' he mused. 'So that you don't spend too much time thinking about things you don't want to think about.'

'I'm lonely.' She shook her head sadly. 'I'm not sure I'm brave enough.'

'You are.' Stuart reached out and covered her hand and

she moved to curl her fingers around his. Her hand was tiny, the skin cool to the touch, the bones barely padded, but her touch was surprisingly firm. 'You're braver and stronger than a hell of a lot of other people I know.'

'When I walked out of here, I wanted to leave everything behind, you know, every bit of Harold and our life together. I couldn't do it when he was alive, so I was determined that I would once he was dead. I bought new things, things that I'd picked, were my choice.' She pursed her lips, but he could feel the quiver in her hands. 'He would never listen when he was alive, he always thought he knew best.'

'Maybe,' he said tentatively, 'it was his way of showing he cared. Buying things he thought you'd like.' He felt the small smile touch his lips as he thought about Jo. 'But maybe he forgot to ask?' He'd always done what he thought was best for Jo, but maybe far too often he had forgotten to check whether she thought it was best? 'It's arrogant and patronising but it happens a lot with us older men you know. We think we know best.' He knew he was talking about himself, not Harold. And he had time to change, even though Harold hadn't.

Hattie made a tiny harumph noise and didn't comment. Maybe she thought he was a fool, and he shouldn't reflect his own shortcomings onto her departed husband.

He gazed around the room. She was packing her previous life away, *giving* it away, and he wasn't sure she was ready even if she had thought it was the easiest thing to do. 'You don't have to do this yet; we can put the estate agents off.'

'Did you do that for your parents? Put things off?'

'It was different,' he said softly, ignoring her slightly dismissive tone. He knew that it came from fear, not derision.

He'd cleared out his parents' house after his father had died and his mother was lost. Sometimes she thought *he* was her husband, at others her grandchild, occasionally – very occasionally – she recognised him for who he was. She had moved a bit further away from him every day.

'I was putting it off for me, not them. Dad was gone, and Mum remembered more about her childhood home than our family one. I lost her months before she passed away. It was my memories of the person she'd been that I didn't want to give away.'

'I'm sorry,' Hattie said with a sigh, but she was obviously distracted and not listening as she usually did. Her normal direct gaze was restless. Drifting from him to the room and back again. 'It wasn't like that with Harold. He was there one day, his normal self, moaning about interest rates and the state of the country one minute and gone the next.' She paused. 'He'd be happy if he'd known that was how he'd go. If he ever could be happy.'

'Could he?'

Hattie paused. And this time looked directly at him. 'Once upon a time, when we were children. I don't think he coped with the responsibility of growing up very well. It soured him. Or I did.'

'I'm sure—'

'I used to think it was me, but recently I've begun to wonder if he didn't know how to juggle life. There were too many things that worried him, that he couldn't control.

And he really liked to be in control. When you're young it's simple, isn't it?' She nodded as though it was the first time she'd thought of him in that way. 'And he'd had Peter,' she finished sadly.

'I think that's my problem,' Stuart said with a wry smile. He'd always been in control at work. He liked it. The routine, the responsibility. But now there was nothing left to be in control of. Jo had built her own life; she'd had to as he'd devoted so much of his time to work. 'Not the juggling bit, I like to juggle. I just don't seem to have any balls in the air these days, but I do like to know where I stand. To be in control.' Except for the one time he hadn't been. Maybe that was what he had to come to terms with – not being in control, not just the fact that he'd not been more empathetic. Not cared enough.

'Well, if Harold had dropped a few balls he might have been happier,' retorted Hattie. 'And I'm sure you can find something to do if you apply yourself. You're a bright man and you shouldn't waste your time. I've done far too much of that. No point crying over spilled milk, though.'

'There isn't. My mum used to tell me that you didn't get rainbows unless you'd had rain. Maybe your rainbows are just round the corner, Hattie.'

Maybe he needed to talk to somebody – talk to Jo – about his rainy days.

'Well, you may be right,' she said. 'But in the meantime, to go back to your question. I do have to do this now.' Hattie rose to her feet surprisingly quickly. Her backbone straight. 'I do, Stuart. Now, shall we start at the top and work our way down?'

They made their way up the narrow staircase and Stuart felt like he'd entered a different world. He was surprised to find that the rooms upstairs were furnished in an altogether different fashion. The rugs were rather threadbare, laid on floorboards that Jo would have said were in need of a good polish.

He felt the smile lift the corners of his mouth. He'd not really realised it before, but he thought of Jo at every turn. She was a part of him, and she'd know what to do about all his problems if he'd talk to her. Share. Sharing it seemed, wasn't just about practical things, it was about emotional things as well.

'Harold wanted it this way,' Hattie said.

Jo had never waited for the rain to clear before she saw rainbows. It was time he made things happen rather than hanging about. Reprioritise the different parts of his life. Since retiring he'd wallowed in his own unhappiness, carried on along his parallel path. He didn't want them to lead separate lives, as Harold and Hattie seem to have done – doing their own things. He didn't just want Jo to be happy – or to help him be – he wanted to make *her* happy.

'Harold spent his money where people could see it,' said Hattie, reading the look on his face. 'He used to say, "what's the point if there's only us to see it?" – which I thought was altogether the wrong way of thinking. My new bedroom is lovely, very cosy. It's a place I want to be, rather than…' She shrugged, then walked into the bedroom and pointed to the imposing wardrobe. 'Can you get the box down from the top, please? I used to keep it in my bedside cabinet, but the day he died I decided I didn't want to look at it, so I got the undertaker to put it up there.'

Stuart pulled a wooden chair over, and climbed on it so that he could easily reach the top. The cardboard shoe box had been pushed right to the back so that it could barely be seen from the floor, unless you were particularly tall, which Hattie was not.

He placed it carefully on the bed. 'Would you like me to…?'

'Oh no, you sit down, and we shall see if there's anything in here worth keeping.'

Her tone was brisk, but her face had gone pale. This box was obviously important, the reason for her reticence, the reason – he suspected – she'd been glad of company.

It sat on the bed in front of them. An ordinary, old, slightly scruffy box.

She sat down next to the box. Her fingertips resting on the top of it.

'Have you ever been unkind to Jo, Stuart? Harold could be very unkind.'

Stuart thought. 'Not unkind in the way you mean, I don't think. But maybe unkind in that I haven't considered her as much as I might. I have rather taken her for granted.'

'Well, you have plenty of time to rectify that, and I'm sure you will.'

'I will, Hattie. Sometimes it takes somebody else, or something to happen, before you realise what it is you have done wrong. I think I've been guilty of selfishness and complacency.'

'I think,' Hattie said, 'I've been guilty of loving the

wrong man.' She paused, her hands still on the box and Stuart wondered – did she mean she should have loved Peter? Or did she mean she had loved Peter, and forgot to love Harold? 'Could you arrange for one of these – clearance people, did you call them – to come?'

'I shall.' He stood up. 'Would you like some time on your own?'

Hattie shook her head. 'I think I may take this home to look at. Harold always thought he knew best…' she mused, but her words had a different tone than when she'd uttered them earlier. They were muted now.

'You're right there. He always did.'

They both looked up at the voice. There was an elderly man standing in the doorway. He smiled. 'But he always meant well, even if he was sometimes wrong. The door was open, Harriet. I was told by a young chap at the library that I might find you here.'

'Peter!'

Chapter Twenty-Five

WILL

Ghosts - Past, Present and Future

Will jiggled the door of the library, as he always did, to check that it was locked properly, before dropping the key into his bag.

A shadow fell across the path, and he glanced up, about to say, 'Sorry, we're closed' when he realised who it was.

'I've found more than Mandy. I've found my ghost, my mum.' She was slightly out of breath, her words almost on a whisper, but he heard them. She laughed. 'I had to run; I thought I might miss you!'

The low sun was behind her, a hazy light shining through her hair and masking her features for the moment it took his eyes to adjust, but he was pretty sure he'd know Avril even in the dark.

She was smiling in a way he couldn't remember seeing her smile before. She looked nervous but elated all at once, and it made his heart pound.

'I wanted to catch you before you left and let you know.' Avril sank back against the low wall and leaned over with her hands on her thighs, catching her breath.

'You could have rung,' he said, grinning. 'But I'm glad you didn't!'

'Can we go for a drink?'

'I thought you'd never ask!' Things had seemed stilted between them since Lucy had turned up at the library, and he'd hated it. He'd half expected her to disappear, but Hattie had told him that Avril wasn't the type to let people down, and she was a member of their team, their writing group. She had a story to finish. Talking on the phone had been good, but no substitute for seeing her. For watching the expression on her face, knowing things were okay between them.

'Have you had a good day?'

'Quiet. Hattie and Stuart went to look at her house, and you were out so it's been a much quieter Thursday than normal.' It was funny wasn't it, how quickly something new became the norm. In a few short weeks, he'd come to expect – rely – on the writing group, and the library wasn't the same without them. But they only had one more chapter each to write. What was he going to do when the story was done, when they all dispersed. Go back to his bookshop?

His parents didn't really need him around now. But something was keeping him here and he'd been kidding himself that it was his job.

The truth was, it was Avril.

'Oh, my God, I'd forgotten about Hattie's house! I hope

she's okay, I forget sometimes just how old she is. You did say Stuart went with her? She wasn't alone.'

'No, she wasn't alone. And … there wasn't just Stuart.' He paused.

'What? What's the matter?'

'I hope I did the right thing, but this man came in asking for her and I told him where she was.'

'This man?' Avril frowned.

'Peter. It was Peter. Not some stranger,' he hastened to reassure her, and at the words the worry melted from her features. She grinned. 'He decided that it was better to see her face to face than waste time on trying to work out how to say things in an email.'

'Wow, really?' She straightened. 'Oh, my God. I can hardly believe it! I mean we emailed him, but I didn't really expect him to get in touch. I wanted him to, for Hattie's sake, but he could have been ill, or married, or not really check emails, or he could have…'

'Died?' Will finished for her. 'But he hasn't. It was him. Definitely.'

'That's amazing. I wish I'd been here, though.'

'I wish you had, too. I wasn't really sure what to say, I told Peter that Hattie was at home as far as I knew, and he said she'd told him she'd moved. But when I told him she was at her old place he seemed to know where her house was. He obviously knew where she lived with Harold. I hope he's not caught her too much by surprise. I'd not got a phone number for either Hattie or Stuart, or I would have called one of them.'

'Well, at least Stuart was with her,' Avril said, 'Are you positive it was him?'

Will nodded. 'Oh yes. Even before he said his name, he looked just like the photo.'

'What was he like?' They fell into step and set off down the street. Avril was gazing up at him, desperate for any information he could give her. 'Did he seem nice?'

'I only saw him for a couple of minutes, but he seemed polite, friendly. Not one of Hattie's axe murderers anyway.'

'I should hope not!' Avril grinned, then it faded. 'Do you think we should stop by her place now and check she got home all right? I don't want her to think we're interfering, but I think she'd already be upset about emptying the house so seeing him again could be too much, it would be a bit of a shock seeing he's not been back in touch after we emailed.'

'If he found her, then she might not want any interruptions.'

'True.'

He glanced at his watch. 'It wasn't that long ago. Maybe go round after we've had a drink? I've got her old address as she left it for you in case you got back early. But I think Stuart would have come back to the library to tell us if he'd been worried. Or he'd tell Jo. He definitely wouldn't leave her on her own if he didn't think it was the right thing to do.'

'You're right. But I'll pop by before I catch my train home. Just so I know she's not upset.'

'I'll come with you.' Will held the door of the bar open and followed her in. 'Now, grab us a seat and give me two minutes to get us a drink and then you can tell me about the ghost.'

Her frown faded away. Avril didn't sit down; she followed him to the bar – her excitement returning now he'd reassured her about Hattie. 'I wasn't imagining things! I was being watched. I know everybody kind of said it was fine, me thinking I'd seen her, but it felt weird. I felt like I was losing the plot or something. But I wasn't.'

'I never thought for a moment you were.' Will handed her the glass of cider, and they walked over to a quiet corner of the bar. Avril had a great imagination, she was fun and different, and he couldn't imagine her sticking to boundaries, to what people expected – her clothes, hair, her style was pure Avril – but they were choices she made. She'd always struck him as down to earth, not somebody who'd see things that weren't there. However much she wanted to.

'So … who was watching you?'

'Mum's friend Mandy! They look so similar, I mean Dad had told me they were very close and had similar tastes in everything, but they really are. I nearly died when I first saw her! I know I don't know what Mum would look like now, but in my head she'd be somebody like Mandy. They could be sisters. I'd not really seen it on that photograph you sent, 'cause you kind of expect that people will all have the stuff that was in fashion at that time, you know, the same hairstyles, clothes?'

Will nodded.

'But I looked again, and close up Mandy *does* look different, I mean her nose isn't quite the same shape, and her eyes are a bit different, but I think it's just'—Avril paused—'her style, it's like I imagine Mum's would be.'

'And she was looking for you?'

'Oh yes, she said she's kept an eye on me over the years, but after Mum died, Dad shut himself off from her and all the things Mum used to do. Mandy said she got that. She knew how hard he'd found it, so she kept her distance, she didn't want to upset him. But she wanted to know I was okay, and she wanted to feel a connection with Mum still. Isn't that lovely? She wants us to meet up again!'

'Fantastic!' He smiled at her. She was beaming, her cheeks flushed. 'Have you told your dad?'

'I told him I was meeting her. He was with me when you sent that photo, and he said he's got other stuff that belonged to Mum. He's sent some more pictures to me, and some bits and pieces.' She stared down at her drink for a moment, then looked back up at him. 'I think he's okay about it now, but I'm not going to tell him about her being my ghost'—a smile lifted the corner of her mouth—'until I've seen her again.'

'Soon?'

'Yep, we're going for a drink and pizza, a week today.' She seemed to hesitate for a moment. 'I was wondering if you fancied coming with me?'

'Sure.'

'Don't worry if you're busy.'

'I'm not, I'd like to come.'

'It's just a bit weird still, and I'll forget what I want to ask and…'

'Avril.' He put his hand over hers. 'I'd love to come. I'd love to meet her and hear about your mum.'

She stopped talking. Their eyes met and for a long moment they sat there, in silence.

'Thanks.'

He'd never been this close to her. She was beautiful in a way that was different to just pretty. There was something about her that was slightly fragile, slightly ethereal, he supposed the word was. Otherworldly, magical. She was delicate, but strong.

'What are you thinking about?' She tipped her head to one side.

He suddenly realised that his hand was still over hers. It felt right, it felt normal. And she hadn't moved away.

'Sorry.' He pulled back reluctantly, laughed self-consciously. But he wanted to keep looking at her, touching her. He wanted to hold her. Instead, he wrapped his fingers round his glass. 'Avril, I'd like us to go out again.' He studied her face, half expecting her to brush him off, come up with some excuse – which she'd give in the kindest possible way. 'I meant it when I asked before, when we went out for coffee.' Before Lucy turned up.

'That would be cool.'

'Really?'

She laughed. 'Of course really! Why did you ask again if you didn't think I'd say yes?'

'I just thought…' He shrugged, tracing the tip of his finger through the condensation on his glass, but couldn't keep the grin off his face. And he couldn't help looking straight back up at her. 'Well, last time—'

'I like you, Will.' Her voice was earnest, and she touched the back of his hand with her fingertips.

'I like you, too. I really missed seeing you today at the library.' He had. After Lucy had turned up, she'd withdrawn, which was why he'd felt compelled to message her. And he wanted to help her find out more about her mum, of course he did, but he also wanted to keep a connection with her. He didn't want to lose her.

'Hey, when we've finished these drinks do you want to come and feed the ducks with me before I have to catch the train? I got some bread from the café – apparently Mandy always gets some from her daughter so she can feed the ducks.' A flush of pink tinged her cheekbones. 'Mandy and mum used to do that together.'

'How can I resist an invitation like that?'

'You can tell me about your bookshop.' Avril's tone was light, but he could read the question in it. The question he didn't have an answer to: when was he going back?

'I will.'

She pushed her empty glass into the centre of the table and stood up. 'I missed you too today.' She said it simply, and Will suddenly felt more positive. About the shop, Lucy, even Jake. If Avril could face her past, and her ghosts, if Hattie was brave enough to forge a new future, then surely he could work out his present and who was important in it?

Chapter Twenty-Six

HATTIE

Parting is Such Sweet Sorrow

'Hello, Harriet. It's been a long time.'

Hattie stared at the man standing in front of them and the pang of disappointment stung the back of her throat and prickled behind her eyes. Maybe it was just shock, that he was finally here. But she knew instantly that it was more than that.

This moment wasn't how she'd imagined it.

She'd expected to feel like she had as a girl. She'd imagined a pause between them; a delicious pause before they rushed into each other's arms. There would be no need for words, but they would all tumble out anyway. They would share the kisses that they had been deprived of. She would feel that this was what she had been waiting her whole life for. That she'd known she had been right.

Instead, he was just a man. A familiar man, a man she instantly felt that she knew, that she could feel comfortable with in the way an old pair of shoes would always slip easily onto your feet. But he was just a man. And a part of him was a stranger. The part that had grown without her.

Despite his age, his voice was still rich, deep with a slightly cultured edge that hadn't been there when he was younger. He held himself upright, with the help of a stick. His thinning hair was neatly cut, and his gaze still held that hint of mischief.

It was Peter. She was glad that he was finally here. But he was not the man she'd been waiting for.

'Hattie. I prefer Hattie these days.' Why couldn't she think of a single thing to say? She'd been waiting to see him for all these years and now that the moment had come, every question that had haunted her had flown straight out of her silly old head. And the first thing she did was correct him!

'Hattie. I like that, it suits you.' He leaned forward, lifted her hand and kissed the back of it. 'As does your hairstyle. Very chic.'

She'd been right. He'd grown up to be quite the gentleman. He'd always had good manners, but she'd never really known him as a man.

'Is this your son?' Peter glanced towards Stuart and Hattie shook her head.

'Harold and I never had children. This is a friend of mine, Stuart. We're doing a writing project together, aren't we?'

'We are.' Stuart looked a bit awkward. 'Would you like me to go, Hattie?'

'Of course not,' she said firmly, then turned back to

Peter. 'Stuart is also helping me sort the house out. I'm selling it. It's too big,' she babbled on, as he quietly watched. 'Now I'm on my own. And too many bad memories.'

'Bad?'

'Life wasn't always easy with Harold.' She looked him directly in the eye to see if he'd contradict her, correct her. But he didn't. Instead, he gave the smallest of smiles, more an acknowledgement, and understanding, than a proper smile.

'Ah. Can I take you for a cup of tea, Hattie? And you too, Stuart, if you have time?'

'I will get back, if that is okay with you, Hattie?'

She looked at Stuart and tried to give him her most confident stare. He was a good man, a kind man, and she didn't want to use up any more of his time, but she was suddenly unsure.

Peter was a stranger. She had played this moment, this meeting, out in her head many times and it had always been different. They'd both been how they were when they parted – in manner if not physically. There had been no awkwardness, no distance. They'd simply taken up where they'd left off.

But now, in reality, she wasn't sure who Peter was. She wasn't sure who she was. She most definitely wasn't the innocent young girl whose heart had broken when he'd left.

'Actually, you know what? If you both don't mind me tagging along, a cup of tea would be rather nice.' Stuart's voice cut into her thoughts. He knew, he understood. 'Jo will still be busy; she'll be pleased I'm out of her hair! I'll carry this for you, shall I?'

Hattie noticed Peter's gaze kept being drawn back to the box. 'It's a few bits and pieces that Harold gave me,' she explained. 'I think we should go back to my apartment; it will be more comfortable.' She didn't want to take the box to some café, to a place full of strangers. 'It's only around the corner.'

She pulled the front door of the house closed behind them and looked at Peter who was waiting at the bottom of the driveway, then she glanced up at the bedroom window. It felt as though Harold was looking down on them. Was this wrong? Was she betraying him, her wedding vows?

'Hattie?' Stuart was holding his arm out, and when she slipped her hand back into the crook, he held it briefly. Reassuringly. 'He seems nice,' he whispered.

'He always was,' she whispered back.

'And he came, so he must have something to say.'

They walked the short distance between her home with Harold and her home without – her new flat. The short distance that had been a huge step for her.

Inside, she put the kettle on, because it was normal, wherever she was. And she poured the tea and put the biscuits on a plate and looked at the man that had been her past, the man she'd always hoped would be her future.

He met her gaze. And as Nutmeg pressed his cold nose against her hand, all she could feel was the present.

'I'm sorry I didn't get back in touch earlier, Hattie. I just thought it was easier.'

'For whom?' Well, she was certainly braver these days, she would never have voiced that question in the past.

The silence stretched. Peter sat perfectly still; he didn't

reach out to stir his drink or move his plate. She remembered that about him. His stillness. Peter had never let life rush him into corners he didn't want to go to. It was this steadiness that had first drawn her to him. Nothing had been steady in her life until Peter came. Her father had been volatile, her mother had scurried away like a scolded mouse if her father as much as raised an eyebrow. Her home had not been a place to relax, it had been a place where you were on edge, waiting for an eruption of harsh words, of violence.

Hattie had learned to be quiet, but it was not the same as the quiet that Peter brought. It had been accompanied by a rapid heartbeat so loud that she was sure *he* could hear it. A rush in her blood, her body, that was waiting for the trigger. For her to act.

When Peter finally spoke again, they were not the words she had expected.

'For Harold. I thought it would be easier for Harold if I stayed away,' he said.

This made sense, because Peter had never been selfish. He had always been a giver, not a taker. She'd always hung on to the thought that he'd either disappeared for her or for Harold. That he had a reason.

Peter smiled, then gestured towards the box that Stuart had put on the table in front of them. 'I never gave you anything, did I?'

You didn't because I had you, Hattie thought. But only shook her head.

'But Harold tried to give you everything,' he said, the gentleness of his voice sending a quiver to her heart.

'He was cruel.'

'He was afraid.' Peter sighed. 'He would never admit it, but he was only human.'

'What do you mean?' She frowned. 'Harold was never afraid!' She could hear the tartness in her tone, but Peter didn't react. He waited. Hadn't she recently suspected that Harold's dislike of the library, the clever clogs who thought they were better than him, was driven by a fear?

'He was scared, so he was overprotective. It was the only way he knew.' Peter's gaze met hers, and all she could see was a need to speak the truth. 'He was scared of losing you.'

Hadn't she thought that maybe Harold, and her father, were worried that if she went out, if she read, she'd learn new things? Have new ideas of her own?

'You were the only person I ever saw him trust, Hattie.' Peter reached out and took her hands in his. She could never remember holding his hands before. It had all been looks between them, fleeting touches. 'You were the only person I ever knew him to want. And we all need at least one person to love in our lives, so I let him have you.'

'But he must have had…' she trailed off.

Peter sat back. 'He never told you about how we met, did he?'

'At school, primary school.'

'It was before then. You knew I was at the children's home?'

She nodded. She knew Peter was an orphan, that his friends were his family. He'd never complained, never acted hard done by.

'Well, that is where I met Harold.'

'Why would he visit that place?'

'He didn't just visit; he lived there for a while.'

'Harold didn't live there. He had family.' She frowned. Harold often told her he was better off without his family, but he had never said that he didn't have any. She had assumed there must have been some big fall out, that it had been his choice to shut them out of his life. And he had very firmly closed the subject, it had not been up for discussion. She had known better than to pry.

This visit wasn't turning out how she'd expected at all. All Peter wanted to talk about was Harold, and it would seem that he didn't know him as well as she'd thought he did.

'You're right. He did have family, of a sort.' Peter took a sip of his tea, then replaced the cup and saucer carefully down. 'I'm sorry if I seem to be going round the houses, Hattie, but I need to tell you everything or I don't think you will ever understand or forgive me.' He gave her a small smile.

It was familiar, that smile. It knocked the years away, took her back to their teens. They'd had laughs, Peter had been funny as well as kind, but he'd often paused. Like he was doing now, he'd been serious, so earnest even when he'd been young. And he'd always smiled like that, even when he was saying he didn't want to do something.

She didn't contradict him, and say there was nothing to forgive, because he was right. He'd left her. He'd taken the decision out of her hands. That was hard to forgive. She wanted to forgive him, she wanted to know he had a reason – but saying he had sacrificed their future because

Harold had nobody else to love was not a reason that sat easily with her.

It was too easy to say.

Too hard to believe.

'Harold never knew his father,' Peter went on. 'Sometimes his mother told him he'd been killed in battle, sometimes she'd say he'd pissed off the moment he saw Harold.' His tone softened. 'She drank, you see, and one day she disappeared, and somebody took Harold to the home. Then a while later his mother came and took him home again. But within a few months he was back. He'd stayed with an aunt and uncle for a while, but that didn't work out. The uncle abused him from what I understand, but he didn't like to speak about it. He was passed around like a parcel, Hattie. Nobody really loved him. Each time children left that home, but then returned, it got harder for them. The lucky ones went back to family or found nice foster homes. But Harold could never be adopted, and he'd often end up with some relative and see his mum now and again. But he wasn't brought up with love. He just existed; I think it was quite a sterile existence from the little I saw. That home was a hard place to grow up in, though, and I'm glad it's gone now. Bulldozed, it was, knocked to the ground.'

'That's tough,' Stuart put in, the first words he'd spoken since she'd made their drinks. 'Really tough.'

Peter nodded. 'It was. The place didn't hold any good memories, well, apart from the people. I like to remember some of the people, but not all of them. These days I think they'd say a lot of the children were "damaged", and sadly I think many of the adults weren't there for the right reasons.

Burying the past is sometimes the best way, don't you think? Even if those that don't understand say otherwise. But'—his smile broadened, and Hattie could see a glimmer of the naughty, mischievous, Peter—'there were some good parts, some good friends, like Harold and'—his smile was directed at Hattie now—'Hattie. And I was placed with a lovely family when I was twelve.'

But then you left me, was all she could think. *Abandoned me.*

'If I'd stopped Harold marrying you, it would have been selfish, Hattie. I didn't want to be selfish. And we were still kids, you hardly knew me.'

'I loved you,' she said, and there was no crack in her voice because it was true. It was a truth she'd known for a long time, a truth she'd hung on to.

'You grew to love the idea of me, of us. It wasn't real, because we never had a chance to find out if it could be. Harold only had you. Everybody else had let him down.'

'And who did you have?'

He shrugged. 'I knew I'd be okay on my own, I knew I'd survive because I'd had love in my life, but I didn't think he would.'

'I missed you; I was very lonely.'

'I missed you, too. We can be friends, Hattie; we were good friends back then.'

They had been. Peter had been the best type of friend.

'I've always kept an eye on you, you know. I didn't move far. Well, I travelled for a short while because I thought I hadn't got roots, but I was proved wrong, so I came back.'

'Are you married?' She had to ask.

Peter nodded. 'I did marry, but my wife hasn't been well.

She is in a hospice now – our daughter insisted. She said it wasn't doing either of us any favours carrying on as we were. But I go in to see her regularly.' He paused. 'You said you didn't have children?'

Hattie shook her head. 'He wouldn't let me.'

'He was probably frightened of bringing a child into the world and them suffering like he did, and I think'—he paused—'I think the responsibility of looking after you—'

'I didn't need—'

'In his eyes it was his duty, Hattie. He *wanted* to look after you, I'm sure. You meant a lot to him, but I suspect he was worried he'd get it wrong. And he would be worried that he'd make the same mistakes his own parents had, with a child. He thought the damage was in him, that he'd curse the next generation. He wouldn't have, though.' He shook his head with a confidence that Hattie would not have felt. But had she not known Harold at all? Had their whole marriage been a façade with no depth, two people who didn't know how to communicate? Who had no idea how to mend what had gone wrong?

'I'd like you to meet Sophie, my daughter, if you want to, that is. If you don't, I quite understand. She has a little boy, I'm a granddad!' His cheeks were slightly flushed with pride.

'I'd like that.' And Hattie realised with a certainty that she would. It was wrong to harp on about the mistakes of the past, the 'what ifs', it was time she lived in the present and the 'what is'. 'I think I might open the box now.'

'And I think I have a train to catch. But…' Peter took a pen out of one pocket and found an old receipt in the other. He turned the receipt over and scribbled down his number.

'Here'— he held it out to her—'I mean it, I'd very much like to stay in touch, if you'll let me, that is?'

'That would be nice, Peter.' Hattie smiled at the tall, handsome stranger in front of her. Harold had been the worn-out sweater that sat comfortably, familiar, around her shoulders. The one that didn't quite fit, and had thinning patches. The one that sometimes felt scratchy. Peter was the shiny new boots that she'd admired in the shop window for months, that she'd yearned for, but now wasn't sure they wouldn't give her blisters. The boots that she had to try on for size. Just so that she knew.

'I've made a right fool out of myself, haven't I?' she asked Stuart after Peter had left.

'You most certainly have not. You've been brave enough to find a man who meant a lot to you, and now you'll be able to meet his family. And he's brought you answers you could never have imagined.'

'But all this time … I thought I loved him!'

'And you probably did.'

'And I thought that I disliked Harold. But now I don't know. I'm eighty-seven and I don't know if I liked my husband. I killed him you know.'

'What?' Stuart frowned.

'Oh, don't look at me like that! Can you see me actually killing a man?'

'Well, I'm not entirely sure how to answer that,' Stuart admitted.

'I meant in the story, silly. It was him I was thinking about when I was plotting the body on the beach!'

'Ah, yes, the one we wouldn't let you have! But that was the Harold who had been cruel to you, not the Harold you knew was inside.'

'So, it's okay to kill somebody who is nasty to you?'

'I didn't say that. But you didn't know why he was like that, Hattie, and he hadn't been able to tell you. I admit, that is terribly sad, and such a shame when your lives could have been better. But you can't change the past. Maybe it was a good job the rest of us wanted to resurrect the character?' He smiled, and she couldn't help but smile back at him. He was a nice man. 'You get a second chance! You could always write a chapter where you discover the things you *did* like about him?'

Hattie looked at the box. 'There are a lot of things that I like about him in there.'

'Then maybe you should spend some time with them,' he said gently. 'And maybe seeing Peter again would be rather nice?'

It would, thought Hattie. There was no getting away from the fact that she had been mildly disappointed by her initial reaction to him. She'd always thought that seeing Peter again would make her feel elated. It hadn't. But it would be good to see him again, and it would be good to talk about Harold with him. He was the only person who knew the real Harold.

'It would be very nice. I shall, don't worry, I shall. Now that I have his phone number.'

Hattie showed Stuart to the door and closed it firmly

behind him before turning the lock and returning to her seat.

She picked up the notebook. What was she going to write now?

And then the box caught her eye again. Before she did anything else, she was going to open the box.

Her fingers trembling, she lifted the lid.

There were more than her keepsakes in the box. There was another, smaller package. A package that hadn't been there the last time she'd closed this lid.

Chapter Twenty-Seven

STUART

Rainbows

'You look like you need a cup of tea!'

'I certainly do.' Stuart smiled at Jo, and it hit him. How lucky he was. Luckier than he'd ever taken time to appreciate.

'What have you been up to?' She was taking cups out, switching the kettle on, but still had time to study him with a look of quiet concern.

'I love you, Jo. I really do.'

'And I love you, darling.' She sat down opposite him at the table and took his hands in hers. 'What's the matter?'

'Hattie has found her Peter again.'

'Well, that's wonderful. Isn't it?'

'It is, but she's realised that there were so many things she didn't discuss with Harold. That her life with him could have been so different.'

'Everybody leaves things unsaid, Stuart. Sometimes it just seems best at the time.'

'I know I have, and it did seem best at the time. But there are things I need to tell you.'

'About Stephen?' she said softly.

He looked up, startled, his gaze meeting hers. She was looking at him steadily.

'You know about Stephen?'

'You've talked about him in your sleep, so I asked around a bit.'

'But why didn't you say anything?'

'I knew you'd tell me when you were ready, Stuart. I knew you'd know I was here for you. And you're ready now?' He nodded. He was. 'Was Stephen the person you didn't feel you cared enough about, the one you felt that you let down? The one you didn't pay enough attention to?'

Stuart frowned.

'I've read your chapters in the story, and it made me wonder. It was a good idea, you entering the competition, wasn't it?'

He smiled. Jo was right. She was always right. It had been a good idea. Therapeutic. 'I've never been very good at saying how I feel.' But he'd been able to express his emotions in a story, when he was writing about somebody else. When it was fiction.

'What did you feel guilty about, Stuart?'

He sighed. 'I've never really considered anybody enough, have I? Never taken notice of people.'

'Oh, that's rubbish, Stuart. You've been a wonderful husband.'

'At providing an income, but not—'

'Now that's nonsense. Do you think I would have married a man who didn't care? I admit, you do find it hard to express how you feel sometimes, but I know. I don't need words, Stuart.'

He smiled and squeezed her hands. He was lucky.

'I've felt a bit useless since I left work. You can manage quite well without me, because you've always had to. No, don't deny it, I know it's true! So I've run around thinking that all I needed to do was find a way of filling my time, but I've realised that isn't the solution. I've realised that it's a sticking plaster to cover up the real problem, which was Stephen. And Stephen is just a symptom. There were lots of Stephens. People I didn't really see properly, who I could have stood to be more empathetic with. I failed at work, Jo. That's partly why they let me go early, and I'd been telling myself I've failed at life. But I haven't. I know that. It was just the easy way out, the way to avoid addressing my problems. Facing up to the real issue.'

'Which is?' she asked softly.

'Stephen worked for me. He was a nice man, not one who particularly stood out at work, but somebody I should have noticed. He'd not been feeling one hundred per cent, and he'd told me, but I hadn't done anything about it. I just let him carry on. He was a very conscientious man, Jo. Never had a day off, so he just carried on as though nothing was wrong. But there was. I should have known. He started making the odd mistake, because he was overtired and I should have stepped in, talked to him about it. But I didn't because I was my normal busy self, proving to the world how accomplished I was.' Jo made a noise as though she was about to interrupt, but he ignored it. 'He had a stroke. A major one. Then he had to leave on ill-health grounds.'

'But you weren't resp—'

'I didn't notice, Jo. He'd made some minor noises about feeling off, and he had a very stressful job. I could have lifted his workload, insisted he had time off.'

'It wasn't your fault, Stuart.'

'It might not have been my fault that he had high blood pressure, or was unfit, or whatever led to it, but it was my fault for not caring enough to actually do something to help him. I knew he wasn't himself, but I just let him carry on.'

'Oh, Stuart. You set the bar so high for yourself. I love you for it, but you can't always be perfect.'

'It's not being perfect, caring about people, is it?'

Jo shook her head. 'But you do care, Stuart.'

'Hattie was talking about Harold today,' he said. 'I think she's realised that all the years she resented him, he was actually trying to do his best for her — he just didn't consider what she actually wanted. I've been like that, Jo. But I want to be better at life, not work. I want to do things for you that you actually want, not that I think you should.'

'Oh, Stuart.' She put her arms round him and after a second he wrapped his own around her. 'I've never felt that you haven't considered me. But I'm glad you've left work. I like having you around and I really, really do like the idea of us being able to share our lives more.'

'Thank you,' he said softly. Kissing her.

'And I would really like to go to the mayor's party!' She

laughed. 'And I've made a nice parkin cake, do you fancy a slice?'

Chapter Twenty-Eight

AVRIL

Ducks

'Ta-dah!' Avril dipped into her bag and pulled out the paper bag of bread that she'd got from the café.

'A magician, as well.' Will laughed.

There was something different about him this afternoon. She'd not really noticed the change in him, because she'd been concentrating on her own feelings. But he'd been on edge since Lucy had come to the library. Fighting the feelings she supposed, because that's how it was when you split up with somebody, wasn't it?

Even if it was you who made the break, there was a reason you'd got together in the first place. You couldn't deny the feelings that had been there, even if you had outgrown them. She'd never really understood how people could have a relationship, then afterwards carry on working together, or living together, or watching their ex date somebody else, because that wasn't how a heart worked, was it?

Her dad still had her mum in his heart, and Hattie still had Peter.

And she sometimes thought of the guys she'd dated in the past. Not in a romantic way – because none of them had been that important, none of them had been the one. They'd not had the power to break her heart, just bruise it a little. When she thought about them, it was just memories, things that had shaped her past, her future. What had shaped Will?

The past always seemed important to Avril, maybe because she was always looking back at it for clues about Phee. Because she had loved her. She knew she had.

Had Will loved Lucy? He said not, he said they'd been drifting apart before they split up. And to be honest, he'd seemed more annoyed, irritated, than broken-hearted when she'd turned up. But why?

Whatever the reason, he seemed happier today. Lighter. More, well … carefree, like he'd been when she'd first met him. She didn't want to spoil it, lose it. But she wanted to get to know him – before he headed back off to his bookshop. To his life.

She threw a piece of bread towards the group of ducks that had been eyeing them up with interest.

'How's your dad doing?'

'Good, good.' He nodded.

'That's great.' Did that mean he was on the countdown to leaving? 'Do you have any other brothers or sisters that help out?'

There was a silence, so she glanced up at him. She hadn't noticed just how close they were together. Their shoulders practically touching. His mouth within kissing distance. The unexpected thought made her breath hitch.

But was it unexpected? She'd liked the touch of his hand in the bar, she'd told him she wanted to see him again. She'd asked him to come here.

'Sorry, ignore me and my questions, it's just—'

'It's fine.' He smiled at her.

Did any of it matter? He was leaving at some point, but why couldn't she just make the most of the time he was here? She wanted to kiss him; she wanted to see him. 'Sorry it's not like I need to know your life story!' But she did want to know, because the past was important. The past shaped the future. If she kissed him without knowing who he was, the thrill would be followed by doubts. She didn't want doubts. She wanted to enjoy the moment, but know it wasn't a mistake.

'I know quite a bit about your history,' he said softly. He traced his thumb over her lips, then cradled her chin in his hand. 'I'm sorry, I'm not trying to be mysterious, I'm just crap at talking about myself.'

'Some would say that's a benefit. I hate self-obsessed people.' She smiled. 'Although they came in handy at the hair salon. With some clients you didn't need to think up stuff to talk about, they would just go on about themselves for however long it took.'

'I bet. I get people like that in the library sometimes. They ask about a book, but before you get a chance to say anything they start talking again, offering their opinion with no room for anybody else's.'

He moved away slightly, leaving her cheek feeling cold as his hand dropped on to his own knee.

'I've got a sister. Sarah,' he said.

He was leaning forward, watching the ducks, his forearms on his knees, but from the tone of his voice she could tell Sarah was important to him. She'd never had a sister to care about. Her stepsisters could have been aliens, they were so different to her.

'But she's abroad, in Australia.'

'Wow, a long way to go!'

'She wanted to get away.' His smile was rueful.

'Not from you, I hope.' She tried to lighten the atmosphere, but it didn't change the look on his face.

'From Jake.'

Then he turned, so that his gaze met hers.

'I don't hate Jake because of Lucy; I hate him because of what he did to my sister.' He took a piece of bread from her hand and started to break it into smaller bits and throw them. 'I don't want anything to do with him, and I really wish Lucy didn't either.' He glanced at her, and she could see he was being sincere, telling the truth. 'I don't love Lucy, I don't think I ever really did, but I do care for her, as a human being. I don't want her to get hurt like Sarah did. But she's not going to listen to me, is she? She just thinks I'm jealous.' He threw a scrap of bread with a force that made her wince.

'Hey, are you trying to stun the ducks?'

The smile was fleeting. But he brushed his hands together, then sat back. 'Sorry.'

'Tell me about Sarah. I'm not interested in Lucy,' she

said softly. 'She's a grown woman, Will, you'll have to let her make her own mistakes.'

'You could be right. I knew Jake at school. Only vaguely, he wasn't somebody I wanted to be friends with, but you couldn't miss him. I think he was born confident; he had a very high opinion of himself. He was good-looking, I guess, and well off, and even though he didn't get the grades he needed for the uni he'd picked he managed to get in somewhere through clearing. If he hadn't, I'm sure he would have charmed his way in somewhere.'

'Woah, you really liked him then!'

The fleeting smile came and went again. 'We both did English degrees, then I stayed down south to help my uncle out.'

'With the bookshop?'

'Yep.' He smiled. 'I didn't want a gap year, but my uncle did! He wanted to try travelling and see if it was for him, or a "stupid old man's dream" as he put it. He said I could modernise the shop, do what I wanted with it.'

'And did you?'

Will raised a questioning eyebrow.

'Modernise it?'

'Oh God, no. It's perfect just the way it is. I'd like to show you sometime. I mean, I know you're not keen on books, but it's wonderful.' His voice had a wistful edge.

'You miss it?'

'I do.' He nodded. 'And I miss Sah. She's five years younger than me, I've always felt I let her down.'

'How? You were in Cambridge.'

'Exactly. If I'd been at home, then I'd have been there

for her!' He sighed. 'Jake finished his degree then decided to do a post-grad for a year. After that he got a job in Manchester as a journalist. That was when Sah met him, or rather he sought her out. She was smitten, but for him it was just a game, and she was easy prey.'

'A game?'

'He was using her for some series about dating that he was writing for the publication he worked for, going full out. He didn't just want to impress his boss; he wanted to get noticed by the nationals.'

'And she didn't know?'

'Nope. Not until her story was plastered over social media. "A warts-and-all account", he called it, of cringey dating lines through to fumbled first kisses and knickers off.'

'Oh, my God, surely he should have told her, warned her, asked if it was okay even?'

'He changed her name, but she knew it was her, and so did all her mates. Basically, everybody that she knew, knew it had to be her. She was just about to take her A levels and completely messed them up. She was embarrassed as well as heartbroken, so'—he shrugged, and she could see the pain on his face—'she ran away. She took a year out to travel and ended up in Australia.'

'As far away as she could be.'

'Yep. She met this guy out there, a really nice guy, so she stayed out there. She's having a great time, but I miss her, and I know Mum and Dad do, too.'

'Maybe she's in the right place, where she's supposed to be, and Jake helped her get there.'

'By being a shit?'

'Yep. It sounds like she's happy.'

He sat back. 'Well, yeah. I guess that's one way to think about it. She is. Maybe you're right, that's where she would have ended up anyway. She'd have missed her chance of meeting the right person if her life had gone how she'd planned it. But I can't give Jake any credit for that.'

'Sounds like he doesn't deserve any credit for anything.'

'He's done it again, used people for his career. He's always been a user, even at school. In Jake's life only Jake matters.'

'So he's still a journalist?'

'Yep, and an aspiring writer.'

'Ah, so that's the issue with the competition.'

'He'll use Lucy, and he'll use this competition to raise his profile and get himself noticed.'

'Isn't it a bit beneath him?' Avril threw the last bit of bread and half turned to look at Will properly. 'I mean he's a journalist, a writer, why would he do something like this?'

'Jake will do anything, whatever it takes. His name is on the entry list, but if he decides not to do that, he'll still make sure he's involved. I just know it. He'll persuade Lucy he can be an advisor, or'—he paused—'God help us, a judge.'

'Well, I hope for our sakes that entries are read anonymously!'

'Me too.' Will rolled his eyes. Then he leaned towards her. 'Lucy isn't important to me, we'd never get back together. We shouldn't have been together in the first place. I'm not quite sure what throwing her arms around me was about, but I don't love her.'

Avril nodded. 'But you do love the bookshop,' she said gently.

'I do. Will you let me take you there?'

'That would be nice. Thanks.'

She wanted to know Will better; she wanted to know the things that meant a lot to him. But if the love of his life was a bookshop at the other end of the country, did that mean he'd be disappearing soon?

She checked her watch. 'I never had time to see Hattie,' she said. 'And I'd better get going, I suppose, or I'll miss my train.'

'I'm sure Stuart would have let us know if she needed us. She might well need some time on her own?'

'True. I don't want her to feel I'm prying.'

'I don't work on a Friday. You don't fancy…?' He left the question open, hanging, and she couldn't help but smile.

'Meeting up tomorrow? Sounds good to me.'

He was on his feet first, holding out a hand towards her. She slipped hers in his and it felt the most natural thing in the world to walk hand in hand with him to the station.

Chapter Twenty-Nine

HATTIE

Pandora's Box

Hattie hadn't expected a surprise when she opened her box. It had, after all, always been *her* box. Harold had never touched it, he had no interest in her belongings, and besides, it had been safely tucked away for years.

But there was no other answer, it had to be Harold who had put this package inside.

She had no idea when, or why, but she supposed she wouldn't unless she opened it.

It was surprisingly light when she lifted it, so she put it on her lap.

Nutmeg jumped up beside her. He sniffed the corner then looked up, as though asking her what she was playing at.

'I suppose I should open it?' He stared at her for a long moment then curled up, his tiny body pressed against her.

She lifted the flap, then slid out the contents. On the top, obscuring everything else, was a large sepia photograph. It was of the children's home on the other side of the town. The home that Peter had lived in.

Hattie reached for her spectacles then peered at it more closely. There was a ragtag group of children of all shapes and sizes, wearing an assortment of ill-fitting clothing that had seen better days. She remembered the clothes that Peter had worn. The other children at school had not noticed when they were young, but as they got older there had been teasing, and sometimes downright cruel comments. She knew it had affected him; she'd hated to see the bright colour scar his cheekbones, but he'd held his head up high and ignored them. No wonder he was so sharp and smart now. Sharp suited him, he was a handsome man, it must have hurt to have had to wear the hand-me-downs that people had donated. She looked again. Although the children were all different ages and heights, they were in tight rows, and all standing to attention. It wasn't a comfortable photograph to look at, it spoke of discipline and cruelty, not home and happiness.

There was a slightly shorter, stockier figure standing next to Peter, that her gaze was immediately drawn to. A familiar figure. Harold.

She had never thought that Peter would lie to her, but it had been hard for her to imagine Harold in the home. But here he was, in the regimental line. Standing to attention.

She turned the photograph. There was a date on it, written in Harold's neat handwriting. He would have been four years old.

A letter caught her attention.

My darling Harriet,

She knew that this would not be a declaration of undying love, or an apology, or any kind of real explanation of who her husband really was and why he was the way he was, because that had not been her Harold. This was him putting things in order.

> *Please forgive me for not disclosing my health problems. I did not want you to worry. Fretting would not have changed anything, and so I have focused on trying to ensure that your needs will be met.*

Hattie shook her head but couldn't help the small smile. How very Harold. Her emotional needs, her loneliness, would not have been his main consideration. His worry would have been her financial situation. But now maybe she could start to understand why. Men of their generation were not used to expressing their feelings, but for Harold supressing everything had probably become a habit that was impossible to break.

> *I love you, Harriet. You have always been my everything. I know that it is fashionable these days for women to refer to their husbands as their rocks, but in my case it was the other way round. Without you, I would have had no purpose.*
> *As you know, letters, words, are not my forte.*
> *In this package are the few things that I have kept over the years as reminders of my early life – my life before you. They may be of interest. I am aware that we never talked about my child-*

hood beyond what you saw. To me the past was the past, and better left there.

My heart condition is between myself and my doctor, but I will leave everything in order, so you are not inconvenienced.

I always felt that I curtailed your freedom and the life you could have had. I apologise, but keeping you close was the only way that I could live.

Seek out Peter. He liked you and was the only other true friend I had. I wish we could have been closer again, but he always said that his going was for the best and that we would be happier without him. I am unsure if that is true. But Peter came into my life like the big brother I desperately needed, and I have always trusted him and followed his lead. I know he will always ensure that you are safe.

Hattie glanced at the date at the top of the letter. Three days before he had died. He knew the end was near, but even death had cheated on him. Caught him when he wasn't expecting it. But it had probably been better for him that way. He had not been waiting. Harold hated to wait.

She laid the letter to one side. There were so many things that had been left unsaid between them. She supposed that these days that would not be allowed. People talked. They talked and they listened.

Had Peter been right? That Harold's cruelty had been unintended, that it had been overprotection? Had the idea of another responsibility – a dog, or heaven forbid a child – been too much for him to cope with, so he had simply forbidden it?

Her father had never been one for discussions, and it

seemed Harold had been the same. What did they say about the sins of the father?

Her gaze was drawn to the notebook. The lives of those two important figures in her life, their worlds, had been so limited, so restricted.

When she has started to write this story, she had been sure that the truth had never escaped her – it had been love that had been missing from her life. She had been so wrong.

She could feel the heat of unshed tears in her eyes. She'd never been one to cry. It wasn't the done thing. It was for babies. But she wanted to cry for Harold. For everything he hadn't had, everything he hadn't allowed himself to be when he was older.

For everything *they* hadn't had.

He'd done everything he had for her, and she hadn't been able to appreciate it because she didn't want her own life to be small. Like his had been.

She had only been able to see Peter, and the optimism and kindness, the love of life, that he'd had. That she had thought would be hers to share.

But Peter had never given her gifts. Peter had never declared undying love, or even marriage.

She closed her eyes. And now Harold had given her his blessing to find Peter.

Her hand rested on Nutmeg's head. She wanted to live the rest of her days more like the little dog did. Expecting nothing, living each day as it came and enjoying it. Not thinking about what might happen tomorrow, or what had happened yesterday.

She'd look through the rest of the papers and

photographs he had put in the package tomorrow. She would learn more about the man she'd shared her life with in the morning, when she had had some time to mull over the day. She was tired.

Instead, she reached for the notebook. What had Avril written? And what, she wondered, had she found out about her mother today?

Dead or alive, everybody left a trace, didn't they? Fiona and Gerald were out there somewhere. A person could be anywhere in the world, could be uncontactable, or simply lost, but somewhere on the internet there would be something about them. They would have friends, job, relatives.

And if you could find even one little thing it meant you had the start of the chain. Something to follow.

Hattie shook her head. She was sad that Avril was so fearful about finding out the truth – scared of what she might find and having her hopes dashed. But wasn't it like that for everybody – the truth was seldom what you wanted or expected. And yet it could bring good in unexpected ways. It could reveal things that could enrich your life. If you let them.

And in her latest chapter, Avril was talking about being brave, about battling on to find out the truth regardless. She was a determined young lady and Hattie really hoped she did find what she was looking for. Without Avril, where would Hattie have been now? She probably wouldn't have found Peter, or the truth.

Hattie turned over to a blank page and picked up her

pen. She knew where she wanted the story to go to next. She'd told Stuart that everybody made mistakes, but it was what you chose to do about them that was important. And now she wanted to make amends with Harold. She wanted to apologise. Not in as many words of course, that would be silly and not fit the story at all. But she could hint at it. She could make sure that everybody knew that she hadn't killed Gerald off. That there was a reason for everything.

Chapter Nine

(Hattie)

Nothing is as it seems, thought Sam as he packed his fleece into the rucksack. The pictures that had been painted of these people may have been accurate in isolation, but they didn't fit together. It was like looking at a collage. Random pictures from different parts of their lives.

There were gaps, the parts of these people that they had kept private. Their real feelings and motivations.

Was it just his job that led him to see people this way, or was everyone like this?

He put the bag on the passenger seat of his car, then started the engine and pulled off.

Eliza's impression of Gerald had been formed by reading her mother's letter and diary. A man who had been involved in an adulterous affair. A man who might have good reason to disappear.

Marie's view had been informed by her life as his daughter, growing up. A father who was always there, had a routine. A man who would have never left his family.

But he had a wife who had left – who wanted her freedom. And possibly a lover who had also pushed him out of her life.

Was he a man who had been driven by the strong women in his life? Or had he attracted such women because at heart he was good, strong, himself?

Sam knew that you should never judge a man – anybody – until you knew them, and there are many people that we only get to know, to understand, when they have gone. When the emotional distance lets us see them for who they were. Not the person we'd wanted them to be.

Everybody that Sam had talked to thought that Gerald was a decent man. Suicide, or disappearing, wasn't what they'd expect. He had no money worries, no health issues, a loving daughter.

If the suitcase had not turned up, would they have let more time pass before jumping to conclusions?

Sam wanted another person's view. He wanted to know who Fiona thought she had married, and he had a lead.

After seeing Eliza yesterday and reading through her mother's diary he had been more determined than ever to unravel the puzzle for her. She needed to know who these people were. She needed to know what kind of life the most important person in her own had lived. She'd said her mother had done everything for her, and Eliza hadn't appreciated her sacrifices — she'd felt guilt for ruining her life. For tying her to a relationship that was wrong. But Sam wasn't sure.

Sam knew that a mother would do extraordinary things for the children they loved. But he wanted Eliza to see that her mother had been good, and happy — had lived a full life — so that Eliza could give herself permission to be the same.

He couldn't give her a fairy-tale ending, he could only give her the truth. He hoped that would be enough.

He'd stayed up all night after she had left. He'd called in a colleague who was an expert at doing the job he needed doing — finding somebody. Together they spent hours trawling through CCTV footage, examining number plates, looking at maps.

From the start, he had felt that Fiona was important. That she might be the key to this. She was the common link between Gerald and Sally.

Sam joined the motorway, turned the radio off, and prepared for a long drive.

He wasn't sure if he was looking for a dead body, or a death by misadventure. Things weren't always how they appeared. People weren't always who you thought they were. He was sure that this investigation was about loyalty, about love, and about the lies that had been used to protect.

This was also about more than his job now. Like it or not, he knew that this was about him, his heart. He'd fallen for Eliza, and his only fear was that the answers he'd bring home could ruin his chances with her forever.

Chapter Thirty

STUART

All Animals Are Equal

S tuart folded his newspaper and put it on the table in front of him. He was glad that he'd got in slightly earlier than normal and had time to catch up with Hattie's chapter before the interruption.

'Morning!' Will said. 'This is Lucy. Is everybody okay for a drink before we start? Hattie?' He glanced around the table, not quite his normal comfortable self.

'I have my cappuccino, thank you, Stuart made it for me. And very nice—'

'Wonderful.' Lucy's smile didn't look genuine to Stuart. 'Well, good morning, everybody, I'm Lucy Martin.'

'Will has said,' Hattie said dismissively. 'As I was saying, this coffee is quite excellent, the chocolate on the top is perfect. Thank you, Stuart.'

'My pleasure.' Stuart smiled at her and tried not to glance Avril's way. Her eyes were shining with laughter, and he was determined to at least attempt gravitas, for Will's benefit.

'Great.' Lucy seemed slightly perplexed. She most probably thought they'd be quite a tame bunch. She looked around the table and then tried to continue. 'I'm the manager of this group of libraries and I'm very excited to be launching our fantastic competition this year. How lovely to meet you all.'

Hattie made a huffing sound before taking another sip of her coffee.

Stuart agreed with her conclusion. He wasn't sure that Lucy was pleased to meet them all, she seemed rather too pleased with herself and her prepared speech. Although that could be unfair.

'We've got quite a few teams entered, so it will be a stiff competition, but I'm sure you'll give it your best.'

Stuart looked across at Hattie, who had started to drum her fingernails lightly on the table. 'Parkinson's,' she explained with a bright smile.

'That's a twitch, not a tapping,' Avril, who was sitting on her other side, whispered.

Stuart's fingers were itching to pick up the newspaper again. Lucy seemed incredibly patronising, which he knew was doing more than getting Hattie's back up, it would be propelling her towards greater things. She had already declared they had to win, to save Will's reputation – and now he was sure this would make her even more determined. He foresaw a dramatic conclusion in the future chapters.

'Well, er'—Lucy looked down at her notes—'we are

lucky to have some accomplished writers taking part. We have the well-known Jake Trent—'

'Jack Train, the actor? He died a long time ago, dear.'

'Trent. Jake Trent.'

'Never heard of him. Have we any more of the Bourbons left, Will?'

Will rushed off to the corner of the room with a haste Stuart had seldom seen. He'd not seen his shoulders shaking like that either. Their librarian was either having a fit or trying his hardest not to laugh out loud.

'Well, you must have, he's—'

'He's a journalist,' Stuart said wearily. 'Specialises in the type of article that translates to the worst of daytime television.'

'Sorry?' Lucy's tone was one of shock. She'd forgotten to be patronising.

'I'm sorry, dear, but I'm about as impressed with that type of journalism as I am with politicians. Untrustworthy and all smoke and mirrors. Padding. Writing a book now, isn't he?'

'Well, yes, he is. But he's entering as part of a team as well.'

'Is that allowed?' Avril asked, the first words Stuart thought she had spoken. 'If he's like a professional writer?'

'He's not a published author. We've tried to make this as inclusive as possible.' Lucy's bright smile was back.

'All animals are equal,' muttered Hattie, which made Stuart smile again and Lucy frown.

'Animals?' Avril reached for a biscuit.

'George Orwell, dear. It's a quote from a book, all

animals are equal, but some animals are more equal than others. I'll tell you about it later, it's a paradox.'

Hattie, Stuart decided, was a constant surprise. She feigned ignorance, and a life of missed opportunities but she probably had done more, and knew far more, than she realised.

'So, this Trent bloke is like an animal?' Avril asked, the look of innocence on her face making it hard to fight the threatening smile on his own.

'A pig,' Hattie said in a stage whisper.

'Something like that,' Will said drily, putting a fresh plate of biscuits on the table.

'I think you've misunderstood,' Lucy said, her tone tight. 'Now, I'm afraid I've got another library to go to, so I'm going to have to rush. But does anybody have any questions about the competition?'

'None at all.' Hattie snapped a biscuit in half. 'As long as we know there isn't any cheating going on, we'll be fine,' she finished brightly.

'Are you accusing me of cheating?' Lucy asked, her cheeks flushed.

'Not at all, dear. But when the competition organiser is shagging an entrant, it can be hard to be objective I'd imagine?'

Stuart almost choked on a stray biscuit crumb that tickled the back of his throat as Hattie uttered the words.

'I'm the organiser,' Lucy spat out, just like Stuart would like to do to the crumb, but instead he coughed into his handkerchief keen not to miss a single word of this exchange, 'and I'm here to help whoever wants it.'

Hattie smiled sweetly; her head tilted to one side. 'Help. What a nice idea.'

'The entries will be judged independently by the mayor and a literary agent, and some local, *anonymous*'—she stressed the word—'volunteers—' She held a hand up to stop Hattie speaking. 'Who the head of the judging panel knows the names of, but I don't. Satisfied?'

'Oh, that sounds lovely, dear. How clever!'

Stuart tried to resist mopping his brow or hiding behind his newspaper.

'Well, if that's all, I will leave some...' Lucy glanced down, then frowned. 'Oh, where's my bag? It's got all my things...'

'You're not suggesting somebody has stolen it? In a library?' Hattie raised her eyebrows in surprise. 'Are you accusing one of us?'

'Well no, I...' Flustered, Lucy stood up and looked round.

'If it's a big red tote bag thing, then I think you will find you left it in the ladies. Very dangerous.' Hattie tutted. 'I nearly tripped up over it. If I'd had an accident who would have been responsible, would I have had to sue Will. Or you? Or the council? Now that would be something for a journalist to report!'

Lucy muttered something that Stuart couldn't catch, but didn't sound pleasant. 'One minute.' Then she trotted off to the ladies' room, her high heels slowing her down considerably he would have thought.

'Good job you spotted it!' Stuart remarked to Hattie as Lucy returned, then he stared at her.

'Er, yes, thank you. Wonderful. Right, I'll leave these, then.' Lucy straightened up, placing – rather forcibly Stuart thought – some papers down. 'The team members should complete them with some personal details that we can use should you, er, win.'

'Well, we'd better make sure they're good, shouldn't we?' Hattie said brightly. Then she glanced up at Lucy, almost as though it was an afterthought. 'Will this Jake of yours be writing the article announcing the outcome?'

'I doubt it.' Lucy spoke through gritted teeth, and then with a forced smile flounced out of the library.

'You lot will get me the sack!' Will sat down next to Avril, shaking his head.

'She was rather up herself,' Hattie declared, making them all laugh. 'I think she just wanted to suss out the opposition for her precious Jake.'

'You may be right. Though you do realise she'll probably tell him, and Jake will no doubt write about this. You'll all be caricatures.'

'Only if he wins,' said Hattie. 'So it's simple. We don't let him.'

'This'—Stuart put his phone down on the table—'is the infamous Jake Trent.' Avril picked it up, then held it out so that Hattie could see the picture on the screen. 'Always good to know the enemy.'

'I suppose he is a bit swoony,' Avril admitted.

'My sister thought so.' Will sighed. 'And I already know the enemy.'

'Looks a bit greasy to me,' Hattie said dismissively,

bringing a smile to Will's face. 'Now, young Avril, I need to hear how you got on with that woman you went to see.'

'And I need to hear about Peter,' Avril responded.

'But first…' Hattie paused, then looked Will straight in the eye. 'Now that we have got rid of Lucy, and we've given her time to definitely get out of earshot, I think it's time you told us all about this sister of yours, and I'm sure she must be lovely if she's your sister. Because this Jake is the root of your problem, not a broken heart over Lucy, isn't it?'

'It is.' He sighed and glanced over at Stuart's phone, the photograph still on display. 'I was just worried that Jake will treat Lucy like he did my sister, Sarah. He broke her heart, but maybe Lucy is different. Maybe she'll use him like he'll use her. She is very ambitious.'

'Oh, I think we know that.' Hattie's tone was tart, and Stuart couldn't help but smile.

'Lucy's the type to trample over the bridesmaids to catch the bridal bouquet.'

'That's funny.' Avril laughed, though Will had sounded serious.

'I've seen her do it, it would have been quite funny if it hadn't been tragic.'

'And Sarah?' Hattie asked softly.

So, Will told them, and Stuart searched Jake on the internet. 'I told you he wrote trash, but this takes the biscuit. This man needs taking down a peg or two.'

'But how do we beat him in the competition?' Avril looked glum, and Stuart could see why. 'If the man writes for a living we don't stand a chance.'

'I think you may find we do.' Hattie smiled.

'Oh?'

'Well, he hasn't *exactly* cheated, but nor have I.'

'What have you been up to, Hattie?' Will sounded frustrated, but Avril was grinning.

'Well, you know me and my weak bladder…'

'You did manage to make a lot of toilet visits in the time Lucy was here,' Avril said, her eyes narrowed. 'You've never complained of a weak bladder before.'

'Old age, dear, old age. It comes and goes. Well'—she leaned in closer—'I just happened to glance in that big bag that Lucy had left in the ladies' room.'

'Oh, you did, did you?'

'Several times. I'm not as quick as I used to be.'

'I do sometimes think we've got a spy in our midst, a modern-day Mata Hari, I'm just glad you're working for our side, Hattie.'

'So am I.' Avril laughed. 'You are, aren't you?'

'Of course. But, well, let's just say you might be better not knowing. Ignorance—'

'Is no defence.'

Hattie glared at Will's interruption.

'Well, it isn't bliss!' said Avril.

'Well, as I was saying before Will interrupted, there was a notebook in there. Not the official notebook like ours, but it had a story in it. And there might, might have been something in there that was slightly incriminating. And I might have taken some photographs of it.'

Avril groaned. 'You've got to tell us the rest, Hattie! You can't leave us hanging. What was it? What did you see?'

'How will photographs help us?' Stuart frowned. 'I don't understand…'

'All will be revealed if there is a need!' Hattie held up her mobile phone. 'I never thought that this camera thing would have a use, but I think Harold might have anticipated that one day it might have!'

'Clever Harold,' Avril said softly, and Stuart could see Hattie's features actually melt.

She didn't speak, she just nodded.

'A secret weapon up your sleeve, just in case we need it.' Stuart smiled. 'Oh, look who's here.'

They all looked up, to see a smiling Jo.

'I sent her a text while that woman was droning on, I thought we might all need something sweet with our coffee to help us recover!' said Stuart.

Chapter Ten

(Stuart)

Eliza felt her spirits lift as she read the text from Sam. He'd had to go away for a few days, 'following a lead', he said. But it wasn't the words that made her feel better, it was just the fact that he had messaged. She was beginning to feel as though he was always there for her, a friend, and she'd started to share more of her feelings and thoughts with him. She knew the saying that a problem shared was a problem halved, and she was starting to understand what that meant. Having somebody to talk to really did seem to make it easier — less of a burden.

She hadn't realised just how isolated she had started to feel after she had received the letter and diary from her mother. She hadn't been able to talk to anybody, because it felt like she would be betraying her mother. But Sam was different.

He seemed to understand about the guilt that kept her awake at night, the thought that she was responsible in so many ways. For the years her mother had felt obliged to stay in contact with the man who was breaking her heart, for not realising the way her mother felt, the guilt she had herself carried. For not seeing that she was tormented and insisting she share her thoughts.

But her mum had now admitted to her feelings, was trying to right the wrongs and Eliza wanted to do the same — even though it was too late for her mother to see.

She knew that she couldn't move on with her own life until she could forgive herself. But she had to understand what had happened, what had driven her mother, before she could understand what her own role had been. How she could make amends.

Eliza glanced down at the photographs that she had downloaded from the internet. Gerald, Fiona and Marie. She'd found very little else. The family, it seemed, kept themselves to themselves. Very much like her and her mum had.

Even the pictures gave little away. She hadn't even solved the first clue that her mother had left, because she couldn't find the people involved.

Making a sudden decision, she popped the photos into her bag and pulled on her jacket. The one person who had always helped, always supported her, that she'd always trusted was her mum. She needed her, she'd always needed her, and maybe that was how she'd find the answers.

The graveyard was quiet, and the bench in front of her mother's grave was empty. As it always was. Eliza hadn't come here for a while. Not since the letter. She'd pulled away, and maybe that was what had left her feeling so sad and alone.

'Oh, Mum. I can't believe that what you did was as bad as you think it was. You weren't a bad person. You were perfect. Totally perfect.' Eliza leaned forward, her forearms on her knees and looked at the headstone. And it was then she noticed it. Something that had been here when she'd visited last time but hadn't registered with her.

A miniature rose in a pot. The soil slightly dry, but the flowers still bravely blooming. She took the step from the bench to the stone, then stooped to pour the water from her bottle into the pot.

She'd seen a rose like this before. She recognised it.
But from where?

Chapter Thirty-One

WILL

Getting to Know You

'Hey, have you got a minute?'

The library was quiet after Lucy had left. Stuart had been busy scribbling away in the notebook like a man possessed – something about the meeting had obviously inspired him – and Hattie and Avril had their head together at one of the computers.

Will looked up from his desk, pleased to see Avril.

'Sure.'

'It's about tonight.'

She looked nervous, but there was excitement in her smile as well. Tonight was the evening they were going to meet up with Mandy.

'It's just…' She put her hand over his. 'It's nothing to do with Lucy and all this, it's just…'

'You don't want me to come?'

'It's not that I don't want you to, it's more that I don't

think you should. It's something I need to do on my own I think, and'—she shrugged—'I know I can now.'

'You always could, Avril. You're one of the strongest, most independent women I know. I know that you don't need me tagging along.'

'I don't need you.' She grinned, the dimples showing at the corner of her mouths. How come he'd never really noticed those dimples before? 'But I do want you to be there.' She paused. 'Apart from—'

'Now. For this.'

Her smile was apologetic.

He smiled back. He got it. But she'd just said she wanted to be with him.

'I want to be there with you, for you, as well.'

'I'm glad you told us all about Jake,' she said simply. That was Avril all over, direct, straightforward. Fair, kind. A million miles from anybody he'd ever dated before. Then she smiled, a bright wide mischievous smile. 'Hattie is going to well and truly kick his butt!'

'Looks like it.' His gaze met hers and she fell silent, her lips slightly parted. 'I'd quite like to get a bit physical with you, seeing as this seems to be a day for being open.' He swallowed to clear the sudden dryness in his throat.

'That sounds nice.'

They were inches apart. Any other time, he'd close that ground and kiss her. He so wanted to kiss her.

'I'm going to go now.'

Could he hear the same tremble in her voice that he felt in his own body?

'I'll call you later.'

He nodded, his gaze never leaving hers.

'Then maybe we can set a date for you to take me to see your bookshop?'

'I'd like that.'

'Cool,' she said softly. The corner of her mouth lifted, and then it dropped, and she covered the small distance between them and settled the smallest of kisses on his mouth.

Will watched her go. He didn't want this to end. He didn't want her to walk out of his library, let alone his life. He wanted to get to know her, to watch her getting to know herself. He wanted to show her who he was.

Chapter Eleven

(Will)

Sam stared at the woman who had just walked into the pub. It was unmistakeably Fiona. She was instantly recognisable from the photograph that they had found in the suitcase, despite the fact that it must have been taken many years earlier, and she was – if anything – even more beautiful.

She smiled, and strangely it reminded Sam of Eliza's smile. Different, of course, but similar in the genuine welcome it seemed to carry. In its kindness. His heart gave a little spasm. She hadn't said a word and yet Sam instinctively felt like she was a good person. That he might finally find the answers that Eliza needed.

He wanted to. He wanted to see her smile like this. He wanted to find all the answers, so that he could close the case and get to know her. If she'd let him.

He wanted her to be happy so much it hurt. Despite her fears, she was searching for the truth, for the past, and it suddenly hit him – he loved her for it. And the feeling was wonderfully scary. She was beautiful, independent, free and clever. He wanted to know who she really was, what made her heart beat faster. What made her laugh.

He blinked as he realised that Fiona was studying him with concern. He had a job to do. He had to concentrate.

'Hello, Fiona.'

If Sally had loved Gerard, then he could see how she might be tormented that he was married to such a woman. Could her hurt stem from the fact that she felt guilty about causing somebody like Fiona harm? Had she caused her harm, caused a rift between husband and wife?

'How can I help?' said Fiona. 'It sounded urgent, but I'm afraid I can't stay long, I'll be in trouble if I don't get back.' She waved a hand towards the waiting taxi.

'Of course, of course, I understand and I'm sorry I had to drag you over here, but it is important.'

'Is Marie okay?'

'She is. This is not about your daughter.'

'Oh, good.' Relief flooded her face. 'But I've got a letter here for her. I was going to post it, but it's so unreliable and I thought if you're going to be seeing her, would you mind—'

'I can drop it in, no problems at all,' he interrupted her. 'But Marie isn't why I'm here. I'm looking for your husband, or is it ex-husband?'

'Gerald? Why on earth are you looking for him? What's he done?'

'I'm not quite sure. But your daughter reported him as missing.'

'Oh!' She looked alarmed.

'Please, sit down. I'll try and explain. She tried to contact you, but couldn't.'

'Reception is terrible here, everything is, but I get in touch when I can.'

'It could really help if you could tell about when you last spoke to Gerald. He hasn't been gone that long, and we wouldn't normally worry at this stage, but then we found his suitcase.'

'Suitcase?'

'On a beach.' Sam suddenly realised that Fiona didn't look worried or upset. She appeared more perplexed. Confused.

She nodded. 'You're right. We need to talk. And I think I might be able to help.' She took a deep breath and then glanced at her watch. 'I've got until the tide turns.'

Chapter Thirty-Two

AVRIL

Family Matters

'Oh, my goodness, Hattie sounds a real character! Your mum would have loved her.' Mandy grinned.

'I love her.' Avril smiled back. 'She's amazing. Will said she's been even more amazing since I came along, though, she's really come out of her shell.' She shrugged self-consciously but was obviously pleased by the thought. 'I think we're seeing the real Hattie, the girl she was never allowed to be.'

'I'm sure you've helped her loads. It's the type of thing your mum was good at, and didn't realise she was doing. You don't always realise how lucky you are, do you.' Mandy twirled some pasta on her fork and then lightly touched the back of Avril's hand. When she spoke again her tone had softened. 'I really wish things had been different for you growing up, but your dad did a good job. Phee would be proud of both of you.'

'I told Dad we were meeting again, and he was really pleased. He said you must have been upset when we lost Mum, and he feels bad that he just upped and left.'

Mandy shook her head. 'I get it. I was sad, but I know it tore him apart. He was in bits, but it would be nice to see him again one day.'

'I think he'd like that.' Avril frowned. 'I kind of get the feeling that he might be ready to talk about her more, but I think he's worried about upsetting Lisa.'

'A lot of time has passed since Joey and Lisa got together, you'd hope she felt a bit more secure but'—she took a sip of wine, giving herself some time—'I think maybe she's always been scared she'd lose him. I mean, I don't want to talk out of turn, and I don't really know her, but any woman with half a brain would know that Joey would never be one hundred per cent theirs, that your mum will always be in Joey's heart.' She put her cutlery down and pushed her bowl to one side. 'Anyway, tell me what you've got up to over the years.'

'Well, I…' Avril wasn't sure where to start.

'Sorry, it's a massive question, isn't it? I just want to catch up on all those missing years.'

'It's fine.' Avril nodded slowly. 'It's nice to talk to somebody about all of this, it's just…'

'A lot?'

'A lot.' Avril smiled. 'Tell me more about Mum.'

'Okay, so'—Mandy pointed at Avril's plate—'that is just what Phee would have done, ordered a pizza like that, then picked off the anchovies! It's so strange watching you do the same thing. The only time she ate them was when she was pregnant, she told me.'

'Makes sense.' Avril laughed. 'They're not a flavour you should submit your unborn child to though!'

'And your mum was dyslexic, did you know that? She struggled with reading at school, but she loved stories so much and she enjoyed books when she was older. She wanted you to, as well.'

'I hated school, too. I just felt so slow and, well, inadequate. And I didn't think I liked reading, either, but I've really enjoyed doing this competition, and I even borrowed a couple of books from the library.'

'Oh, wow, that's great. What kind of books do you like? I can probably lend you some. I'm into my thrillers, but Phee always liked a bit of romance in hers. She liked James Bond movies, a bit of tension, a bit of romance and a few laughs.' Her smile was gentle. 'She liked to laugh. That's where you get those dimples from.'

It wasn't too late when they left the restaurant, so Avril decided to walk home. She liked to walk. Walking gave you time to think. To mull things over.

She'd relaxed quickly in Mandy's company. She could understand why her mother had liked her so much. There was no pressure, no agenda, just a casual, natural exchange of information. She'd confided in Mandy about the diary, the letter to Phee. Told her about work, and why she'd left, her doubts about what she'd do next. She talked about her dad, and the worries she had with him. She also told her about Will and how she thought she was falling for him and didn't know what to do about it, or how she'd handle the short time they had before he'd leave. Avril told Mandy things that she'd kept to herself because she hadn't had the right person – a mum – to tell before.

Mandy had listened. Had offered stories of how she'd handled similar situations. Had held her hand and talked about missed opportunities and chances. 'You'll never regret failing, but you will regret it if you don't try in the first place,' she'd said as they hugged goodbye.

Avril suddenly realised that she was turning into her own street. She'd been so wrapped up in her thoughts that she'd hardly been aware of her surroundings.

She spotted Lisa's car immediately. She must have come to visit Chloe and not been able to park any closer. Her pace instinctively picked up. She didn't want her evening spoiled by an encounter with either Lisa or her stepsister. She wanted to be able to close her front door, put her feet up and run it all over in her head again.

'Hey.' Lisa was standing at her front door. Avril felt a sudden pang of irritation. Then stopped herself. Smiled. What had Mandy said about Lisa? Lisa had always felt second best to Phee. And she might not like Avril much, but she'd stuck by her dad. She'd loved him for what? Most of her life? Whereas Avril had never managed to really love somebody, commit to them, take a risk. Because she didn't want to lose anybody else.

But Lisa had done it. Taken a chance, before she missed the opportunity.

'Hey. Er, sorry I've been out. I didn't…'

'I know. Your dad said you'd been to see Mandy; you shouldn't need to do that.'

'But I wanted to see her!'

'Sorry, that came out wrong. I meant that there's nothing wrong with seeing her, and I understand why you'd want to, and you shouldn't have felt you had to go and find somebody you didn't know to tell you about your mother. I should have been here for you, answered your questions.'

'Oh. Well, it doesn't matter. She's nice.'

'It does matter,' Lisa said quietly. 'That's why I'm here. But if this is a bad time or if you're too tired…'

'No, no, I'm fine. Erm, is everything okay? Dad?'

'He's fine. Sorry, I didn't mean to worry you, it's just … I feel like we should talk, well *I* should talk.' She fiddled with the strap of her handbag. 'I owe you an explanation.'

An explanation?

'Come in,' said Avril. 'Would you like a coffee or'—she paused, glancing again at Lisa's face, at her hesitant words—'something stronger? I've got a bottle of wine in the fridge.'

Lisa sat down at the kitchen table, and her gaze settled on the notebook, which Avril had been planning on reading when she got home.

'Ah, is this the library competition you're doing? Your dad told me all about it. He's really proud of you; he says you always were the clever one when you were at school!'

Avril set the two wine glasses on the table. 'Clever? You're kidding. I couldn't read!'

'But you could tell a story, you had a right good imagination you know. You're so like her, your mum.' Lisa sighed. 'I can't make stuff up to save my life, and nor can the girls.'

'But they passed all their exams and got proper jobs.'

'Your job at the salon is a proper job,' Lisa said, her tone soft. 'And there's more to life than passing exams, Avril.'

It was time to confess. 'Well, I haven't got any kind of job now, which is why I've got time to do the competition.'

'Ah, well. You'll find something better. You always do, you take after your mum.'

Avril didn't know what to say. So she took a sip of wine and waited.

'I envied her, you know, your mum. She was a free spirit. She wasn't always what you'd call sensible, but she didn't just do daft impetuous stuff, she thought about it and decided it was what was best for her. A bit like you I suppose. She wasn't ordinary like I was, and most of the other girls at school. She was different, extraordinary I suppose. Yeah, extraordinary. That's why'—she pursed her lips—'Joey fell for her like he did.' She glanced up, and her gaze caught Avril's. Avril couldn't ever remember Lisa looking straight at her like that before.

'But I was never good enough,' Avril blurted out. 'I never stuck at stuff.'

'You were always good enough,' Lisa said softly. 'Look, I'm sorry, Avril. That's what I came here to say. I'm sorry that I always spent more time with my own girls, and'—she took a steadying breath—'I let them make fun of you and did nothing—' She held a hand up to stop Avril interrupting. 'And I know I made your dad feel guilty about talking to you about your mum. I just couldn't stand being reminded about how wonderful she was, how he'd have always chosen her ahead of me. How I was second best. But you were always there, Avril, and you are so like her. I've been small-minded and selfish, ridiculous, I'm a grown woman and I've been jealous of you right from when you were a little girl.' She paused, took a drink of wine. 'You'll always be your dad's priority, as you should be, you're his daughter. I'd do anything for my girls, Avril, so why shouldn't I understand him being like that with you? Look, I know I'm going on a bit, but I need to say it. I know you had to go off to talk to Mandy about your mum, but me and your dad are here and should be telling you about her as well. We need to do this together. As a family.' She nodded. 'Family is important.'

Avril topped up their glasses as she processed what Lisa was saying and tried to think of how to respond. As she tried to think of something smart to say.

'Thank you,' was what she settled for. She met Lisa's gaze. 'So, Mum must have been rubbish at something? Was it maths, like me?'

'Oh yeah.' Lisa laughed. 'She was total rubbish at maths, and PE. She was so uncoordinated.'

Avril grinned. 'Just like me, then! Do you remember when I got a black eye in that dance class and tried to pretend that I'd been a fight, because it was so embarrassing?'

'I do! Don't hate me for saying it, but you were so ungainly, you were like Bambi, with your long legs going in all directions! In our day we had to climb these rope ladders in the gym, and your mum got all tangled up and had to be rescued.' Lisa smiled, and this time it looked like it was a happy memory. She patted Avril's hand, very briefly. 'But she was good at so many things, just like you are. She used to paint pictures that were pure fantasy. I'd be copying some vase the teacher had brought in, and she'd have turned it into a peacock or a unicorn.'

Avril gazed at her. 'You really love Dad, don't you?'

Lisa's smile was gentle. 'Always have done, love.'

'And you'll always be there for him. I know you will,' Avril said, as though to herself.

'Why, what's wrong, Avril? You're not ill, or...'

'Oh no.' She laughed. 'Sorry, I didn't mean to sound dramatic. You see, there's this guy I fancy, and I think maybe I need to take a chance, find out if it could work.'

'But?'

'He's going back to Cambridge soon.' She looked at Lisa. Not a wicked stepmother, just an ordinary woman, who'd always loved a man who had given part of his heart to somebody else. But a woman who'd learned to accept it, who would rather have part of him than none. 'I think I should go, at least for a bit, but I worry about Dad. We've always been there for each other.'

'And you always will be, love, just like Phee is always there for you, even now. I think she'd want you to be happy, to follow your heart. You can always change your mind and come back; we'll always be here, I promise. And this lovely place of yours will always be here.'

'True.'

'But please don't think I'm trying to get rid of you,' Lisa added hastily. 'Come round for tea tomorrow. We can have a chat with your dad. I know he'll miss you if you're not on the doorstep, but it's easy to stay in touch with each other on your phones, isn't it? And I always did fancy going down to Cambridge. It would be a good excuse – to come and see you!'

'Tomorrow would be nice.'

'Good. I'll get out of your hair now, I'm sure you're tired, but I wanted to get it off my chest, to tell you I'm sorry, because it's well overdue. Don't worry about your dad, I'll look after him, I promise. It's time you started to think about yourself, Avril. I know you didn't go to university because you didn't want to leave him. But he'll be okay.' She walked towards the front door, but then paused before going through. 'This might sound a bit weird, love, but I want to help you be whoever you want to be. I guess I was always afraid that when you found yourself, you'd remind us all of your mum, but that's wrong. I want you to be happy. Honest. You will be, won't you?'

Avril smiled and nodded. 'I'm getting there. I think I wanted to see Mum because I felt a bit of me was missing, but she can't tell me what to do. She wouldn't even if she was alive. What I do with my life is my choice, isn't it?'

'You are like her you know. *So* like her.' Lisa's voice was barely more than a whisper, and the small smile on her face looked sad rather than bitter. 'Perfect.'

Avril closed the front door behind her stepmother. She felt exhausted, but in a good way. It had been a strange day, a strange few weeks, if she was honest.

She went back into the kitchen and picked the notebook up.

Could she put some of herself, some of today into her chapter? Could she convey her realisation that though you couldn't understand everything, that there isn't always an answer – or a right one, the one you wanted – that was okay.

Chapter Twelve

(Avril)

Sam started up his car engine, ready for the long drive home. He'd texted Eliza, but not told her where he was or who he'd been to see. He had not wanted to disappoint her, if he didn't find the answers she was looking for. He did feel slightly guilty, though. He did not like to deceive people. And specially not Eliza.

He wasn't sure if he had found what she needed. But he knew that not everything has a rational explanation and there isn't always a right answer, or the one that you are looking for. Uncovering the truth can be messy, and it can be unexpected – because that is the nature of life, of people.

Eliza had thought she'd known her mother. But do we ever really fully know anybody else? And surely the bits we do know are the important bits, the main part of a person's character, morals, beliefs, emotions?

Sam had not discovered anything that he would call shocking. He had just uncovered another facet of Sally's life – the part that wasn't a mother, but an adult who had lived through the emotions and feelings that most of us do. He had, he decided, been proved right about his hunch. He'd driven up here thinking that those three things that guide so many lives, and can cause so many problems, can lead to good and bad, were important in this case. Love, loyalty and lies. Three emotions that are bedfellows, one is not often present without the others.

Would Eliza be happy to learn what he had to tell her? He hoped so. In his heart he thought that this was good. That her future could be the one her mother had wanted her to have. Hoped she would have.

He glanced to his left, shared a smile with his passenger and then he indicated and pulled off the motorway.

'Okay?' He got a nod back in response, and the briefest of smiles.

Chapter Thirty-Three

HATTIE

The End

Hattie hung her coat up, then went through to her small kitchen to make a cup of tea. They had finished their lunch off with a pot of tea, but one made with her own brand, and her own water always tasted better. Harold used to say that.

She put the radio on, so that it was a low background noise to keep her company, and then sat down at the small kitchen table she ate her meals at.

Peter's daughter had been quite a surprise. She was tall, as Peter was, but there the resemblance ended. Maybe it was just her age, but she was very assertive. Bossy, Harold would have said. She'd told the waitress off for spilling the tea and, it seemed to Hattie, had been intent on finding fault – and correcting it. Not at all like her father. Peter had always been very mild-mannered.

She was nice enough, well meaning, but had left Hattie

thinking. If she had taken a different path in life, would she have ended up with a child like that?

Instead of a daughter, Hattie had found a friend. Avril. Who was far nicer. Did it matter that they weren't related? Maybe Hattie had had the best life, the life she was supposed to have. Which reminded her, poor Will's sister might (as Avril had told him) have always been meant to find her way to the other side of the world – but finding the path because of heartbreak didn't seem right at all.

She put her handbag on the chair next to her and pulled out her phone. She was quite pleased with herself – at one time she wouldn't have dreamed of seeing herself as a sleuth and she certainly wouldn't have peeped into somebody's personal possessions. But the outcome justified her actions, she felt. If Lucy and Jake were as cavalier with other people's lives as it appeared, then they deserved what they got.

'Thank you, Harold,' she said out loud, with a small smile. When he had bought her the phone, she was sure she would never ever use the inbuilt camera. She had no use for a proper camera, so why would she use this one? But it had proved very useful indeed.

Seeing the notebook sticking out of the top of Lucy's bag had been a gift she couldn't reject. And when she had furtively read it, well, it certainly was an eye-opener. She'd been tempted to rush out and whisper to Avril, but then she'd had a better idea.

She smiled. Maybe Harold did sometimes know best, but it's the way you tell people, isn't it?

'It was just his manner that was wrong,' she said to

Nutmeg, whose eyebrows twitched in response. 'He didn't know how to talk to people properly, without causing offence.' She looked again at the photographs she had taken of the pages of the notebook, all written in a beautiful, elegant hand. At least there was that to admire. Then she switched the phone off and put it on the table. 'It's time to write the final chapter, I think, don't you, Nutmeg? Closure can be good.'

It was over two hours later, when her hand ached with holding the pen for so long, that Hattie closed the book and reached for her coat.

'I think we shall go for a walk, Nutmeg. I've just got to make a quick phone call first, then there's somebody you need to meet.'

And with that, she picked up the small bag that she had packed earlier, clipped on his lead and headed for the elevator.

———

Hattie sat down on the bench in the garden of remembrance and carefully unpacked the container from the bag and placed it next to her.

'I'm glad I didn't rush into a decision,' she said softly, then turned to Nutmeg. 'This is Harold. I think he might have grown to like you, if he'd let himself take the risk. But I suppose the trouble for him would be that he would have known he'd lose you. He didn't like to take risks like that, you know.' Nutmeg tipped his head to one side as though he was listening. Understood. Just as she was beginning to do.

'I didn't take him to the pub, like I've been telling people. He's been on the bedside cabinet, on his side of the bed, from the day I collected him. We shared too much together to just let him go.' She shook her head.

'He'd have been pleased about that.' She turned to see Peter sitting down on the other end of the bench, so that Harold was between them. Like he'd always been. But this time, Hattie didn't mind. It felt right.

'I was so angry at him after he died,' she said. 'The more I thought about how he'd controlled my life, how I'd lost you, the angrier I got. But I do wonder if I was also angry at him for leaving me. Well'—she sighed, and stroked Nutmeg's silky ears—'maybe that was the biggest reason of all.'

'We all need somebody in our life, and you were his somebody, Hattie. Never forget that. He probably didn't want to share you, and he definitely didn't want to lose you.'

'I just wish he'd been able to talk to me.'

'I think he'd given up on expecting people to listen. If you feel like nobody has ever done that, then sometimes you stop trying.'

'I suppose it's that thing they say: if no one sees you, then do you exist?'

'Harold didn't think he did exist as far as the rest of the world was concerned. And he felt safer if he wasn't noticed. At least he knew what to expect.'

'Nothing,' Hattie said softly.

'Until he had you.' Peter leaned over Harold and placed his hand on top of Hattie's.

'I think he'll like it here. It's quiet, but very well maintained. He liked things to be neat.'

'He did. He liked order, to have things just so. To know that if he went away and came back, they wouldn't have changed.'

'I've changed. He might not have liked that.'

Peter smiled. 'He might not have been brave enough to like the idea of that happening, but I'm sure he would have loved to see it. He'd be proud if he could see you now. And maybe he can.'

'Will you do it? He'd have liked you to do it.' Hattie smiled. 'He wouldn't have considered it a job for a woman.'

'I'd be honoured.' Peter stood up, lifted the container with one hand and held his arm out so that she could slip her hand into the crook of his elbow.

Together they made their way towards the solid old oak tree in the middle of the garden.

Halfway there, Nutmeg stopped. Hattie waited for him to cock his leg, or some such nonsense. But instead, he lay down and rested his chin on his paws.

'Is this not a job for you?' Hattie asked gently. The dog glanced at her, then towards Peter, and Hattie had to blink the tears away. 'Is this a ridiculous old woman talking, or do you think Harold might have sent Nutmeg to me?' she asked Peter.

'You're never ridiculous. And you could be right. You could be right.'

'You be good.' She told the little dog, and then walked on to stand beside Peter, who had undone the lid.

'Ready?'

'I am.' She looked into the familiar eyes. 'And if I go before you, will you bring me here?'

'Of course I will, Hattie.'

He tipped the container and Harold drifted out, caught on the gentle breeze that seemed to swirl around the tree. They didn't have to move; he danced his own dance as he'd always done – but close to both of them.

'Free at last,' Hattie whispered softly.

'But not alone.'

Chapter Thirteen

(Hattie)

Eliza reached the top of the steep incline and looked across towards the bench. Sam was standing there, gazing down at the cove as she so often had done. As she had been doing the day that she had met him.

It felt like she had known Sam for a long time – all her life, even – but it had only been such a short time. And yet any contact between them had been nothing more than a gentle touch, an unbroken look. That was the way it had to be, she knew that. She had longed for him to cover the short distance between them, to caress her face. To kiss her. Though she knew he was being professional, still she hoped he felt their connection, too, and that in different circumstances he would have reached for her. But who knew? She could be wrong. He could just be empathetic, caring. He might feel none of the feelings that flooded her body when she saw him.

When she had received his message earlier in the morning, her heart had stuttered at its oddly formal tone.

'Can you meet me on the headland today? There is somebody I need to introduce you to. Sam.'

She had of course said yes, but even as she drove over, her pulse was skittering, and her throat was dry. Is this when he would tell her that they were closing the case, he was moving on, and that she would never see him again? Or maybe he had guessed how she felt and was going to tell her that they needed to distance themselves from each other. That he would introduce the person who would replace him as her contact.

As she drew nearer, Sam seemed to sense her presence and turned.

And it was only then that she became aware of the other man. Sitting on the bench.

'Eliza, I'd like you to meet somebody.' Sam's face was solemn, but there was something in his face that told her this was important. He gestured at the man, who stood up. 'This is Gerald Old.'

Eliza stared. She didn't know what she had expected Gerald to be like (most likely dead, if she was completely honest), but in her head he had been either some handsome cad who had swept her mother off her feet and destroyed her life, or a murderer (whatever one of those looked like). However, Gerald was very much alive, and very – for want of a better word – normal. He was slightly taller than Sam, and of a fairly lean build, with greying hair, kind eyes and a tentative smile. Sincere seemed to be the word that fitted him best.

Could this really be the womanising rake she'd thought might be her father?

She had built up a case against him, had grown close to hating him and blaming him for her mother's death. But the truth was she didn't really know ~~Harold~~ Gerald.

'It's lovely to meet you, Eliza.' Gerald held his hand out to shake hers, but she couldn't move. She could only stare.

'But you're missing, you're…'

'I'm not dead or missing.' His tone was soft. 'I was away, I didn't know all this was going on.'

'But the suitcase. You left the suitcase, the clothes.'

He shook his head. 'I didn't leave anything. I've just been away for a bit.'

Eliza sank down on the bench and covered her face with her hands. None of this made sense. She thought that she'd lost all hope of meeting Gerald. That she'd lost him before she had found him was bad, but now he was here, alive and well, saying that he'd never been missing at all. And that the clues had nothing to do with him.

'But Marie was looking for you. She thought you were dead, or something.'

'I know.' He glanced at Sam. 'I feel terrible. I went to find Fiona, to try and sort things out between us. Life is too short for misunderstandings.'

You can say that again, thought Eliza.

'But your daughter said your passport was still in the house, and the police checked flights.'

'But they couldn't check small boats. I didn't go abroad; Fiona is on a remote Scottish island. She's looking after it, caretaking. I didn't really think it through, I went on an impulse.' He grinned as Eliza stared at him. 'I know, I know, I'm a man of habit. But sometimes acting out of character is good for you. I never considered the fact that Fiona can't contact Marie, so therefore I wouldn't be able to either. I guess I didn't think much at all.' He looked out to sea, an expression of gentle acceptance on his face. He looked happy, thought Eliza. Content. He turned to look at her. 'But to be honest, I didn't think she'd miss me. Marie's got her own life and we don't talk that often, really – and I didn't expect to be there as long as I was. The first time I'd planned to come back, the sea was too rough for them to pick me up. Then me and Fi got talking and I didn't want to leave. I wasn't ready. Then this lot'—he tipped his head towards Sam—'tracked me down and told me I'd got to come back and answer for myself.'

'But you're going back?'

'I will do, yes. It's beautiful. Fi has only got another couple of months, then her tenancy ends and she's thinking about coming back here for a while, and maybe we'll find somewhere else and go there together. Maybe.'

Eliza watched the emotion flit over his face. This was the love affair that had escaped her mother.

'I don't understand about the suitcase, though,' she said softly. 'It's got a photo of your wife ... it's your things.' She paused. 'Your diary. Your diary with your name in it.'

'I'm sorry, the detective told me all this, and those things aren't mine.' He shook his head again, this time more vehemently. 'I think your mother left those, or rather got somebody else to. The suitcase was hers.'

'But it had your things in it! And how do you know her anyway?'

'I'm sorry, Eliza. They're things that meant a lot to Sally, things that she didn't want to forget, that she wanted to pass on to you. The case wasn't left as a sign of what I'd done, I think she'd left it so that you would try and track me and her sister down. It was clues for you. That was how she wanted to make amends. She wanted you to know your family.'

'My family? Her sister?'

'That photograph in there is of my wife, Fiona.' He paused. 'Your aunt.'

'Aunt.' She blinked. 'You mean she's Mum's sister.'

He nodded. 'That's why she looked familiar to you. She's your aunt.'

'So, you're not...' Eliza couldn't finish the sentence. She barely dared to ask. If this man was her father, then her mother really had done something unforgivable.

'No,' he said softly, 'I'm not your father, Eliza. There was never anything romantic between us. Things aren't always how they appear.'

She looked at him straight, and could see no trace of deception, no sign that he was telling a lie.

'Your mother was a lovely woman; she would never have done something so cruel. The terrible thing she did was to fall out with her sister, Fiona. My wife. I tried to keep in contact with her, to make sure you were both okay, but Fiona hasn't seen her for many years. Since you were born.'

'But what was so terrible that made Mum stop talking to her sister?' Eliza was confused. Her mother had always been so even-tempered, so caring. So wonderful. She never had a bad word to say about anybody, or very rarely, just if a person had been bad.

'It all started because'—he paused, and looked Eliza in the eye— 'Sally wanted a baby.'

Eliza frowned. 'But that's not….'

'Sally had no partner. She asked if I would help, but Fiona wasn't happy with the suggestion. We had Marie, she was only a baby, and it seemed so complicated.' He sighed. 'You would have been cousins, and half-sisters I suppose. But Sally was so desperate. She wanted a child so much and Fiona thought it was wrong.'

Eliza swallowed down the lump in her throat. 'So … my father?'

The gaze that met hers was soft. Caring. She could see why her mother had liked this man so much. Her brother-in-law. Why she would have liked him to have been Eliza's father. 'This is difficult. You need to understand that she thought it was for the best.'

'It's not the person she refers to in her diary, the one she actually fell in love with.'

'You were the person she fell in love with, Eliza. You were all she needed. But to have you, she decided to choose a donor. A man she wouldn't know, but who had a "CV"; somebody she picked using logic, not emotion. The one who could be the perfect man she wanted. The perfect stranger.'

Eliza blinked, and when she spoke her voice had a harsh edge even to her own ears. 'My father is a sperm donor?' She couldn't quite believe it. Her mother's diary had talked of love, of passion. They'd moved to start again, after her decision to free herself. 'But in her diary, it's you she's talking about. I'm sure it is. She was'—she paused—'very fond of you, wasn't she?'

Gerald nodded. 'But it stopped there.'

'I don't think it did in her head.' Eliza frowned. 'I think falling out with her sister wasn't just about wanting a baby that my aunt didn't think she should have. I think it was about not being able to have you.'

Gerald blinked at her words, and the look on his face was shock mingled with something else. Maybe a recognition that her words were the truth, that his eyes had suddenly been opened to the realisation.

'I think that was her terrible thing, it was loving you, and not being able to do anything about her feelings so she broke up her own family. Started again.'

'My God, Eliza.' He looked like he was about to cry. He stared at the crashing waves. 'But she never said. I never—'

'Like you said, my mother was a lovely person,' Eliza interrupted softly. A lovely person who'd only lived half the life she could have had.

Gerald wasn't some terrible man. Her mother hadn't really done a terrible thing. Apart from hope. And love. And not always get it right.

'She was.'

'I think she was obsessed with the idea of you. Infatuated. And the more she knew that she couldn't have you, the worse it got. Until I was born, and she finally felt she could stop herself.'

'Oh, Eliza.' Gerald shook his head sadly. 'How can life get so complicated? If only we'd known.'

'If only I had,' Eliza said softly.

There was a long pause.

'I need to get back, explain to Marie and Fiona. You will stay in touch, though? I'd really like that, and I know Fiona would. Though I quite understand if you can't.'

It was too late to tell her mother that it was okay, too late to try and understand her better than she had. But it wasn't too late to make amends with Gerald, Fiona and Marie.

'So would I.'

Eliza and Sam sat in silence after Gerald left. They watched the waves crash in then retreat, taking the debris of the day with them. Cleaning the beach. Preparing for a new day. A fresh start.

'We did look into your mother's death, Eliza. The day she died, Fiona had been in touch, trying to patch things up. It was bad weather for driving, visibility would have been terrible and on top of that she could well have been emotional… They had arranged to meet.'

'I wish they had.'

'That's why her sister fled. Not because of Gerald and their marriage, but because she felt responsible for Sally's death.'

'But she wasn't. Mum made a choice; we all make our own choices.'

'She did.'

Eliza paused, as a realisation suddenly hit her. 'The rose!'

'Rose?'

'There was a rose left on Mum's grave, I've just realised where I saw an identical one. In the photo I found of Fiona. She must have been to see her, before she left for Scotland.' *She smiled.* 'She forgave her.'

Sam laid his hand gently over hers. 'So your mum gave you the answers even before I could?'

'She did, but you filled in the gaps. Thank you.'

'You're very welcome. It's been a tough day.' She loved the sound of his voice, its gruff edge. Its warmth.

'A weird day.'

'So … I don't know if I should say this now or not, but the case is almost closed. Just a few loose ends to tie up.'

'You're going.' She closed her eyes. Waiting for the inevitable. Not wanting to see the end.

'I don't want to go, Eliza. I was wondering, would you come for a drink with me? I can do that now. Now that there's no conflict of inter-est. I mean, I get it if you want nothing to do with me after all this, but—'

'I'd love to have something to do with you, Sam. I would.' Her gaze met his.

She had loose ends of her own to tie up. She had family to get to know. But most of all she wanted to get to know Sam. To make sure she lived her life properly. As her mother had wanted her to. 'I really would. Will you kiss me?'

His lips were dry, firm. He smelled of good things. He tasted of the sea. And Eliza realised that you didn't have to have all the answers if you were happy. Sometimes just being with the right person was enough.

THE END

Chapter Thirty-Four

WILL

Love, Lies and Loyalty

'Well now, isn't this exciting!' Will had never seen Hattie look quite as happy as she did today. Her eyes were positively twinkling, and she was sporting some new, more colourful, streaks in her hair. They matched her summer dress.

Will had worried that she would want to bring Nutmeg to the centenary celebration party, as it was rather a long time to leave the little dog at home on his home – but she'd told him that Peter's daughter had insisted on looking after him. 'Don't say anything to Peter, but I find her a bit of a bossy one,' she'd confided. 'I think her heart must be in the right place, though, or Nutmeg wouldn't like her, would he? He's a good judge of character and he's quite happy with her. Maybe she's one of those people who is better with animals than people.' Then she'd looked Will in the eye. 'Peter is coming to the party with me, or he'd have looked after Nutmeg. He's my plus one. Harold would have liked him to be.'

'He would.' Will had agreed. 'I'm sure he'd be really pleased, having his two favourite people together. And he'd be pleased you're happy.'

Hattie was happy, she was in her element, thought Will as he looked at her now. She might be a different Hattie to the one Harold had left, but maybe that was why he'd fallen for her in the first place. Why he'd married her. Because he'd seen who she was inside, and he'd wanted that – even if he couldn't let himself allow her to be the real Hattie while he was alive. Maybe he knew that Peter would take care of her, would let her be the woman she should be.

'It's very exciting!' Jo grinned. 'I think it's amazing that you're one of the top three, though I never doubted it for one moment.' Will saw her squeeze Stuart's arm and couldn't believe the difference in the man. When he'd first come to the library, Stuart been very distant, he'd hardly said a word to anybody and had stuck to his routine religiously. Now he seemed to have blossomed, if that word could apply to a man. He seemed bigger, braver, happier. And everybody loved him, especially Hattie. 'But it's a bit nail-biting, isn't it?'

'Well, it is, and it isn't,' said Hattie, winking at Stuart. She patted her handbag. 'I have my mobile phone in here, and if the wrong team wins, I will have something to say to the judges.'

'I really think you should have told us what you saw.' Avril wagged a finger at Hattie. 'You're very naughty.' Then she winked at Will. Why had it taken him so long to get to know her? He felt like he'd wasted so much time, and as Hattie kept telling them, life was too precious to waste. If Hattie loved Stuart, she positively adored Avril. Just like he did.

'When you're my age you can do what you like. I could even murder somebody and get away with it!'

'Can we wait and see if we've won first?' asked Stuart.

'Oh, my goodness, look!' Hattie was suddenly distracted and waved wildly in the direction of the makeshift stage that had been assembled at the side of the marquee.

'What?' Avril frowned.

'Look!' Hattie waved again. 'It's a sign!'

'It's a suitcase,' announced Stuart, suddenly catching on. 'Look, at the side. A navy blue suitcase.'

'Petrol-blue, not quite navy,' Hattie corrected. 'Like the one in our story.'

'I think that could be a coincidence.' Will shook his head. 'Don't get too excited, there are lots of cases like that. Anyway, shush, the mayor is here!'

'And so is that booby woman!' announced Hattie in a stage whisper that carried remarkably well.

Avril tutted, and the booby woman – Lucy – leaned forward to the microphone.

'Good afternoon, everybody, I'm so thrilled to see you could all make it.'

'I'm sure you are.' Hattie was not to be silenced.

'I er, yes, well we were delighted with the fabulous entries, so without further ado I will hand over to the mayor to announce the winner.'

There was a smattering of applause, and a middle-aged

man with a very large mayoral chain resting on his stout chest took centre stage.

It made Will smile. Were the mayors selected partly with events like this in mind? The chain would have looked ridiculous on Will but it might have suited Stuart – who was currently trying to look nonchalant but was gripping Jo's hand so hard she was wincing.

'Thank you, Miss Martin. I'm honoured that you let me be involved with the competition and help compile a short-list. And I was particularly pleased that you have given me the chance to select the winner from the three top entries. As you know, I, in common with many other people, have dreams of becoming a famous novelist but I think that may have to wait until I retire! This competition was particularly wonderful, though, in that the guidelines allowed entrants from all walks of life to take part. The task was not onerous, and was, I hope, fun for the contestants. The results definitely showed you all rose to the challenge. Right, well, enough of me. Let's talk about you! There were some excellent entries, truly wonderful ones. There was one in particular that was cleverly structured and beautifully written with all team members maintaining the same voice.'

Hattie gave a strangled squeak, and Will put a hand on her arm to stop her leaping forward and waving her photographic evidence at the mayor. 'Hang on, let's see what he has to say,' he whispered.

'But that is not what this competition was about.' The mayor waved a chastising finger, and Hattie visibly relaxed.

'I should hope not!'

'We didn't want one voice'—the mayor was in full flow

now, his voice strengthening as he built towards a crescendo —'a story driven by one person. We wanted something diverse, original, a demonstration of collaboration, and evidence that the writers were able to adapt depending on what other people wrote. We wanted originality, we wanted the individual voices to sing, to add something special in a way that a single author could never achieve. We wanted to hear those voices—'

'I think he wants to hear his own voice,' muttered Hattie.

'He could be stirring the troops,' agreed Stuart.

'Or addressing a rally.' Avril shook her head. 'I wish he'd just get on with it.'

'It's his moment, we'll have to let him have it.' Will squeezed her hand.

'—as you would in a fireside story in the past,' the mayor continued, 'with control being passed around the fire. This was *our* written fireside story. Therefore, the very accomplished work produced by the team headed by Jake Trent slightly misses the mark and will take third place.' He peered over the microphone in Jake's direction, and Will couldn't help but grin. Jake looked very uncomfortable.

Avril nudged him in the ribs, her grin broadening.

'Which leaves two standout entries.'

Jo gave a little squeak, then put her hand over her mouth.

'We are therefore awarding them as joint winners. The first team, led by Mrs Hattie Jamieson, had me hooked with their little whodunnit. They sneaked in a couple of hundred extra words but that final chapter was a corker and well worth it, so if the team would be good enough to join me over here. And the second—'

The second name was lost as the team cheered…

'Many congratulations to both teams,' said the mayor once order was restored. 'Now, we have a grand unveiling. It's quite exciting! In this suitcase'—he smiled at Hattie—'which one team might find quite appropriate, we have something wonderful. Mrs Jamieson, if you would be kind enough to do the honours.' He lifted the case, a petrol-blue, dark but not quite navy, onto the table and held out a hand, inviting Hattie to open it.

Will smiled. It was perfect, but he was sure it had nothing to do with Lucy or Jake – who now appeared to have left the party. The mayor, it seemed, liked a bit of theatre. Maybe he was a frustrated actor, as well as a frustrated novelist.

Hattie lifted the lid. 'Oh, my goodness, how wonderful. Books. Our books!' She picked a copy out and held it up. 'Look, Avril, look.' There was a distinct quiver in her voice.

Avril looked, and then hugged her. 'Oh, Hattie. I wish Harold was here to see this. He'd be so proud.'

'I think he would, wouldn't he.'

'And so is Peter. Look at that smile on his face!'

'Now isn't this just perfect?' asked Jo, slipping her hand through the crook of Stuart's arm. 'I'm so proud of you.' Stuart glanced down at her.

'It is. Thank you, darling.' He dropped a light kiss on her

lips. Then raised his glass of champagne. 'I'm so proud of all of us, actually. Who would have thought we could have done this and won!'

'Well, I had the utmost faith in us,' replied Hattie. 'We make a splendid team.'

'We certainly do.' Stuart nodded.

'But I think you need to tell us now, Hattie.' Avril took a sip of her drink. She looked even more beautiful than normal, thought Will. Finding her mother's friend had made her happy, they met regularly for a catch-up and she seemed to grow more in confidence every time. But it was more than that. She'd told him all about Lisa's visit, and it was that that really seemed to have made her happy. She could chat about Phee openly now. It wasn't a secret.

She glanced his way, met his eye, and smiled.

If he hadn't been sure before, he knew for certain now. He'd fallen in love. Neither of them quite knew where their future journeys would take them, but for now he just wanted to make sure he saw as much of her as he could. The future would take care of itself. Maybe it was already mapped out. Maybe they couldn't do anything to change it – just as, maybe, his sister Sarah couldn't, and Jake was just a bad interlude – but they could make the most of each moment.

'Tell you what, dear?' Hattie asked, all innocence. But they all knew that she knew what Avril was asking.

'Hattie!'

She laughed. 'Oh, if you insist!'

She was quite the performer, thought Will. She'd been transformed since that first visit to the library. It was funny how writing this story had affected all of them in one way or another.

'Well.' Hattie reached into her bag and got out her phone. 'You may look at the photos.' She handed it to Avril. 'They are the only ones on there so it's not hard to find them!'

'Tell us,' Stuart said, his tone soft. He knew, thought Will, that Hattie would relish telling the tale.

'Jake wrote their whole story. Every page of that notebook was written in the exact same handwriting.'

'Wow, are you sure, Hattie?'

'Of course I am. I have the photographic proof, don't I?'

'That's cheating.'

'It most definitely is. He must have then got his team members to copy out a chapter each into the notebook that they submitted to the judges. But I saw the original! I did imagine that any judge worth his salt would see it immediately, as long as they weren't some gormless lackey of the booby woman.'

'But the judge wasn't gormless,' said Will with a smile.

'He most certainly was not. He's a very nice man. And I rather like that mayoral chain, don't you? It suits him.'

They all turned to look at the mayor who gave a cheery wave and a thumbs up.

Epilogue

AVRIL

Every Story Paints a Picture

Avril looked at the display in the shop window and smiled. Who would have guessed that a book would have led her to the library, and one collaborative story would have changed her life so much? Is that what people meant when they talked about 'the power of storytelling'? She felt a sudden rush of emotion that made the tears prickle hot in in her eyes. She was a storyteller. They all were.

The book was slim, and their story was only a part of it, but it didn't matter. It was the lead story; it was what they'd created – and learned from. In some way they'd all told their own stories within that novella. Is that what writing let you do? Express emotions, grow? It was why she'd written her diary, her letter to her mother, she supposed. But this was greater. More powerful, because their stories, their feelings were entwined. Stronger together than they would have been on their own.

Wow, she was getting a bit philosophical! But the book was beautiful. The same deep red cover that their notebook had been. Almost a copy. And the title, *The Storytellers*, was perfect. We are all storytellers, wasn't that what it had said on their notebook? And it had been right.

'Are you coming back in?' Will's question drew her away from studying the window display of the bookshop.

'Sure. It looks great, doesn't it?'

'Amazing.' He kissed her lightly, then slipped his hand in hers and drew her back to the door. 'But they'll all be here in a few minutes. I want a proper kiss before our peace is ruined!'

She laughed. 'It won't be ruined! They're our friends!'

'I didn't mean it. I do like having you to myself, though. Anyway, look.'

Inside the bookshop there was another display with more books, and a sign with photographs of the four of them, announcing them as joint winners of the East Cheshire Library Competition.

———————

By mid-afternoon the small bookshop was crowded. Avril glanced around. They were friends – all of them. And she'd been sad to leave them and move down to Cambridge. But as she said, she'd be back regularly. She had a family to visit. Her dad, stepmum, her stepsisters and their children. Then there was her friend, Mandy, and of course the team.

'Well, now, isn't this splendid.' Hattie smiled at Avril then moved forward to hug her.

'Where's Nutmeg?'

'Oh, he's here, we stayed in a hotel picked specially for him. Sophie, Peter's daughter, found it. She's clever at things like that. Very efficient.'

Avril grinned. Hattie was quite capable of making 'efficient' sound like a disease, but today it sounded more like a compliment.

'Here they are. Sophie, this is my good friend Avril.'

'Hi! Oh and lovely Nutmeg!' She stroked the little dog, who was in the arms of a woman, who she had to admit, looked 'efficient'.

'And this is Peg. She lives in my apartment block; I'm helping her research a friend she's lost touch with,' Hattie continued.

Avril shook hands. She vaguely remembered Hattie talking about the terrible twins, Mabel and Margaret – Peg – when they'd first met. Peg, it seemed, must have grown on her.

She glanced across the display. Will had his arms around a young woman, his sister Sarah. She liked Sarah, and she was sure her brief return had finally reassured Will that Jake's betrayal was firmly in the past.

How could one story have brought so many people together, righted so many wrongs, made so many people happier?

'And this was when we were diving with stingrays when we were in the Caribbean.' Stuart was showing her dad his photos.

'Wow, that's amazing. Can we do that, Joey?' Lisa took

the phone from his hands. Then saw Avril watching and winked at her.

'You should,' Stuart carried on, ignoring Jo's warning dig in the ribs. 'We do love a cruise, don't we, Jo? We realised that one thing we both wanted to do was travel. Jo has plenty of time to paint, and I do a bit of scribbling. We can share and do our own things as well, it's splendid.'

'Peter is helping Peg as well.' Hattie drew her attention back. 'We've been researching the children's home and found out a bit more about Harold and his mother. She wasn't really horrible, you know, I think she had a difficult life, like he did.'

Avril glanced at Peg. She seemed quite enamoured with Peter, standing so close that their arms were nearly touching.

Hattie saw her watching and grinned.

She knew. But she'd moved on. Peter wasn't the love of her life. He never had been. But he was a good friend.

She moved closer to Avril.

'Are you happy in Cambridge, Avril? Do you think you'll stay?'

'I am. Are you happier in your apartment?'

'I am now. It's okay. Better since Mabel went into care!' The note of mischief was back in Hattie's voice. 'Me and Peg might go on a cruise. Not the Caribbean, but they do nice shorter ones. And Peter can look after Nutmeg.'

'Not go with you?'

'Oh no, I don't want any shenanigans, I want to enjoy it!'

Avril laughed. 'What if Peg wants shenanigans?'

'She can do that another time.'

'You are happy, Hattie?'

'I am. I'm sad that I wasted so much time thinking about Peter, when I could have been working out what Harold's problem was. But I can't change that now, can I?'

'True. I think we all waste time on the things we shouldn't. It's just the way things are.'

'Yes. You can't relive your life; you make your choices and follow the path you're given.'

'I'm glad our paths all came together, Hattie.'

'So am I, dear.'

'Did I tell you that Dad, Lisa and all the family are coming down for the wedding? I hope you'll all come, too?'

There was a shriek from Jo. 'Wedding! Stuart, Stuart, they're getting married!'

'Well, I must say, I had my suspicions when I spotted that engagement ring.'

'Engagement ring? How did I miss that? Oh, my goodness, show me, Avril!'

Avril held out her hand, just as her father wrapped his arm around her shoulders. 'Okay, love?' he asked softly.

'Very.'

'You won't be a stranger?'

'Of course not, Dad.' She loved Cambridge, and it had surprised her how quickly she had felt at home. But maybe that was down to who she was with, rather than where she was. She loved Will, she loved the bookshop. And she knew that her mum would be with her wherever she was.

'I wish I'd not put all the books away,' said her dad.

'It didn't matter. I found them again.' She'd learned just

how much her mother had loved books. Mandy had told her how much Phee had read to her as a child.

'And I'm sorry I didn't realise that the girls' banter was more than that, and that it hurt you.'

'It's fine, Dad. Honestly.'

'Ah, here's the man of the moment.' They watched Will walk round the book display and head in their direction with a bottle of champagne. 'I'm glad you found him, Avril. If you're half as happy with him as I was with your mum, then you'll be okay.'

'I'll be okay, Dad. I know I will.' She smiled up at Will as he leaned in, his mouth close to her ear.

'They're fabulous friends, but I'll be so glad when it's closing time and I've got you to myself again!'

She laughed.

Sometimes you found your happy ever after in the place you least expected to.

Acknowledgments

Biggest thanks of all to my wonderful team of two – Charlotte and Amanda!

My amazing editor, Charlotte Ledger, I couldn't do this without your support, inspiration and never-ending patience. Thank you also to the lovely HarperCollins and One More Chapter team – so many wonderful people have played a part in producing this book and I'm very grateful to you all.

Amanda Preston, my agent, what can I say? You're a star, and I'm so thankful that you're always there for me, fighting my corner, listening to my woes and brainstorming ideas with me.

Thanks also to my family, my dogs – who drag me away from my desk at regular intervals for exercise and decompression – and all the lovely readers and bloggers who get in touch and during the tough times remind me why I do this wonderful job.

ONE MORE CHAPTER

The author and One More Chapter would like to thank everyone
who contributed to the publication of this story...

Analytics
James Brackin
Abigail Fryer

Audio
Fionnuala Barrett
Ciara Briggs

Contracts
Laura Amos
Laura Evans

Design
Lucy Bennett
Fiona Greenway
Liane Payne
Dean Russell

Digital Sales
Laura Daley
Lydia Grainge
Hannah Lismore

eCommerce
Laura Carpenter
Madeline ODonovan
Charlotte Stevens
Christina Storey
Jo Surman
Rachel Ward

Editorial
Janet Marie Adkins
Kara Daniel
Charlotte Ledger
Laura McCallen
Jennie Rothwell
Sofia Salazar Studer
Emily Thomas
Helen Williams

Harper360
Jennifer Dee
Emily Gerbner
Ariana Juarez
Jean Marie Kelly
emma sullivan
Sophia Wilhelm

International Sales
Peter Borcsok
Ruth Burrow
Colleen Simpson
Ben Wright

Inventory
Sarah Callaghan
Kirsty Norman

Marketing & Publicity
Chloe Cummings
Grace Edwards

Operations
Melissa Okusanya
Hannah Stamp

Production
Denis Manson
Simon Moore
Francesca Tuzzeo

Rights
Helena Font Brillas
Ashton Mucha
Zoe Shine
Aisling Smyth
Lucy Vanderbilt

Trade Marketing
Ben Hurd
Eleanor Slater

**The HarperCollins
Distribution Team**

**The HarperCollins
Finance & Royalties
Team**

**The HarperCollins
Legal Team**

**The HarperCollins
Technology Team**

UK Sales
Isabel Coburn
Jay Cochrane
Sabina Lewis
Holly Martin
Harriet Williams
Leah Woods

**And every other
essential link in the
chain from delivery
drivers to booksellers
to librarians and
beyond!**

Read on for an extract from
The Secret Ingredient!

Chapter One

April 22nd
Before

Sooner or later, most people will come across their 'day that will change everything'. For Kate it was April 22nd. Not this particular one – though the aroma drifting through from the kitchen as she opened the front door held quite a promise – but the one four years ago when she met Eddie.

She had just turned twenty-six and he was joking about his own thirtieth birthday looming over him. But the age difference was irrelevant; that first shared smile unlocked some deep desire inside her that she didn't know she had.

She had never wanted anything, or anybody, as much as she wanted Eddie.

When she was little, and told her mother that she *needed* something, her mum would say she *wanted* not *needed*. But by her third date with Eddie, Kate knew with a certainty that this was the guy she *needed* to spend the rest of her life with.

She didn't tell anybody how she felt because just knowing herself was enough.

'Wow, that smells amazing!' Kate pushed the front door shut and took a deep breath, letting the luscious smell of chicken fill her senses. Coming home was definitely her favourite part of the day; parts of her she didn't know were tense seemed to relax as the smell of Eddie's food wrapped around her.

She slipped her shoes off, and slid them neatly into the rack, giving herself time to savour this moment.

'It's going to taste amazing as well!' His deep voice made her glance up from the shoes. He was framed in the kitchen doorway. His chuckle brought her out in goosebumps, just as it had on that first date.

There was a broad smile on his broad face – everything about Eddie was broad. Strong. Dependable.

His long, curly hair was tied back, the chef's apron she'd bought him smeared with spices and tomato.

Eddie was a hands-in, rather than a hands-on, type of cook. He used every knife, every chopping board, every spoon, and then he used his fingers. He sprinkled and tasted as he went. He'd always wiped his hands on any tea towel that was handy, or the front of his T-shirt, which was why she'd bought him the apron. Well, two. One to wear, one in the wash.

He closed the space between them, his hands reaching for her waist. 'Happy anniversary, Mrs Shaw!' His touch made her pulse skitter; his steady gaze made her happy-dance inside. Those words were still the best ones in the world.

Kate couldn't ever remember feeling like she belonged, that she was with somebody who accepted her as she was and didn't expect more from her or want her to change.

And then Eddie had asked her to marry him, twelve months to the day after their first date, and Kate knew she'd been right about him. Them. He had no expectations, he loved her just the way she was. In a world full of uncertainty and rubbish, Eddie was the constant, the good.

Of course, they'd got married on April 22nd, and on this particular day it was their wedding anniversary, their second.

'Happy anniversary to you too, Mr Shaw.' She grinned back at him, her hands reaching up to his neck as his lips skimmed lightly over hers. A promise of something more later.

He pulled her closer, the warmth of his palms over her back, the gentle rub of his thumbs sending a tingle to the base of her stomach – in the same way it had the first time he'd touched her.

She called it the Eddie-effect.

'I'm starving.'

'For me or my food?' His eyes were dark, but his tone was teasing.

'Well…' She drew the syllables out and he laughed.

Tightening his grip until her body was snug against his. 'When you put it like that!' Her stomach rumbled and he loosened his grip, laughing.

'You're always starving!' He kissed the tip of her nose, then was still for a moment, long enough for her to appreciate the gorgeous smile, the deep chocolate-brown eyes, the smell of him. Her man. The man she was so lucky to have.

Eddie wore life like a comfortable blanket. Where Kate fought her way through every step, he moved easily with it. They were the perfect combination; he was good for her.

'You can't blame me! It's the smell that does it. I didn't realise I was this hungry until I opened the door. What are we having?'

'Surprise.' He tapped the side of his nose with his forefinger, then took both her hands in his. 'Come on – I need you to taste something. Close your eyes!'

Eddie might leave the toilet seat up, his guitars (yes, plural) in the living room and his shoes in exactly the right spot for her to trip over – but she could forgive all the things he did wrong, because of all the things he did right. And that included knowing that one way to her heart was through her stomach. She ate like a goddess, and he even sometimes washed the pots and pans up as well. The kitchen was his domain, and she was more than happy to have it that way.

She closed her eyes, let him lead her into the kitchen. 'No peeping!' She stood still as he let go of her hands. Listened to the sound of the oven door opening and closing, of pan lids being lifted. Stirring.

The familiar aromas hit her senses, making her stomach

rumble. Roast chicken, tarragon, mushrooms, garlic. It was roast dinner at her grandparents, mingling with the smell of the glorious buttery-garlic potatoes that Eddie had served the first time he cooked for her. The comfort food of her childhood mixed with the tantalising flavours that her husband knew she loved.

Her mouth watered; her stomach rumbled louder. 'Arghh, you're torturing me, feed me!'

'Shh!' His rumble of laughter rolled over her. 'Open up!'

The taste was even better than the smell. A spoonful of creamy sauce, soft chicken, the sweetness of leeks.

'Mmm, oh my God, how can food do this to me?'

This was different from that first meal he'd cooked for her, but the flavours were the same. She was right back there, in his tiny flat, gazing into his eyes – watching his face break into an enormous smile as she nodded her approval.

Their first proper dinner together. The first time she'd stayed over. The first time they'd made love.

'Nice?'

'Nice? Soooo good. Better than an orgasm.'

'Really? Are you sure about that?' The spoon clattered onto the board, and he was there – his arms wrapped tight around her.

She opened her eyes. 'It's awesome,' Kate said, her voice turning throaty at his intense stare as their gazes locked.

'I'm going to get you cooking one day.' His tone matched hers, as his eyes searched her face.

'But you're so good at it!' she joshed gently, but he didn't smile. 'Maybe, one day when I've got some spare time.' She'd not grown up with home cooking; her mum never had the time. Oh hell, she was beginning to sound more like her. *Be* more like her. She was not going to let that happen. 'How about tomorrow?' The words tripped out before she had time to think, but his lazy smile made her want to repeat them, say the words again. Make him happy.

'Tomorrow sounds good.' The light touch of his finger-tips on her neck sent a shiver through her.

'How long until dinner's ready?'

'It needs a bit longer, but nearly there.'

'How much longer?' She knew she was teasing, asking him another question, but this familiar pang of hunger was nothing to do with chicken.

'Long enough,' he paused, 'to test out that statement of yours. I know my cooking is good, but I think you've forgotten just how amazing I am in other rooms of the house!' He swept her into his arms. Ignored her laughed shouts of protest.

'What about my dinner!'

'It's fine. It's simmering nicely.' He gazed into her eyes, raised an eyebrow. 'Just like me!'

'But I need a shower, to get changed.'

'I might join you. Everything,' his voice had turned throatier, in a way that made her pulse race, 'is bubbling away just how I like it.'

They lay naked on the bed, on their sides facing each other. His hand resting in the dip of her waist.

'That was good.' His voice was soft, post-sex languid.

His fingers traced a line over her rib cage, his caress light as he reached up to tuck a tendril of hair behind her ear.

Kate smiled lazily back, wanting to snuggle in, but knowing they had to get up and dressed.

'We should do it more often.' His gaze was steady, and she knew what he was going to say before he said it. She half-reached out, to put a finger on his lips. Stop him. But he caught her hand and spoke again before the words could come out. 'As often as we can, before—'

The sigh broke free before she could stop it. She pulled away slightly, rolled onto her back. It was a reflex action; she couldn't help it, even though she hated herself for doing it. She stared up at the ceiling, tried to swallow the frustration away. 'Aren't you happy the way we are? Just the two of us?' She risked a glance towards him. 'What's the rush?'

'No rush.' His hand rested easily on her stomach. A light steady pressure. 'It's just…'

'If it happens, it happens. If it doesn't it isn't meant to.' She couldn't keep her tone light; a defensive note had drifted in. Kate hated it when that happened. It wasn't Eddie's fault.

'We can afford to give—'

'It's not about money,' she snapped, then instantly regretted it. She closed her eyes for a moment. 'IVF just seems so,' she hesitated, 'clinical.'

His smile was gentle. 'Yeah, guess it is clinical.'

'If we're going to have a baby, I'd rather give it time, let it happen naturally,' she said softly, resisting the urge to wriggle away. But her whole body had tensed. It was a defence reflex that she hated.

'We've given it time, Kate. I don't want to be an old

dad.' His tone was soft, but she could hear the disappointment. The quiet determination. This was important to him.

'You've got years left in you!' She tried to keep her tone light, teasing.

'I want to be young enough to kick a ball around, to be in touch when my kids are teens. Don't you?' She shrugged. 'Wouldn't it be great to have kids and really enjoy it, not be knackered all the time, then still have years of fun left after they've grown up and gone?'

'Wow, that's some fast-forward. There they were, gone!' This conversation got worse every time they had it, or should she say Eddie tried to have it. Didn't he realise that life wasn't always how you wanted it? That kids didn't fit into every life. That parents could wish they'd never had them?

'We've got options, Kate. We should take them.'

Kate wasn't sure she wanted options. But was that fair? They'd never discussed having a family before they got married. It hadn't come up, because everything else had slotted into place so perfectly. They wanted the same things. She'd never questioned it, never dreamed that there would be something major that they didn't agree on.

But now she knew that what her grandad had said was true – two of the most important things that you need to discuss are money and children.

Kate and Eddie hadn't talked about either, because as long as they had each other everything would be fine.

And they'd got enough money; she'd always worked hard, earned enough to support herself. Earned enough to support both of them, if he followed his heart – ditched his job and retrained as a chef.

She swung her legs off the bed, her back to him. 'Maybe it's not the right time…'

'Lots of people say it's not the right time, but you just have to make it be.'

She moved away just far enough so that his fingers skated her body and his arm fell to the bed.

'I don't have to make it be.' She could hear the tightness in her voice as she struggled to do up the clasp on her bra.

He reached over again, his hand over hers. Stilling her. 'We, Kate. We, it's not just you.'

'And it's not just you. You can't make the decision.' She bit back the 'It's my body'. She was being unfair, she knew she was, but it always made her feel defensive. It always made her pull away from him, withdraw. It was too hard to explain. That was what it wasn't the right time for. Explaining.

'I'm not trying to make any decisions, I just want you to open up, talk to me, like we do about everything else. What's different about this? I don't get it.'

Everything is different, she wanted to shout. We don't need to pay out a ton of money so that some doctor can *make* me pregnant. I know why I'm not pregnant.

She didn't shout. Instead, she said, 'Please, can we not? Let's not spoil tonight. We can talk about it tomorrow.'

'Sure.' His finger traced a line down her spine, and she shivered in response. 'It's no big deal.'

But it was. There was a note of defeat in his voice that she hardly ever heard, and she hated. She'd done that.

Kate felt the bed bounce as he rolled off, came round and squatted in front of her.

She couldn't help but smile. He always knew how to make her smile.

She laughed with him, loved him, shared her secrets, her body, her hopes and dreams. Her life. So why was it so hard to talk to him about this?

He bounced on his haunches slightly, and she shook her head – unable to stop the smile broadening. 'You look like a giant frog!'

'Ribbit!'

This time she laughed.

He stood up, kissed the top of her head.

He had made her laugh, tried to lighten the atmosphere again, but she knew she'd spoiled things.

'I'm sorry I…'

'I'm sorry I keep pushing it.' He ruffled her hair. 'You're right, there's no rush. I don't know what it is.' He laughed as he pulled his jeans on, but he had his back to her now. She couldn't see his face, and she knew there would be disappointment on it. 'Maybe it's a mid-life crisis looming?' He shrugged. That boyish, cute shrug that she had fallen in love with.

'You're not mid-life!' She stood up, wrapped her arms around him. Buried her face in his back.

'Getting there.' He untangled himself, took a step away, but kept hold of one of her hands. To show he forgave her.

'I'm sorry, Eddie. I just can't—'

He interrupted her; maybe he didn't want to hear her say 'do this', or maybe he agreed that it was a conversation for another day. Not today.

'Hey, I've cocked up.' His voice had changed to more

matter of fact, but with a thread of hurt running through it, a slight tremor in his normal steady tone. 'There's some stuff, a couple of ingredients I forgot. I'll pop and get them, won't be long, dinner will be ready in,' he glanced at the clock, 'twenty minutes, so I've just got time. Have a chill for a bit! Anything you need me to get?'

Kate shook her head. She knew he probably didn't need to go out. He was giving her some space; he was giving them both time.

Pressing the reset button.

She tried to swallow the lump in her throat at his happy-sad wink. Eddie never could hide his feelings; it was one of the things she loved about him.

Kate listened as he went down the stairs. 'Hey, I love you!' she shouted out, just as the front door clicked behind him. Pretty sure he'd not heard, or he'd have shouted back. He always shouted back.

She slowly pulled the rest of her clothes on and sat at her dressing table.

She took her time putting her make-up on, styling her hair, and then decided to make more effort − picking out a dress he liked, to try and make amends for being such a wet blanket.

She put on some music, their favourite playlist. Pottered around the kitchen, his kitchen. She loved sitting at the island, watching him cook. She loved him; she loved their home. She loved their life.

It was as perfect as it could be, as good as she'd ever hoped. She just wished he'd hurry up back though. Then they could kiss, open the wine. Then she'd know it was okay between them.

Kate's mobile bleeped. The image brought a grin to her face instantly. A selfie Eddie had taken this time last year of them both grinning, holding up champagne glasses.

There were bumps in the road with any relationship; it would be plain weird if they never argued. They were good.

And tomorrow she'd help him cook dinner. She'd share that particular passion in his life, and maybe stop feeling so bloody guilty about this.

Still smiling she tapped out a reply.

'Love you, hurry back home! I'm ready and waiting [winking emoji] Xxx'

Her gaze stayed on the screen, wanting to know he'd seen the message, he knew how she felt. One tick, sent. Two ticks, delivered. She waited for them to change colour – for the status to change to 'read'.

It didn't.

Available in paperback, ebook and audio!

YOUR NUMBER ONE STOP

ONE MORE CHAPTER

FOR PAGETURNING BOOKS

One More Chapter is an award-winning global division of HarperCollins.

Subscribe to our newsletter to get our latest eBook deals and stay up to date with all our new releases!

<u>signup.harpercollins.co.uk/ join/signup-omc</u>

Meet the team at
<u>www.onemorechapter.com</u>

Follow us!

 @OneMoreChapter_

 @onemorechapterhc

 @onemorechapterhc

 @onemorechapterhc

Do you write unputdownable fiction?
We love to hear from new voices.
Find out how to submit your novel at
<u>www.onemorechapter.com/submissions</u>